ROCKS

WAGES

Vivian Doolittle

A Black Opal Books Publication

GENRE: MURDER MYSTERY

ROCKS WAGES
Copyright © 2022 by Vivian Doolittle
Cover Design by Transformational Concepts
All cover art copyright © 2022
All Rights Reserved
Print ISBN: 9781953434432

First Publication: JUNE 2022

Published by Black Opal Books **http://www.blackopalbooks.com**

Chapter 1

It is in your moments of decision that your destiny is shaped. ~ Tony Robbins

1975

The cotton in his ears, legacy of state-of-the-art speakers in an acoustically perfect concert hall, was second only to his cottonmouth, brought on by too much pot and not enough whiskey. But he was well on his way to correcting that imbalance. At a minimum, he could slake his thirst. The muffled hearing might take a while longer, as it nearly always gave way to unabated ringing. Tinnitus, the medicine man had called it. No doubt the first in a series of fees assessed by the devil, aka the record company, to whom he'd sold his soul.

Windy City's sellout concert at Seattle's Paramount Theatre ended just before midnight. His watch now said it was a quarter to three, but Ricky Harris didn't feel like it had been more than about half an hour since they'd ended the show.

He had a cigarette in one hand and half a bottle of Jack Daniels in the other, and he was trailed by three giggling groupies, the eldest of whom couldn't have been more than about fourteen. A part of him wanted to just give in to their silly whining and let them give him the very best bj's they could manage, but he only had Angie on his mind. He wanted to take her to bed and just get lost in her dark exotic beauty. The hard-on he sported through most of the concert was for her. The girls in the front row could think it was for them, the sycophantic fags who worshipped his unfuckingbelievable guitar could think it was his love of the music that got him off, but he knew better. He only had doing Angie on his mind, and the rest of the concert was practically on autopilot.

He shook his head and turned around, smiling his best boy-next-door smile.

"Ladies, I'm flattered, and I am so tempted," he said to a chorus of giggles. "But I can't. My heart belongs to Angie. I think you know that, don't you?"

The girls looked disappointed, but one of them held out her ticket stub hopefully. "Would you autograph it?" she asked.

Ricky was charmed. "Sure," he said with a grin. While he wrote, the other two produced their ticket stubs and fresh pens, and, before long, he had them all autographed and on their way.

He patted the pockets of his jeans, self-frisking in search of their room key. He found the keys to the rental car, but no hotel key. Shit. Most likely Angie was still partying with the rest of the band, wondering where the hell he was.

Even though Ricky could barely recall what city they were in, he had really liked the venue. He stayed behind to watch the roadies put it all away for transport to the next town, Portland or Vancouver, he couldn't remember which. He chatted with the management guy for quite some time before he realized that the rest of the group had long gone, even Angie.

Ricky was left with the rental car; the limo took everyone else back to the hotel. They stayed at the Edgewater

Inn because it was where the Beatles had famously stayed back in '64, so it had a kind of rock and roll cachet that couldn't be ignored. Funny, security wasn't nearly as tight this night.

He got to the room and knocked. No answer, of course, since the noise and music coming from inside were deafening even through the closed door. He tried it, and it opened so he walked on in. The cloud of smoke that wafted out reeked of pot, hash, and cigarettes. *Ah, sweet perfume!*

"Hey, Rick-ay! Join the party, man! Where you been, dude? We are way ahead of you, man!" Don was sitting cross-legged on the floor with Craig and a couple of the bodyguards, along with an assortment of groupies. Don was wasted. They all were.

Ricky smiled and took a long pull off the Jack. "I'm catching up quick, my man, be patient." He scanned the room. No Angie.

"Hey, where's Ange?"

"I dunno. She and Rufe left a while ago. Rufe had some acid." Don shrugged.

Ricky looked around again and sure enough, Rufe was gone too. Ricky's well-earned buzz started to fade a bit.

"Where'd they go?" Ricky hoped he sounded uninterested. Don shrugged again.

"Don't know. Sit down, man, the bong's coming around again." So saying, Don proffered a rapidly shrinking joint to fill the gap until the bong finished its appointed rounds.

Ricky took a hit off the roach, then extinguished it on his tongue and swallowed the remains.

"Wow," said Don from somewhere far away. "That's not even a Bogart, man, that's just…that's just wrong." His disappointment didn't last long, as the bong had arrived and he fired her up after the chick on his right repacked the bowl. Don took a good long hit. Much raucous laughter followed, but Ricky was still mostly deaf, from standing between the speakers all night, and he really needed to find Angie.

On a most unwelcome hunch, he walked down the hall to Rufus's room and tried the door. As expected, it was unlocked. He walked in to discover that all lights but the lamp by the bed were off. By the light of that one lamp he saw Angie, naked and astride a recumbent and equally naked Rufus. In their coital ecstasy, they hadn't heard him walk in.

For the first time in his twenty-three years on the planet, Ricky understood emotional pain. The loss of his mother had occurred at too young an age to really grasp the implications of growing up motherless. His father's emotional abandonment had come so close on the heels of that loss that it too, failed to register very deeply on his young psyche.

No, this was abandonment on a much grander scale. What was the line from that Jethro Tull song? "*His woman and his best friend, in bed and having fun...*" Yeah, pretty much.

Without conscious thought, Ricky threw the Jack Daniels bottle across the room. It shattered on the heat register adjacent to the bed. They must have been pretty high indeed—the two of them reacted in slow motion. They stopped moving together and both turned to look at Ricky.

"Right then," was all he said.

He tossed his still-smoldering cigarette butt at them and left, fumbling for the keys to the rental car. He grabbed an as yet unopened bottle of whiskey from the table to the left of the door on his way out. Halfway to the elevator, Angie caught up.

Her round face was flushed with recent sex and strings of her dark brown hair crisscrossed it in random patterns. She had wrapped herself in a white sheet that now trailed behind her like a ragged bridal gown.

"Ricky," she began, but he forestalled further comment with a raised hand. He didn't look at her.

"Please don't try to mind fuck me with any sort of explanation, you cheating cunt. You were fucking my best friend, there is no 'not what it seems' explanation for that. Fuck you, Angie. Fuck you, fuck *you*!" Mercifully, the elevator arrived and he got in and hit the L button, rapidly followed by the Door Close button, which he kept slapping until the bloody thing finally drew slowly closed. His last memory of Angie as he left the hotel that night, was her beautiful face, marred by heavy stage makeup that was running down her perfect cheeks in wide black tears.

Ricky found the rental car, a brand new, fire engine red '75 Dodge Charger, and got in. He didn't start it right away. He sat staring through the windshield at a creeping fog that was rolling in off Puget Sound.

The dark January Seattle sky had been clear and cold when he got back to the hotel, what, twenty minutes ago? Now there was a frigid pea-souper roiling around and driving could become treacherous in the near-freezing temperature.

He was enormously glad he'd grabbed another fifth of Jack. He wanted to take another slug from that bottle to see if it would dull the growing ache in his heart or, failing that, at least blot out the image of Angie and Rufe together that was all too detailed and clear in his mind.

He opened the bottle and took a swig. The warm liquid burned a trail down his throat like the trails left by the tears streaming down his cheeks.

"Jesus Christ," he said. He turned over the engine of the rented Dodge Charger. Ricky wasn't stupid. He had been noticing how Rufe looked at Ange. How they shared the occasional joke to the exclusion of the rest of the band.

Ginger, Brillo-haired motherfucker! Rufe knew that

Ricky was planning to ask Angie to marry him. *My best friend*, he thought. *That back-stabbing sonofabitch!*

Ricky shook his head and, as he did, his shoulder-length blonde locks rubbed against his neck. He felt another tear leave his eye and, with it, a renewed wave of anguish flow through his heart. The betrayal was more than he could bear.

He drove out of the parking lot, having no idea whatsoever where he was going. He just needed to go. He needed to drive, and drive he did, aimlessly and for a long time.

The fog seemed like the perfect soft counterpoint to the ringing in his ears and the unrelenting dryness in his mouth. At this hour the streets were deserted, the clubs were closed. Ricky drove without direction, barely registering anything as he drove past. The sight of the two of them together had thrown him for a loop and he could not get the image out of his mind.

He cried for a while, and then he got angry. He was already sick to death of touring—sick of unwelcome edits from the suits at the record company—sick of always having to get Don's help to write.

It was no longer about the money. Ricky had more money than he could spend in a lifetime. Somewhere along the line, it had ceased to be about the music, too. He wondered for a moment why he did it. Why he even bothered. Angie was the answer, of course. She loved the whole singing with the band thing, the whole rock star vibe. And Ricky had to admit he loved that she loved it.

He looked down at the dashboard and realized he was only going about 25 miles per hour. He straightened up and looked around. No cops. Good. He sped up just in time to round a corner and come to a large, weird intersection. The light was red, so he stopped and looked around. He could go straight, but there didn't appear to be much down that way. If he went left, it would be a hard left, nearly 180 degrees and that would most likely take him back to town and back to the hotel. No way, man.

The light turned green and Ricky took a right. In the fog-softened glow of a streetlamp, he saw a short bridge. It was fancy wrought iron, painted green and the lettering on the top railing read "Fremont."

As Ricky slowly rounded the corner, he saw figures on the bridge. He didn't have to get any closer to see that there was a struggle taking place. He pulled the Charger onto the grass to the left of the bridge, dousing the lights as he did.

Had Ricky been one toke less high, one pull off the bottle of whiskey more sober, he probably would have had the sense to make a U-turn in the intersection and beat feet out of there. But he wasn't, and he didn't.

Instead, he cut the engine and watched, fascinated, as two big ol' boys beat the holy bejesus out of a smaller guy. The victim-dude was a young-looking guy with long blonde hair, not unlike Ricky's own. He was dressed in jeans and a leather jacket. His attackers wore dark suits without ties.

Men in black, Ricky thought. But there was no humor in it. He wondered what the dude had done to so piss off the two hulks that were having their way with him. There was quite a bit of argument and shouting to accompany the beating, but even after cracking his window an inch, Ricky couldn't make out what they were saying.

Was it a debt unpaid, perhaps? A drug deal gone bad? Ricky didn't have time to think much beyond that because the two goons picked up the smaller dude and tossed him over the side of the bridge.

He sat there watching for a moment until the men got into a big black car and left. He jumped out of the Charger and ran to the edge of the canal. It was lined on either side by a concrete retaining wall. The canal must have been manmade because the wall went as far as he could see into the fog in either direction.

Christ, it's cold! Ricky peered into the foggy darkness of the water and listened carefully. Surely the dude had come up and was swimming for the concrete wall now. But he heard no sound other than the flowing water. As his eyes adjusted to the darkness all around him, Ricky could see the surface of the water. It was unbroken and smooth and doubtless fucking freezing.

With no more thought than to take his own jacket off, Ricky jumped into the frigid wet blackness of the canal.

The deep breath he drew before leaping off the edge of the retaining wall was sucked out of his lungs in an instant by the unbearable cold of the fast-moving water. Ricky pushed up and out of the water sucking in freezing, wet air with a rasping *whoop!*

Unbelievably, the air outside the water actually felt colder than the water itself. Ricky took another deep breath and dove down again, eyes closed and flailing blindly for the submerged victim.

After what seemed like too many long moments, he felt something that could only be the dude's leather jacket. He grabbed the collar and hauled the unresisting guy toward the surface.

In the dim light of the fog-enshrouded streetlamp, Ricky could see very little, but he saw that the dude's eyes were open and he didn't seem to be breathing.

He swam toward the wall, every stroke becoming harder as he slowly froze to death in the bitterly cold water. He managed to get the guy up onto the berm first and then hauled himself sluggishly out of the water right behind. He lay on the grass panting for a moment, but the damp air began to draw the remaining warmth from his body, and he knew time was of the essence.

He rolled the guy onto his back and listened for sounds

of breathing or heartbeat. There were none. Ricky looked up and around for someone, anyone, another car even, just someone who knew what to do because Ricky had no clue.

The frigid water combined with adrenaline had done a bang-up job up of sobering him up. Ricky tried to remember the steps of Artificial Respiration he'd been taught in the seventh grade. Pinch the guy's nose shut. He did. Tilt the head back. He did. Clear obstructions from the victim's mouth. Well, obviously there weren't any, the guy had the shit beat out of him, he hadn't been eating anything.

Without further deliberation, Ricky put his mouth over the dude's mouth and began to rhythmically blow into it as hard as he could. He stopped after a few repetitions and listened again for a heartbeat. There wasn't a sound coming from the guy's chest.

He tried again, about ten more breaths and another good listen, before abandoning his feeble attempts at reviving the guy.

"Dude, I'm sorry," he said. "You picked the wrong hero, man. I have no idea what I'm doing, but I'm pretty sure you're dead."

An involuntary shudder wracked Ricky's body, and he realized he needed to get dry and warm post-haste or he would surely die along with the hapless man in his lap.

It was at that moment that an idea both great and terrible occurred to Ricky. It was perfect in its simplicity. Were he a spiritual man, Ricky might have thought that the Universe had conspired to bring him to this very moment in time. He refused to contemplate the terrible aspect of the idea, there simply wasn't time. He had to get dry and warm or he was going to be in big trouble.

Ricky rolled the body over and checked the back pockets of the guy's jeans. Sure enough, he found a wallet in one of them. He opened it but there was no cash. There was a driver's license and a *MasterCharge*, but that was about it. Thor Swenson was his name. *You have got to be fucking kidding me*, he thought.

Sure in his purpose, Ricky worked quickly now. He put his own wet t-shirt and buckskin jacket on the corpse, substituting the guy's wet t-shirt and leather jacket for his own. He pulled the $400-odd dollars out of his own wallet and then put his now empty wallet in the dead guy's back pocket, placed the cash into Thor's wallet, and tucked that into his jeans.

He also grabbed a small key fob with the name of a tavern on it. The fob held only three keys. Ricky knew he was gambling that one of them was to a place to dry off and change clothes. The address on the driver's license had better be up to date, and it had better be close by.

Fishing the car keys from his right front pocket, Ricky ran back to the rental and opened the driver's door. He grabbed the bottle he'd taken from Rufe's hotel room. He put the key in the ignition and then ran back to where the dead guy lay.

Working as quickly as he could in spite of the bitching cold, Ricky tilted the dead guy's head back and poured some of the liquor into his mouth. He made sure it went down, then dumped a bit onto the wet shirt of the guy. With great effort, Ricky dragged the body back to the car and slowly and painfully hefted it into the driver's side, eventually placing him behind the steering wheel of the Charger. He put the whiskey bottle into the guy's right hand and wrapped the left hand around the steering wheel.

Ricky didn't know if it was the cold or rigor mortis setting in, but the dead guy's hands stayed on the wheel and dutifully clutched the bottle of booze.

He reached in and turned the key, then stepped over the dead guy's legs with his right foot. He pulled it into gear and stomped on the gas at the same time.

As the car leapt out of his grasp, he pulled his leg out

and slammed the driver's door shut as the car flew past. He watched as the Charger jumped the low lip of the concrete wall and dove into the canal.

It was over in an instant. The silence that followed the enormous splash the car made brought with it a new chill. Ricky knew he had to get inside and get warm and right now. He had absolutely no idea where he was going to go, so he began by walking across the bridge from which Thor Swenson had so recently met his demise. If he could find a phone booth, he could find a phone book. The phone book would have a street map in the front and he could find Thor's dwelling with any luck.

There had been only one vehicle in evidence when the men tossed Thor from the bridge. They had driven it away into the darkness. Ricky headed in the same direction. Wherever the three men had come from, they had come by car. *Please god, don't let it be very far*, he thought.

ⱭᴐⱭᴐ

The next morning, the 20-point banner headline on the front page of the January 14, 1975 issue of the *Seattle Post-Intelligencer,* read "Rock Star Found Dead in Fremont Canal."

Chapter 2

No, no, that's not going to work. It's in the key of A, so F# blues runs work nicely. Here, see?" Thor's fingers walked over the strings, lithe, flexible, and accurate as hell. The riff wasn't fast, but it was clean and pure.

"Try again. Do it like I just did." Thor placed his fingers on the fretboard where he began the riff and went through it slowly a second time. Larry followed as best he could, playing a little too fast toward the end.

"Not bad," said Thor. "But slow it down some, like this." He ran through it again. "You're not at Woodstock man, just have fun with it." He laughed.

They must have looked quite comical, the pair of them. They were sitting alone on a Saturday in Thor's Chinook University office, practicing Blue Oyster Cult's, "Cities on Flame with Rock and Roll." Larry had expressed the desire to learn it, in time to add it to his band's repertoire as soon as next week.

Larry could play pretty well and Thor enjoyed teaching him, though it had to be on the down-low. Larry felt his bandmates, also teachers at the university would be horrified to learn he was actually taking lessons. They took their little tavern band seriously. Larry was the de facto leader of the group and had to appear confident in his talent.

"I should let you get back to your real life," Larry said.

"This is hopeless."

"No, not at all!" said Thor. "You're doing great! Besides, this is my life. I teach, I play—I play, I teach. It makes me happy." He smiled to show he was sincere.

"One more time, OK?" He watched as Larry gave it another try. This time went better and he kept the tempo throughout. He even added a little flourish at the end which was quite appropriate. Thor thought it sounded really good. Then Larry froze.

His hands suddenly clenched the guitar so tight it looked as though his knuckles might break through the skin.

"What's the matter?" Thor asked. He looked up and saw that Larry's face had gone an alarming shade of gray. His lips were blue and he was sweating.

Thor set his guitar in the stand and rose. He took Larry's guitar from his clenching grasp and set it on the floor. He knelt in front of the other man.

"Larry? You OK, man?"

Larry responded with a croaking sound and keeled over off the metal folding chair. He clawed at his chest as he hit the floor.

"Heart…" he said in a faint whisper.

Thor stood and pulled his cell phone from his pocket. Fuck. It was turned off, as it would be during the lesson. He powered it up, waited impatiently for it to cycle through so he could make a call. He punched 911 and paced at Larry's feet until finally, an operator came on.

"9-1-1, what is the nature of your emergency?" she asked.

"Heart attack, I think. Please hurry! Send someone! I don't know what to do! The guy is dying! Hurry!"

"Sir! Please try to calm down. What is the address?" He told her.

"At the university?"

"Yes, for fuck's sake! *Hurry*!"

"Is the victim male or female?" she asked.

"What difference does that make? For God's sake, just get an ambulance here!"

"Sir, they are on their way. I need to give them information en route. Please stay on the line with me until they arrive." She sounded so unbearably calm, he wanted to reach through the phone and strangle her.

"Male or female?" she asked again

"Male!"

"How old is the victim?"

"How the hell should I know?" he yelled. "Hurry!" he said again as if demanding she make the EMTs step on it and that would get them there any faster.

Larry was looking pretty bad at this point. His face had made the trip from ashen to blue and he didn't appear to be breathing.

"Uh, mid-sixties I guess," he told her.

"Is he breathing?" she asked

"I...I'm not sure. I don't think so."

"Sir, check to see if he is breathing and if not, put the phone down and start CPR. Do you know how to perform CPR?"

"Yeah. I think. It's been a long time. Let me check. Hold   on."

Thor knelt next to the colorful Larry and felt for a pulse on his wrist. Nothing. He tried to feel for the carotid artery pulse but again got nothing. He rolled the unprotesting Larry onto his back and listened at his chest. Nada. Zip. Zilch. Again, fuck.

He picked up the phone. "He's got no pulse and he's not breathing. Tell me what to do." Thor's own heart was beating fast.

She quickly ran through the steps, and it seemed to Thor that there was a whole lot more pushing on the heart than there was breathing. He remembered that differently but did as she instructed.

The office was on the third floor of the building, and he couldn't hear the approaching sirens, so he was heartily relieved when two firefighters ran in carrying equipment and radios and other unrecognizable things. They went immediately to work, and he stepped back to let them do their life-saving magic.

He picked up the phone and let the 911 operator know they had arrived. She sounded very cheerful when she commended him for a good job and rang off. He felt a little guilty for shouting at her. She was only doing her job, after all.

Thor looked down at Larry. The EMTs were continuing the CPR. Two more firefighters came in. One of them helped the two, that were working on Larry, heft the portly victim onto a gurney. They quickly wheeled him out to the waiting ambulance, one of them rhythmically squeezing the bag that was sending air into Larry's empty lungs, another keeping up the chest compressions as they went.

The remaining fireman asked Thor some questions, and then told him which hospital they were taking Larry to. He asked if Thor knew how to get a hold of Larry's wife or family. Of course, he didn't.

"Um, I guess I can get his wife's number out of the faculty directory. I'll give her a call and meet you at the hospital."

The fireman thanked him and left. Thor stood for a moment, the waning adrenaline in his system leaving him feeling shocked and shaky. He busied himself at his laptop, sorting through pages of faculty info until he found Larry's home number. He had no idea what he was supposed to say to this woman, a stranger to him.

She answered on the second ring.

"Yes, this is Dr. Swenson," he said. "Larry was here,

uh, having a guitar lesson, um…"

"It's OK, Dr. Swenson. I know all about it. Larry only keeps that little secret from his friends. How can I help you?"

"Well, I'm sorry to have to tell you this, but he's really sick. I think maybe he's had a heart attack. The paramedics just left. They're taking him to Northwest Hospital." It sounded as though she may have dropped the phone.

 e

The A-frame simplicity of its architecture belied the splendor that was the interior of Luther Memorial Church in Seattle, Washington. Inside the church itself, the rows upon rows of white birch pews were flanked on either side by stained glass walls that ran the length of the building. Their multi-colored rectangles in random sizes allowed a rainbow of sunlit colors to illuminate the congregation. At the front of the church, behind the altar, which sat on a dais, the wall was made of river rock that climbed all the way to the apex of the steep roof. The rock wall was bisected with copper candelabrums, six of them, each four feet in length.

To the left of the altar hung a crimson glass lamp, suspended from the high ceiling by a copper chain. The lamp housed the Presence Light. The flame therein symbolized the presence of God within the assembly, and it was to remain lit eternally.

At the bottom of the four carpeted steps that led to the altar, a casket sat upon a wheeled platform. The top half of the casket was open and Larry Malone lay within, deceased.

Thor was seated next to the casket and beside him, a young woman sat. He was playing his twelve-string guitar, and the woman deftly accompanied on a mandolin. They were singing, and their harmony was breathtaking.

As he sang, Thor looked out into the congregation and noticed the remaining members of Larry's band, Dead Salmon, seated together in the front row to the left of the aisle.

Thor had tapped one of his grad students to perform with him at the request of Larry's widow, Barbara. The student's name was, Eleanor Carmichael, and she sometimes assisted him during office hours. He'd heard her humming once, and mentioned that she had a lovely voice. It was then that he learned that Eleanor was working on her Master's in musicology, concurrent with her Mathematics master.

When Mrs. Malone called to ask if Thor would play "The Battle of Evermore," by Led Zeppelin at Larry's funeral, he immediately thought Eleanor would be a good choice to sing the harmony. They had only practiced a few times, but she was quite talented and he felt Larry would be pleased.

According to Mrs. Malone, that had been Larry's all-time favorite song.

Their voices blended in perfect harmony as they finished. The silence following was uncomfortable for Thor. He hated church, always had. It seemed weird that they could turn in such a beautiful performance and receive not one hint of applause.

He stood and held the chair for Eleanor as she rose. They returned together to their place on the front row pews on the right of the aisle. The officiating pastor said a few more words and then offered the pulpit to anyone who wished to say something in remembrance of Larry.

The widow was in no shape to say anything, it appeared, so Thor was not surprised to see one of the Dead Salmon bandmates stand and head for the lectern. His steps on the stone floor echoed in the great open space.

The man stepped up to the microphone and pulled a few notes from his breast pocket. As he looked down at them, he paused as though unsure of what was written there. He cleared his throat.

"I'm Eric Jensen," he said. "I considered Larry to be my best friend." He paused, audibly choking up. The depth of his grief was painfully apparent to the rest of the congregation, likely mostly strangers to him. Thor felt a pang of sympathy for the guy.

Although it had been many, many years since he'd performed in front of an audience, he was still comfortable doing so. Mr. Jensen, not so much, it seemed.

Eric took a deep breath and began again.

"We met in high school if you can believe that. We went all through college together and we were sure we would change the world." He smiled. "I don't know if we did, but maybe we changed it for a few people along the way, friends, family, and students.

"What you might not know is that we formed a little garage band a few years ago. I think coming over to my place to practice was Larry's favorite part of his day." He choked up again, then and slid his thumb down the page of notes, as though skipping over a big chunk of them.

"His death was a shock and an unplanned ending for all of us, I know. We'll all miss him, but I think I will miss him more than most. He was such a fixture in my life." He raised his eyes toward the ceiling. "Godspeed, Lare," he said.

Eric returned to his seat, looking self-conscious and casting his eyes to the floor.

So many people got up to speak that Thor decided anything he might have to say would be extraneous, so he decided to skip it. That Larry had been well-liked was an understatement.

It was two hours before they finally left the church and

made the long slow drive to the cemetery. Thor knew that Eric and the rest of the band were only marginally aware of the circumstances of Larry's death.

He'd been on campus when it happened, that much they knew. But what he was doing there was still a mystery to most. It was a Saturday when he had the massive coronary that took his life.

Yes, Larry was a lover of good food. So, what? He surely knew the two spare tires around his midsection were not the healthiest of body parts, but he loved food and drink and never missed a chance to party.

Thor knew that he'd been having fun in his lesson when the big one came, but he couldn't share that with a soul. He'd been sworn to secrecy.

That hadn't stopped the whispers around campus that Larry was not in his office when the heart attack struck. Someone called 911 and it was a good bet Larry hadn't been in any condition to dial his cell phone. So, Thor also knew that he was going to have to fill the band members in at some point. Mrs. Malone was probably in no shape to answer nosy questions of that kind, so it would have to fall to Thor.

The sunlight that had shined so beautifully through the stained glass in the church was occluded by heavy cloud cover by the time the mourners gathered at the cemetery.

The ceremony at the gravesite was mercifully brief, and it began to rain as if cued by an unseen movie director. When the final amens were mumbled, everyone sprinted to waiting cars. Larry's family and closest friends drove in a loose procession back to the family home, nearly an hour to the north.

Thor followed the procession in his car. He had said goodbye to Eleanor after the service at the church. She hadn't known Professor Malone, so there was no reason for her to go to the cemetery.

When they finally reached Larry's house, some of the women gathered around the widow and fussed over her like a clutch of hens. The four men who comprised Dead Salmon stood off to the side, away from the softly chatting gathering of family and friends. Thor knew absolutely no one in this company, although he recognized professors, department heads, and others from school. He decided the best defense was a good offense, so he took a glass of wine from a sideboard and joined the band members. They looked up in greeting but did not speak to him.

"Shit," Eric said. "I still can't believe he's gone." The others nodded in agreement.

Eric was about 6 feet tall and sturdily built. He had medium brown hair that was beginning to gray at the temples. His close-set brown eyes were the unwitting victims of an ever-present scowl.

Middle age had thickened his midsection some, but he was physically fit otherwise, and it showed. Had Thor not known that Eric was the coach of the Chinook University football team, he might have guessed it.

According to Larry, he, Eric, Tom, Roger, and Bert had formed Dead Salmon, their garage band that performed classic rock at taverns on occasion, four years ago on a lark. What had been not much more than a joke for starters, turned out to be halfway decent at playing the oldies, and they developed a local following. Even the band's name was a play on Chinook University.

Now, with Larry gone so suddenly, Dead Salmon might be dead in fact. Larry Malone had been the heart and soul of Dead Salmon, Thor knew. He played a mean guitar, and he had the best voice of the bunch. Nearly all the lead vocals had been performed by Larry. Without him, they were dead fish indeed—washed up on the shore of middle age.

"This so sucks. Let's get out of here," Eric said.

Thor took that as his cue to exit as well. He didn't know

Mrs. Malone and felt terribly out of place. He'd put in an appearance for his friend, that was all anyone could expect from him. He tossed back the last of the wine and after setting the empty glass on the sideboard, slipped out the front door.

Cars lined the suburban street on both sides in front of Larry's home. The rain was still coming down as Thor found his dark grey Hyundai and got in. When he put the key in the ignition, he heard a loud click, but nothing else happened. Frowning, he tried again. *What the hell?* He got out, went around to the front, and opened the hood. Thor really had no clue what he was doing, but it seemed the next logical step.

The Dead Salmon four exited the house just behind him, and it happened that the car they headed for was parked just in front of his. They saw him poking around with the hood up.

"Need a hand?" Eric asked. He and the others went and looked into the exposed engine.

Thor looked up, still frowning. "I need more than a hand, I'm afraid. I have no idea how to fix a car. I can't even tell you what might be wrong."

Eric extended his hand. "Eric Jensen," he said. "Football coach?" He offered it in the form of a question as if Thor might not know who he was.

"Oh yes, of course!" Thor shook the offered hand. "Thor Swenson, Professor of Mathematics."

Eric smiled. "I know." He rubbed his hands together. "Let's have a look here," he said. Eric busied himself under the hood for a moment. "Go try to start it again," he said. Roger, Bert, and Tom looked on as Thor climbed into the car and turned the ignition. Click.

"I thought perhaps the battery was dead," Thor said. "But the lights are on, everything electrical seems to otherwise be working."

"Yeah," Eric said. "I think it's probably your starter. Do you have towing on your insurance?"

"Yes," said Thor. "I think so."

"Good. Let's get this puppy to a garage, and I'll give you a lift."

Thor called for a tow truck, and the other men kindly waited with him for over twenty minutes until it arrived. He made arrangements for the disposition of the car, paid the driver of the wrecker, and followed Eric and the others to Eric's car.

"We are on our way to one of our favorite taverns," Eric told him. "We want to have a beer and a toast to Larry."

Thor nodded, his grey ponytail swinging in time. "Fitting. And absolutely, I'm in," he said.

They drove for about thirty minutes, heading back down south toward Seattle. Eric magically found a parking space at the Southampton Arms on Aurora Avenue. The group took a back booth and Thor followed, taking the last seat. They ordered a pitcher of beer and five glasses.

"Dr. Swenson," Eric began.

"Please call me Thor."

Eric nodded. "Thor, I think it's time for real introductions." He looked around the table.

"To my left here in the corner is Roger Collins, our bass player, who also plays a mean harmonica."

Roger shook Thor's hand. He was six-four and could stand to lose more than a few pounds.

"I teach English Lit but I'm a poet at heart, though I've published little so far," Roger said.

His thinning hair was grey and really just a losing proposition. Thor smiled.

"And this," Eric went on, indicating the man to his right, "is the best keyboard man in all of rock, Tom Morrison!"

Tom was a tenured professor of History at the

acclaimed, if small, Chinook University. He had short, dark hair and appeared to be in average shape for a man in his mid-sixties. He smiled and tipped his glass toward Thor.

"He runs the track with me every morning before first classes," Eric said. "I think he has enough talent that he really should be a professional musician, instead of a member of an old guy wannabe band, but we are thrilled to have him."

"On your left, there is none other than Bert Scott, drummer extraordinaire! He teaches Physics to everyone from freshmen to graduate students. He has a brilliant mind and has been published in some respectable scientific journals, but he won't tell you that. He's kind of shy," Eric said with a wink. Thor reached over and shook Bert's hand.

"And I play rhythm and alternate between backup and lead vocals. We are, collectively, Dead Salmon," Eric finished.

"I'm very pleased to finally meet you all. I wish it could have been under better circumstances," Thor said.

When the waitress brought the beer, they waited until she left, then with Roger leading, they hoisted their glasses high and took turns toasting their lost comrade.

The bar was dark, old oak and leather with a strangely nautical theme that belied the very British-sounding name. Its incongruity was most of its charm. Dead Salmon had played here, as well as drunk many a beer.

"To Larry," Eric began. They all raised their glasses. "He was the heart of Dead Salmon. He will be sorely missed." He got a little emotional at the end and they all took a somber sip.

"To Larry," Roger said. Again, the glasses rose high. "Best lead guitar in the business." They drank again.

"To Larry," Tom said in turn. He looked as though he might add more, but no words came. After a moment, they drank again.

They turned to Bert, but his eyes welled with tears and he just shook his head. They drank again and for a few minutes, they sat in silence, each man attending to his own private thoughts.

Then, as if choreographed in advance, the four band-mates all looked at Thor.

Thor had been lost in his own reverie and could feel their gaze upon him. He looked up and met their eyes, each man in succession. It was his turn, obviously, and they wanted more from him. Perhaps they wanted to know how he was acquainted with Larry.

"To Larry," he said and raised his half-empty glass. They raised theirs in unison.

"The best guitar student I ever taught," he said and drank.

The other four men sat with glasses held aloft, staring at him and clearly thrown off by this revelation. One by one, they each slowly took sips from their beers and set their glasses down.

"Well, that was an interesting toast," said Eric.

Thor sighed. "You know, it was going to come out sometime, it may as well be now," he said.

Eric looked annoyed. "Do tell." He crossed his arms. The others listened intently.

Thor took another deep breath. "I've been dreading this confrontation because I knew it was coming ever since Larry died. I just hadn't had time to think about how to approach it with you," he said.

"Larry didn't want you guys to know. He'd been taking guitar lessons from me for about six months. He was really good, I'm sure you know that. But he had little formal training until he came to me. It was so weird that it even happened, but I couldn't turn him down!"

Eric stared at Thor.

"He took *lessons* from you?" Eric asked, dumbfounded.

Thor downed the last of his beer, just as the waitress brought another round.

"He didn't want you to know," he said again. "He was proud of his ability, and he made me swear to keep it a secret. I didn't have a problem with that because I didn't know any of you guys. It was easy to agree to." He took a sip off the fresh brew.

"You know he didn't read music, right?" Thor asked.

"Yeah," said Eric. "We knew, but we also knew that it wasn't an impediment for him. He had a great ear." The other men nodded in agreement.

Thor nodded too. "You have no idea," he said. "Larry had perfect pitch. Do you know what that means?"

Roger nodded. "Yes. It means if he heard a note, he could tell you what that note was."

"Essentially," agreed Thor. "I'm telling you guys, if Larry had lived, he would have been an incredible musician. You were all playing with an amazing talent. He just didn't learn about his ability until too late in life." He looked at his beer.

Eric frowned, then brightened as a sudden realization dawned on him. "It was you!" he said. "You are the one who called 911 when he had the heart attack!"

"Yeah, it was me," Thor told them the circumstances of Larry's lesson turned heart attack. When he was finished, he stared into his mostly empty schooner. The others were silent for a while. Finally, Eric, the new leader of the band, spoke up.

"How did he come to you for lessons in the first place? How did he even know you play guitar, let alone teach?"

Thor thought for a minute before he spoke.

"One day last spring, I was finished for the week. I took my acoustic out onto the quad and sat under a tree and started to play. Just for fun, you know? It's relaxing, like meditation.

"Anyway, I was sitting there playing and this man walks up. He listens for a bit. I even remember what I was playing, *Mood for a Day,* by Steve Howe.

"When I finished, he applauded, and I bowed and we both kinda laughed. He introduced himself and told me that he played a little, too. So, I handed him the Martin and sat back, and he ran some nice riffs then handed it back to me.

"Larry told me that *Mood for a Day* was one of a number of songs he'd always wanted to learn, but couldn't because he didn't read music

Tom spoke up. "We never worried about it, because once he learned something we could practice it, and he would play flawlessly." The others nodded in agreement.

"I've played the piano since I was five," Tom went on. "By the time I was in high school, I was winning competitions and doing some teaching myself."

"Yeah," Thor said, "I hear that! I paid my way through school by giving guitar lessons.

"Anyway, he asked if I would teach him to play that song, so I said sure and that was the start of things.

"He used to come up to my office at the same time every Saturday and it became a sort of ritual for both of us. I really enjoyed teaching him. What an apt student! I've never seen the like. I was teaching him to read music, but honestly, he was much better just playing by ear. If I played a riff, he'd copy it nearly exactly. We had some amazing jams." Thor stopped and studied his beer for a moment. He was hit with the realization that he would never have one of those jams again and the intensity of the sadness it produced surprised him.

Eric clapped his hands together suddenly and said, "Well! We're men of the world, we can handle another pitcher, eh gents?" A chorus of agreement ran the table and the waitress was summoned yet again.

Fortunately, the next day was Sunday and none of them had class. They sat toasting Larry and sharing stories of his life until closing time. Coach Eric must have had a hollow leg, because he claimed to be sober enough to drive and miraculously, he got them all home with no issues.

☙◦◦◦❧

Sunday was normally band practice day, but the group hadn't been together since Larry's ill-fated trip to Harborview and subsequent demise. It was nine o'clock and Eric sat at his kitchen table looking out at a much-neglected lawn as he nursed his second cup of coffee. His wife wasn't home from the Malone's house yet and that was fine. He wasn't in the mood to talk anymore about Larry, the funeral, or poor widowed Barbara.

Instead, he thought about band practice. Right here in his very own garage, as always. It was time. But without a lead guitar and lead vocal, really what was the point?

Last night, as they all left in a drunken uproar, debating whether to stop at a mini-mart to get more beer, he had exchanged business cards with Thor. He had to be honest with himself: Thor was an aged, but well-preserved Nordic god. He was fit, handsome, and apparently played a mean guitar. It was a given that he could sing, the Led Zeppelin number at the funeral was proof of that.

He wondered if Dr. Swenson would consider joining the band. He would certainly be the perfect person to take over the lead guitar and vocals from Larry. Shit, Thor must be a lot better than Larry since he'd been teaching him. Was that even possible?

Then he wondered whether Thor was already in a band. Maybe he was giving lessons to others, too. If he wasn't interested, perhaps he knew someone who might be. Eric sipped his coffee. It seemed like the perfect solution and asking is always free.

He got up and fetched his cell phone. He called the rest of the guys and told them to come over for practice as usual. It was time to get back to playing, grief notwithstanding. He would run his idea by them and see if they all thought it was the stroke of genius that he thought it was.

Smiling to himself, Eric finished his calls and set about making breakfast. He felt better than he had in a month.

Chapter 3

Mick took another hit off the vodka rocks. He stared off into the middle of the room, focusing on nothing.

"Don't you think you ought to slow down on that stuff?" Stephen asked.

Stephen was thirty-five, an accountant. He broke the family cop line at an early age. Mick and Terri had never once questioned his career choice. Maybe it was time to move away from law enforcement. Stephen's wife, Emily, and their twin little boys, Trevor and Tristan, would never know the sleepless nights a cop's family knows.

Mick retired from the force at age 65 and he didn't feel like that was old enough to just stop. He was not an imposing figure—he'd always thought of himself as an overgrown leprechaun. At 5 foot, 6 he was usually one of the smaller cops in Seattle. Now, much of his red hair was gone and the fringe around the back of his head that remained was silvery-white. His gray eyes looked weary, with little of the mirth that used to light them in his younger days. His fondness for vodka, as opposed to whiskey, might well fly in the face of the stereotype for Irish cops, but it still showed in his generous paunch.

His son, Stephen, proved the adage that the apple doesn't fall far from the tree. He was a little taller than the old man, and his still red hair was full on his head, but the resemblance was clear to anyone who might have looked.

"I'm not finished," Mick said. He assumed that Stephen would know he wasn't talking about the vodka.

"You're not finished with what?" Stephen asked, proving Mick's supposition.

"My job. I'm retired, but I'm not finished."

"Dad, what the hell is that supposed to mean?"

Mick slowly rolled his eyes up to his son who stood over him, puzzling at his behavior.

He thought about the years before Stephen was born. Mick was a young beat cop then, wet behind the ears. His first big case had been that rock star driving his car into the drink at the Fremont Bridge.

He took a deep breath and looked at the glass in his hand, then slowly looked back up at his son. The setting autumn sun sent a weak beam through the den window. It ended in a small puddle of light on the worn carpet. Mick stared into that spot of sunlight as if into a well.

"I'm not done, Steve. "I've left some things unfinished, and I need to finish them before I can really consider myself retired."

Stephen shook his head. "Are you talking about a case, Dad? Because you don't have any open cases. You retired with full honors because you closed every single case over twenty-five years. That, Dad, is quite an accomplishment. How can there be anything you haven't done?" He asked sounding very sincere. The entire city of Seattle had turned out for Mick's retirement party, it seemed. Detective Mick Thorne was a legend in the SPD.

"There's a closed case. A very old, cold case really," he said. "It happened a long time ago before you were born. I was a new cop on the beat. I was the first one at the scene. Well, there wasn't much in the way of a scene, actually," he said. "I was on graveyard shift. I was alone in my cruiser, driving across the Fremont Bridge. Just before I was all the way across, I saw a metallic glint in the water. I stopped and got out of the cruiser. I shone my flashlight into the water and saw what could only be a submerged car." He sighed and looked off into the distance again, saying nothing for a few minutes.

"That's when the circus began," he said after a moment. Stephen came around the side of the couch and sat down across from his father.

"What circus?"

"I saw the car underwater and immediately called it in. I ran to the edge of the canal and peered into the water. My flashlight didn't illuminate much. I wanted to dive in, to see if anyone was in the car. For some crazy reason, I thought there might be someone alive in there." He took another sip of the vodka.

He looked at Stephen again. "You have to understand something. This was in January, at around four o'clock in the morning. It was below freezing out there, never mind the water temperature. There was no way I was jumping in to see if there were any survivors." He set his glass on the table between them.

"So? You called it in. Backup arrived at some point, I presume. How does that leave unfinished business for you? And when did all this take place, Dad? You said before I was born? That's a long time ago. Why are you thinking about it now?"

Mick smiled. "I'm thinking about it now son because a day hasn't gone by in the last forty years that I haven't thought about it. Now, maybe I'll have time to finally close this case, too." He nodded to himself. *That would be good*, he thought. To close this last case before he called it quits.

Stephen smiled. "Now I'm intrigued. "You are going to have to tell me the whole story, Dad. Start to finish."

Mick picked up the vodka and took another drink, then very deliberately set it back onto the table. He took a deep breath and once again focused his eyes on the sunspot on the floor.

"It was 1975. I was a Seattle patrol officer, fairly new to the job. I had my own cruiser and my own beat, but no partner at that time—just me and my thoughts in the car, night after night as I drove. The young guys get the shitty graveyard shift, you know," he said.

↭↭↭

Mick turned right onto the Fremont Bridge. It was so damn cold that night. The fog was threatening to freeze black ice onto the roadway, and surely onto the bridge deck. He carefully slowed down as he turned. The metal bridge deck would be treacherous in this weather. Visibility was minimal as it was, and with black ice, he could likely hit the sides of the span. He didn't want to put a dent in the cruiser, there would have been hell to pay in that instance.

As he crept slowly across the bridge, a bright flash caught the corner of his eye. He rolled to a stop and looked at the black water on the left side of the bridge. Is it possible for darkness to be darker? He wondered about that. The black water flowed, frigid and mute, below the bridge.

He got out of the car and pointed his flashlight into the murk, his breath condensing in great clouds in front of him. He saw another metal gleam. Slowly, he swept the light along the width of the canal and back. There was a car in the water.

Holy shit! Mick ran back to his cruiser and got on the radio. He called it in and backup was on the way. He stood for a few moments, looking down into the fast, dark water. He wondered how long the car had been in the canal before he arrived. There was no question in his mind that the occupant or occupants would have perished in very short order.

It wasn't long before the nascent dawn was accompanied by sirens, flashing lights, and commotion. This was the biggest thing to occur all night, even the watch commander showed up. Two tow trucks pulled in unison and before long a late model Dodge Charger was drawn from the water.

Inside was a young man, alone, still behind the wheel, clutching a bottle of booze. Mick shook his head. *Idiot*, he thought. The ambulance guys pulled him from the dripping car and laid him on the grass. To Mick it appeared as if the guy couldn't be deader. He was a dreadful shade of white, his eyes were open and staring at nothing, and he seemed frozen for reasons other than exceedingly cold water.

One of the tow trucks revved its diesel engine and slowly motored off, the drenched Charger following. The forensics guys were milling about, taking Polaroids, smoking, drying then dusting things. A car full of them followed the Charger, intent on poring over every inch of that car for clues.

Once the car was out of the way, one of the aid cars backed slowly toward the victim who was being placed ever-so-carefully into a body bag. That final zip couldn't have come soon enough, and Mick turned away. He would head back to the station and complete a report. Drunk kid drives into a canal with fatal consequences, so ends the thrill for the evening.

When he got back to the precinct, he found a beehive of activity and excitement. It seemed they had made a positive ID on the decedent. He had been one Richard Allen Harris, Ricky Harris to his fans. Mr. Harris, it seemed, was something of a rock star, or had been. Now he was a corpse on a slab in the Harborview Medical Center morgue. A car had been dispatched to notify the rest of the band, who were staying at the Edgewater. Well, why wouldn't they? Isn't that where all the rockers stay these days?

Mick lit a smoke. He went out a back door and stood behind the precinct, smoking and looking up at the gray January morning. He tried to make sense of what he'd just learned. This young kid, at the top of his game, does a sold-out concert at the Paramount. He goes back to his hotel, supposedly hangs out with his bandmates and roadies or whatever they were called, and gets loaded. That part makes sense. Then, hours later, he's found on the bottom of the canal, deader than a lame excuse. Nobody at the hotel knows where he went or why he left.

The girlfriend is hysterical and inconsolable and therefore incoherent. In other words, she's useless. The rest of that lot is no better. They are drunk, stoned, passed out, or utterly wasted. Miraculously, they can produce copious amounts of booze, but pot and other drugs are not in evidence. Who'd have thought?

Mick lights another cigarette. He looks at the overflowing dumpsters dotting the alley and then back up to the dreary morning sky. His gut clenches and gurgles. Likely, it's trying to tell him he needs to eat, but deep down he feels it's telling him something more. He doesn't know what it is. He can't quite see it, like a star that you notice at night from the corner of your eye. When you look straight at it, it's gone. He feels to the depths of his soul that the young man in the car was not Ricky Harris. But he doesn't know why, and he can't begin to imagine how he could prove such a thing.

ຂໍຂໍ

Mick covered his face with his hands. He'd long since stopped nursing the vodka rocks that he set on the coffee table a while before. He knows Steve is looking at him, waiting for more to the story. But there is no more. That dead end was long gone, and the case closed, and history made and everyone had moved on, lo these forty-odd years gone by. Everyone except Mick Thorne.

In all the years after, he'd never once believed that the man in the 1975 Dodge Charger was Ricky Harris. He didn't know why, but he knew it just wasn't right. There were so many things that night that just did not add up. He had Ricky Harris's wallet on him. Big fucking deal, anyone could have planted that. There was no money in it. No credit cards, either. Did no one but Mick think that was odd for a famous person out on the town?

Oh, and there was so much more. Why were there no skid marks? Harris was so drunk he didn't try to prevent his slide into the canal? OK, that's possible, but then why were there so many footprints alongside those lazy tire tracks? Of course, by the time Forensics got there they added so many footprints over what was already there…well, there wasn't any way of distinguishing one from another.

"Dad?" Steve had been listening intently. How much was just wool-gathering and how much had he said aloud? Mick wasn't sure. He smiled.

"Sorry, son. I got a little lost in my memories. Where was I?"

"You said you thought it odd that no one questioned the lack of skid marks…?"

"Right. So, on top of that, there were the footprints. I saw many footprints around those tire tracks before anyone else got there. I'm telling you son, it was as if someone had put him in that car and pushed it over the edge. It couldn't have been any other way." He finally took another sip of the vodka.

"This was the seventies, remember. We didn't have any DNA or CODIS or anything of that nature. Fingerprints are all well and good if they are in a file someplace. We didn't have AFIS, computer comparisons, databases, all that crap. We took fingerprints. If no fingerprints for the deceased were on file, he was a John Doe until identified by next of kin."

"What about dental records?" Stephen asked.

"Well yeah, sure, we used dental records, if the victim had any on file. Ricky Harris either had never been to see a dentist or had never been to see a dentist who was on the up-and-up, because he had no dental records." Mick shook his head.

"I'll tell you something else about his teeth. He was missing a front one. If anyone looked for it, they never found it. His face looked like he'd been punched out by someone seriously pissed off. A low-speed slide into the canal might force his face into the steering wheel, even with the seat belt. But I'm telling you, I saw that dead man's face and it was swollen and bruised and obviously, the injuries had been inflicted before he ever got in that car. Which, to me at least, explains how his band could have positively identified the body. The woman wouldn't go in, she couldn't look, but the three guys did. They all glanced at the face and said, 'yeah, that's him.'

"Why didn't he have any money on him? Why were his credit cards missing? And why the hell was his face swollen and bruised? Steve, somebody beat the holy crap out of this guy!" Mick said.

"You can't tell me that hitting the bottom of the canal in slow-mo is going to fuck up your face to that extent! No, nothing about this was right from the get-go, and yet, I'm apparently the only one who thought so.

"Here's the thing, drunk out of his mind rock star drives into the canal in the wee hours of the morning after a concert. What's the question? What's the problem? Open and shut, right?

"I don't know why, but to this day I know, I really know, the dead man in the car we pulled from the canal that night was not Ricky Harris. I think Ricky Harris beat this guy senseless, put him in the rental car, and pushed him into the drink. He murdered this man and stole his identity. If I can find out who died that night, I'll find Ricky Harris and I'll find a murderer."

"OK," Steve said. "So where do you go from here?"

Mick tossed down the last of the vodka rocks. "From here, I go to bed. In the morning I'll have breakfast and then I think I'm going to requisition some old records. They'll let me have anything I need. They'll think it's funny and that is just what I would like them to think. It gives me more time to track down some new leads."

He rose unsteadily, and Stephen grasped his elbow and accompanied him down the hall to make sure he got into bed all right.

Chapter 4

F ucking cold, wet, nasty night, it was. Little pissant Thor Swenson was late with his payment and Mory Taglio wasn't pleased.

"There's only so much protection a guy can give, you know?" he said to his boys, Rocco and Tony D. "Little bastard cleans up money for me, OK. I appreciate that. But there's a price, you know?" he asked again. Rocco and Tony D nodded in agreement.

It was a late night in January and the clear sky had given way to dense, dark fog here in the wee hours of the morn. Mory was on a tear and Rocco and Tony D knew better than to cross him. He had to get it all out.

Nixon was no longer in the White House, 'Nam was winding down and the country was still in a mess. Fucking hippies everywhere causing trouble was just enough to put Mory over the edge, you know?

"Thor the Viking hasn't paid the price for some time," Mory said, looking down at his beat-up oak desk. He studied his fingernails for a moment and looked up. "Thor the Viking owes me money," he said. "I don't like anybody owing me money. Makes me uncomfortable, you know?" Rocco and Tony D nodded again. It made them uncomfortable as well, but they were quite reluctant to share that bit of information with Mory. It just might piss him off more.

"I've worked hard to get this little nest egg here in Seattle," he said. "I've made a name for myself in this part of the country. New York got nuthin' of any interest for me now, *capiche*? I like it here. They got good winters. New York winters suck, don't they Tony?"

Tony D tried not to look afraid as he nodded affirmation that New York winters do indeed, suck.

"So, we would hate for me to lose my nest egg, would we not?" Mory asked.

"Yes, boss, we would hate that a lot," said Rocco.

"Exactly," said Mory. "So, it is with a very heavy heart, gentlemen, that I must ask you to pay a visit to our friend, Thor the Viking, and remind him that his payment to me is much overdue."

Rocco and Tony D again nodded in unison and got up to leave.

"Gentlemen, one more thing," Mory said.

They looked at their boss.

"It is important to me that upon collection of the debt owed, that Thor the Viking not survive the encounter. Is that understood?"

Again, the two thugs nodded together.

"On with the show," Mory said, and they were out the door.

"He scares the shit out of me," said Tony D as they hustled down the stairs outside the rundown warehouse their boss called his office.

"Yeah? Well, that makes two of us then, don't it?" Rocco responded. They arrived in the parking garage and climbed into a new, black Cadillac Seville.

Rocco got behind the wheel and Tony D took the passenger seat. Rocco pulled the Caddy away from the curb and headed south toward Thor the Viking's apartment.

Tony D supposed that Thor didn't know they called

him that. It was the moniker they gave him as a cohort and member of the inner circle. In Mory's inner circle, Thor was unique in his Norwegian heritage. The rest of the gang was Italian-American, born and bred. Mostly from the east coast, they were still getting used to the more laid-back, west coast style. But, style notwithstanding, the numbers game was the numbers game, protection was necessary everyplace, and so was laundering the money so ill-gotten.

When they got to Thor's tiny one-bedroom apartment in Fremont, he was in bed asleep. It was going on 3:00 a.m. and they were dragging their feet deliberately. Mory was enough to put the fear of God in just about anyone, but Tony D and Rocco knew they had to absolutely not fuck this up or their days would be numbered as well.

They pounded politely, all things being equal, on Thor's door. Him being asleep and all, he took quite a while to answer.

When he did, his little blonde self was unprepared for the two goons on his doorstep.

Thor pulled his robe around his nakedness and cleared his throat. Straightening, he tried to look fully awake and not shocked to see who would likely be the agents of his demise.

"Rocco! Tony!" he said with mock bravado. "To what do I owe the pleasure?"

He bloody well knew what they were there for and probably didn't have the money anyway. He never had any money, not that such an excuse would make a rat's ass worth of difference to Mory. Thor's ass was grass and he most likely knew it.

"Please come in," Thor said.

He bowed a little and gave a flourish with his arm to gesture that they enter. They did and by God they took up most of the room.

"We don't got time for niceties, Thor," said Tony D.

The D stood for DiThomasso, and it was stuck there on the end of his first name to differentiate him from fellow Taglio employee, Tony Christoforo, who, as might be expected, was Tony C to his friends.

"Mory wants his money," Tony D went on. "You got it or not?"

Tony saw Thor glance around his tiny, one-bedroom Fremont flat. The only potential exit was the front door and Rocco stood blocking that, hands clasped in front of him with an air of disinterest.

The kitchen window was over the sink, and even if it had been big enough to allow a person Thor's size to go through, there was no way he was going to cross that distance before Tony D dropped him in his tracks. Thor was fucked. Big time.

"Yeah, I got it," he said. "There's this guy down across the bridge. He owes me. He owes me seven grand and I told him I'd be collecting soon. I say we go wake him up and make him make good on his debt."

He glanced toward his bedroom again and Tony could smell the mildew growing on long-neglected laundry.

"Let me get dressed and I'll take you there. I know he's good for it, he's a good friend."

Tony D and Rocco had a lot of muscle. What they didn't have was a lot of brains. They bought Thor's story in its entirety.

Rocco looked at his watch. "Clock's ticking," he said.

Thor dressed quickly and donned his prized possession, a leather jacket he was always seen wearing. Rocco led the way and Tony brought up the rear. With Thor between them, he was less likely to make a run for it.

Thor got into the back seat with Tony D right behind him. Rocco drove, as was his custom. They headed down to the canal, and as they got to the Fremont Bridge, Tony realized that there were no dwellings on the other side.

Thor's imaginary moneyed friend didn't live where there were no houses unless he was a troll under the bridge.

Thor looked like he could tell that Tony was scanning the far side of the bridge for dwellings that weren't there. Eventually, even dumbshit goons catch on and such was the case with Tony D. Rocco soon followed.

"Where'd you say your friend with the big debt lives again?" asked Tony D.

"Uh, here, well up the hill there," Thor said. His hand shook as he pointed and the hesitation in his voice was all the impetus the thugs required.

Rocco pulled the car over to the curb before the bridge. He and Tony D hauled the hapless Thor from the back seat and dragged him onto the bridge deck. It was slick with black ice and treacherous, even on foot.

Thor's arguments were weak and futile, and he ended his days beat to a bloody pulp and tossed carelessly into the freezing waters of the canal without so much as a backward glance.

Once back in the Seville, Rocco slid behind the wheel, Tony his front seat passenger again. They didn't bother with safety belts, fuck that shit. Rocco pulled the big black sedan away from the bridge and headed back toward Mory's office. The boss would want an accounting of the night's proceedings.

Just as Rocco turned back in the direction they had come, Tony D tugged on his sleeve. "Hey, wait a second," he said.

Rocco glided to a stop. "What?"

"Check this out," said Tony D. He pointed out the rear window toward the bridge.

It was hard to make out in the dark and fog, but there was a car parked on the other side of the bridge and a guy was diving into the canal just as Rocco turned to look.

"What the fuck?" he asked.

"Yeah," said Tony D. "Turn around, I want to see this."

Rocco turned around and the two goons sat in their Caddy, lights off, engine off. They watched in the dark as some guy risked his life to save the obviously dead Thor Swenson. It was really quite the thing of beauty, and they both had to appreciate the lengths this guy was going to, just to save a dead guy. But what he did next was incredible.

He dragged the body up on the grass and tried some bastardized version of artificial respiration. When he got no response, he did the damnedest thing and dragged the body into his own car, gave it a bottle of some kind, and drove the whole shebang into the canal.

As the car sank out of sight, Rocco and Tony D looked at each other and laughed. The guy who was now wearing Thor's leather jacket was walking, presumably soaking wet, toward the fog-dimmed streetlights of Fremont.

"You think we ought to go after him?" Tony D asked.

"Nah," Rocco replied. "He just made sure that nobody could ever pin this on us! Thank you very much, Mr. Stupid Guy. I hope you catch your death in those wet clothes." The two goons shared another laugh and drove back to tell Mory the good news.

Chapter 5

A little over a week after Larry's funeral, Thor was snuggled under the covers in bed on a Sunday morning, petting his purring cat Tim and drifting in and out of sleep. He would almost decide it was time to get up, then find himself in the middle of a pleasant dream. His cell phone jarred him fully awake. It was Eric Jensen.

Thor answered on the third ring. "Thor! This is Eric. I just had a crazy idea, man. Do you want to hear it?"

Thor coughed, cleared his throat, and groaned. "What time is it?" he asked.

"I don't know! It's like nine-fifteen or something, who cares? Listen, I want to ask you something!"

Thor felt a little more coherent on the second try. "I was asleep, Eric, give me a sec."

"Sorry to wake you but I have to know! Thor, can you sing?"

Thor thought that was a silly question in light of the fact that Eric had heard him sing at Larry's funeral. He cleared his throat. Still rubbing his eyes, he said, "Well I guess that depends on who you ask."

Eric pressed on.

"Not good enough my friend, I already know the answer, I heard you sing in church, remember? Robert Plant got nuthin' on you!"

Thor sighed. "Yeah." He was wondering where Eric was going with this odd line of questioning.

"With Larry gone, we need you in Dead Salmon," Eric said in a rush. "None of us can take his place. Please think about it!" He sounded desperate and embarrassed. Nonetheless, Thor answered without deliberation.

"Well, fuck it. Why not?" Tim head-butted him and he lay back down.

"Practice is at my house this afternoon. We usually get going around one. Will you come?"

"Today? Uh, yeah I guess so. Text me your address," he said and rang off.

ເວເວ

After weeks of unrelenting drizzle, the clouds had dissipated, and the cold October sky was as blue as a raspberry Popsicle. Thor felt good. He hadn't played with a band in so long. He hadn't been sure it was a good idea when Eric first called. But now, the weather was cooperating, and Thor was warming up his voice by singing along with whatever song came on the radio. He was in such a good mood at the prospect of joining Dead Salmon, it made him wonder if maybe cutting himself off from music for most of his life had been a mistake.

He turned into a cul-de-sac in the old-money neighborhood of Wedgewood. Chinook University was small, and the football team was double-A, they didn't play against the likes of the University of Washington Huskies or the Washington State Cougars. No, the Chinook U Cohos were a good, if unsung team. Still, Coach Eric must be well paid indeed to live in this neck of the Seattle woods.

"Your destination is on the right," said the GPS on his phone, courtesy of the Blue Tooth connection in his car.

Thor pulled into a long driveway that bisected a small

but well-kept lawn. Old-growth evergreens towered behind the two-story brick structure that was the Jensen
home. He counted enough cars to realize that the other
members of the band must already have arrived.

He set about unpacking his Martin D-41 acoustic and
the 1972 Gibson Les Paul Deluxe that he had found on
eBay a few months back. It was the same model of a favorite guitar he had left behind many years before and it
was a joy to play.

The centermost of the three huge garage doors swung
open and Eric and the guys were setting up. Near the front
was a nice-looking vintage Fender Stratocaster on a stand.
Thor wondered if it had been Larry's.

He pointed to it as Eric took the Martin from him to
ease his burden. "Was that Larry's?" he asked.

Eric looked at the Strat as if he'd never seen it before.
"Yeah, that's the one he left here most of the time. He had
quite a few others," he said. "Your question does make me
wonder about Larry's guitar collection though. I wonder
what Barbara will do with them."

"Too soon to ask, I'm sure," said Thor.

Tom was on the left, already seated on his piano stool.
He was surrounded by keyboards, an organ, an electric piano, and a synthesizer, plus another very electronic-look-
ing board that Thor was unfamiliar with. Tom looked like
Keith Emerson from long ago.

Roger went about strapping a Fender bass around his
neck and reaching for the amps on the switch.

Bert sat behind his drum set and tapped and adjusted
and fiddled with things. He saw Thor looking at him and
smiled and nodded.

The three-car garage was cavernous and contained
many years of stored family stuff. Bicycles were suspended from the high ceiling, boxes full of who-knows-
what were crammed into every conceivable space, and

tools were hung on a wall above a bench on the far-left side. On the far-right side, a small car sat under a canvass cover. The garage was tidy and clean nonetheless and presented an interesting experiment in acoustics. The space smelled of dust, mildew, motor oil, and other less identifiable odors. It smelled like a home, Thor realized and he felt a little pang of jealousy.

He'd never married, never had a family. There had been relationships over the years and a couple of them lasted for many years, but in the end, he was alone.

He picked up Larry's Strat. It felt good in his hands and he played a few scales, unplugged. "Nice," he said. He realized the others were watching him.

"I can play my Les Paul if you'd rather," he offered.

"No!" It was a four-part chorus.

Eric looked sheepish. "I left it there hoping you would play it. I think Larry would really like that. I'm rhythm, do you mind if I take a turn on your Les Paul?"

"Not at all," Thor said and switched on his amp. He ran a few pentatonic scales again and adjusted the reverb on the Strat. His new bandmates watched in awe. He pretended not to notice, but on some level, it amused him.

"Can we start with one we all know well?" Eric asked.

"OK," said Thor. "Lay it on me."

Tom played a Gm7 on the Hammond organ and then went into a familiar blues intro. About a minute and a half in, Bert began to keep time on the snare.

Thor instantly recognized Lazy, by Deep Purple and tapped his foot to the beat as Tom and Bert got their groove on. At the appropriate moment, he started in on Ritchie Blackmore's classic riff and Roger joined on bass with Eric right behind him and in a moment, they were rocking it like nobody's business.

Thor's mike was on, and when the time came, he didn't miss a beat.

"You're lazy, just stay in bed," he sang.

They played, tight as a tick, all the way through. When they finished, they all stood looking at each other for a minute, then burst out laughing.

"That was awesome!" said Tom.

Eric walked over and shook Thor's hand. "Is there anything you don't know how to play?" he asked.

Thor laughed. "I don't know. I guess I'd have to see your playlist. Show me what you do best."

"I anticipated such a question," Eric said. "I printed out the song list we've used for just about every gig. Larry liked Lynyrd Skynyrd and the Allman Brothers. But your voice goes another direction, man. You sound a lot like Ricky Harris."

Thor looked up from the printed song list. "Really? I don't think anyone's ever said that to me before." He wasn't lying. He hadn't sung in public since forever. In fact, the first time he'd sung in public in over forty years had been at the funeral. He straightened up a bit.

"Nevertheless, I take it as a great compliment!" He smiled and the band all smiled back at him.

They played their way through the printed song list, which ran the gamut from Jethro Tull to Led Zeppelin. Thor managed to get his gravelly tone in gear for "Whippin' Post" and "One Way Out" by the Allman Brothers.

The next song on the list was "Phoenix" by Windy City. Thor saw it and paused. The song title caused a pang in his gut so strong he couldn't name the emotion it elicited. Fear? Nostalgia? His heart started to pound.

The other guys were looking at him. He had to say something or start playing. Hands shaking, he chose the latter.

The Ricky Harris solo at the beginning of the ballad was slow and resonant. Most times, A minor will be the key that brings in the listener. It's mournful and wistful and the very bedrock of rock sound. Any minor key is, really, but A minor seems to grab them most times, kind of like the message in "The Hook," that Blues Traveler song. The hook brings you back, and Thor was brought back to Ricky Harris, someone he had not thought about in over forty years.

He played it just as he wrote it so long ago. He lost track of time as his fingers flew over the fretboard.

The band joined in as the vocals started and they blew that garage apart before they were done. Thor's singing would have made a dead man cry, and by the time they were done all of them were near tears.

They stood for a moment, quiet. Everyone was looking straight ahead, lost in his own thoughts, his own response to the passion of the song they had just shared. Tom spoke first.

"Oh... my... fucking... god!" he said.

"You don't just sound a little like Ricky Harris, man. You *are* fucking Ricky Harris!"

Thor stood staring at him, not having the slightest clue how to respond. His heart hammered in his chest. He couldn't think. Over four decades of not hearing that name and now this.

Suddenly, Eric slapped him on the back.

"I hope to shout!" Eric exclaimed. "He's the very embodiment of the guy! Wow! That was so spot on we sounded like a recording of Windy City!"

Thor smiled. His anxiety level subsided from DEFCON 1 to DEFCON 5 and he was able to breathe again. Tom's exuberance was only that, exuberance. He hadn't meant to accuse Thor of anything other than talent.

Thor grinned and blushed. "You guys have no idea what that means to me," he said. "I'm really flattered. "I thought I'd come in here and step on your toes and be the outsider, but you have all made me feel so welcome."

Bert came out from behind his drum set. "Man, you are a criminal waste of talent! You said the same thing about Larry, but you know what? Larry's gone on to his reward. We are the ones left standing, and man we can use you! Please say you'll join the band!"

Thor knew there was some weird destiny at work here. He felt it. Without sufficient forethought, he answered, "I'd be honored."

Chapter 6

*Your love burned into my heart, but the flames of your
betrayal took my soul.
Now I rise from the ashes of our love like a Phoenix,
yeah, like a Phoenix.
~ Phoenix*, Windy City

Thor played with Eric and the band for six weeks before they finally snagged a gig in a local bar that
had quite a live music following. He recognized the
venue from his early years in Seattle.

Back in the late '70s, it had been known as the Aquarius
Tavern. It was a Mecca for slightly better-than-local bands
and occasionally hosted a headliner in a very cozy, private
setting. Every single night of the week, the Aquarius was
packed to the rafters.

Long since, the Aquarius had given way to the original
name of the venue, Parker's Ballroom. By the late 90s it
was simply Parker's.

In the age of tribal casinos, Parker's went from a ballroom to a card room to a casino with no slots, to a dance
hall once again. And it was at this venue that Thor Swenson made his debut as lead singer and lead guitar of Dead
Salmon.

The venue was enormous for this type of gig. Easily
200 people sat at tables surrounding a great, hardwood
dance floor that could have doubled as a basketball court.

They set up on a raised dais in the center of the dance floor so that the patrons could surround the live music as they danced.

The ceilings were high and painted black so that the lights and wiring therein remained invisible in the darkened room. On the perimeter were four large bars, one on each wall. The former casino had been relegated to a big back room and a few gamblers came and went through the night, but they were not there to dance.

The band started with "Lazy" and finished the first set with "Under Pressure."

The drinks were free and gray as they were, women still came close to the stage and seemed to offer more than fat, middle-aged smiles. The band played on.

At last call, they were near the end of the final set and of course they played, "Phoenix." There were still many listeners at this hour, but most of the dance floor remained empty.

"Phoenix" was a ballad of lost love and lost opportunity. It was a song Ricky Harris had written long before he lived the lyrics for real. The pain in the song was clear in Thor's voice as he sang and there wasn't a dry eye in the house when he finished.

It was 2:30 and the bartenders were cleaning up and closing down for the night. Dead Salmon was packing away their gear and everyone was tired, not in the mood for conversation.

A gentleman of late middle age walked up to the band, his plump wife stayed back, in the shadows. He went straight to Thor.

"I want to shake your hand, sir," he said. Thor took the offered hand and shook it.

"I have never heard that song played or sung as it was tonight. It's our anniversary," he said and indicated the little woman standing in the shadows.

"Phoenix" was the song we lost our virginity to," he said. "It was the song we got engaged to.

"You sir, have made an old couple very happy," he finished. Thor smiled.

"Happy Anniversary," he told the man. "I'm touched that I could be a part of it," he said.

The man smiled and rejoined his wife and they left. Thor stood and watched them walk away. His mind was racing. He didn't know what to think. Math, music, teaching, it was all a blur suddenly. He looked at the guitar in his hand and realized he was supposed to do something with it, but he couldn't remember what. He set it in a nearby case and walked away, just as he had walked away forty-two years prior.

"Hey, Thor!" Eric called. "Hey man, where you going?"

Somewhere, off in the distance, Thor heard someone call his name. But he was lost in memories and he couldn't answer. Alice may have gone down a rabbit hole, but Thor was falling down a memory hole and the scene at the bottom of that hole was not a pleasant one.

He walked out into the darkness that was Aurora Avenue. It was after two in the morning and it was December, closing fast on Christmas. The night was clear and cold and Thor walked past his car in the lot and kept walking. He didn't know it, but he headed south toward the city and away from his home in Shoreline.

In all the weeks of practice with the band, Thor had been able to keep a distance that was comfortable. He had his house in the tony section of Shoreline called Richmond Beach, which he loved. He taught his fall quarter classes with enthusiasm. Finals week was upon him and he looked forward to the Christmas break while his students dreaded final exams.

His navy blue peacoat kept out the chill as the fog

slowly started to roll in off the Sound. The damp air began to work its magic on his thick, gray hair and soon his ponytail felt thicker and frizzier than before.

Thor wondered why just playing that one song, "Phoenix," made his heart race. He wondered why a man about his own age would come and shake his hand as if he'd done something miraculous or special. He thought about why he had deliberately sung "Phoenix" as though he owned it, as though he wrote it. He could have changed it up, ad-libbed a little, altered his voice some. But he didn't. He very specifically sang that song as he had so long ago. He sang to Angie. He wrote that song for her, long before he ever knew she would betray him. He wrote from the heart—he wrote his basest fear into that song. He saw that fear come true and it had colored every relationship he had thereafter.

The temperature started to drop in earnest and the fog was getting pretty serious, too. The streetlamps were old but held their own against the fog, and Thor walked on into the darkness.

He thought briefly about the band, about his guitars and equipment, but he knew that Eric and the guys would take care of those. They might wonder about his car still in the parking lot, but they would give him his space, he did not doubt.

A couple of months back, when he first began this escapade or folly or whatever you want to call it, Thor thought of joining the band as a game. He thought it was a chance to play his guitar and maybe sing a little and have some fun like he used to. He thought it might assuage some of the guilt he still held for not being able to save Larry when he'd had the chance.

Then it hit him like a brick upside the head. He was running away again. The mere thought of Angie, Windy City, Rufe, betrayal, had brought him to this, his only defense against the dark was to run away.

He'd run away from his boozing father all those years ago. Maturity had brought with it the realization that his father crawled into the bottle to escape the pain that Ricky's mother's death had caused them both. She ran off to join a commune in California and left her seven-year-old son and his bewildered father alone. Not long after, they received word that she died when her group's VW van plunged over a cliff on the way to Big Sur.

Ricky's dad got drunk in self-defense, and little Ricky Harris learned to run from abandonment. He sealed himself off from his dad and threw himself into whatever took his fancy.

Finally, at 15, destiny put an old guitar in his path, in a dumpster out behind the ramshackle apartment they lived in. He picked it up, took it home, and wondered how he would get the money to buy strings for it.

With his dad in a state of drunken confusion most of the time, Ricky learned to be self-sufficient early on. He got a paper route and spent his free time outside of school picking up bottles in the gutter along the road.

Sometimes, he'd fish them out of the dumpster too. When he had enough for a few bucks, he'd take them up to Mr. Nelson's store and turn them in for the deposit. He bought strings for the guitar and taught himself to play and pretty soon he was jamming with guys from school and before long, Windy City was born.

A gust of icy, wet wind tore Thor from his reverie and left him wondering where to go from here. He loved Dead Salmon, and he loved playing with them. He knew he couldn't just refuse to play Windy City hits. Aside from being an odd request, it would raise some red flags. They recognized his voice, though none of them realized it. Of all the songs in their repertoire, "Phoenix" was the best. It had to be with Thor playing lead and singing.

He realized he had two choices here, he could quit the band, let them think he was some weirdo, and go on with his life. Or, he could continue to play with this little aging, wannabe rock band as Thor Swenson and get over himself. He was no longer the man who had died some forty-odd years before, just as he'd intended.

When Thor finally looked up, he realized that he had no idea where he was. The fog had settled in for real and he couldn't see much beyond his outstretched arm. He pulled his cell phone from a pocket and dialed 411. He got a cab called and parked himself under a streetlamp so that the cabbie would be able to see him in the haze.

After a few cold minutes, a cab appeared and picked him up. He gave his address to the driver and climbed into the back seat. Thor felt more tired than he had in years. He fought to stay awake until finally, the car pulled into his driveway.

He got out and paid the driver, then dragged his feet to the front door and let himself in. He flipped on the light and was greeted by his fat brown tabby cat, Tim.

"Oh, jeez," he said. "Sorry, buddy." He went to the kitchen and opened a tin of cat food and dumped it into Tim's bowl. Tim purred his appreciation and went to work eating his extremely late dinner.

Chapter 7

Mick alternately loved and hated his nickname. Michael Thorne, as he had been christened, was a fine family name. Mick was a shortening of the name, but also a jab at his Irish roots. Now, at the age of 65, Mick was supposed to be retired. But, like an old horse, he would last much longer if he continued to be of use. He wanted to work. He liked to fish, and occasionally liked to camp, but let's get real kids. Old bones don't do so well in sleeping bags on hardpan, covered only by a canvas tent.

Golf is what some old cops do when they retired, but Mick had never been into golf and the prospect of taking it up now was intensely off-putting.

Mick's forte was investigation. He wasn't about to stop now. In fact, retirement was ultimately freeing. He had no more day-to-day grind, no more policies, and procedures to adhere to. For the most part, Mick was a free man. Free to pursue anything he liked. What he liked was the chance to prove his old theory that Ricky Harris, frontman for Windy City, did most certainly not die in the Ship Canal between Lake Union and Puget Sound on that bitching cold night in '75.

His 2004 Ford Taurus had seen better days, and its once silver paint job had faded to a dull gray. There were dents and dings in it, and it made a little more of a growl when first starting than it used to but it ran, and it got him where he wanted to go. He didn't see the point in getting a brand-new car at his age. Anyway, Stephen would likely take his keys away in not too many more years and that was just fine with Mick.

The interior smelled of mildew and desiccated French fries. The driver's seat was worn through in spots, but Mick still found it cupped his butt comfortably. He listened to the radio as he drove. KZOK still played the oldies, classic rock they called it. It had to be an omen that at this very moment, Windy City's biggest hit, *Phoenix*, was playing and he sang along. The sun was out after a morning-long battle with the marine layer, aka fog, that reliably rolled in off the Sound overnight this time of year.

He drove downtown, straight to the bland concrete structure on 4th Avenue that housed, among other things, the King County Jail, Midtown Seattle Police Precinct, Seattle Property Room, and Evidence Vault. Though written reports and witness affidavits were long since transferred to digital media, there were still some written records from back in the 70s.

The Ricky Harris case had been closed a long time, but Mick had taken special care to make sure that the boxes of scant physical evidence were never sent to storage, and when the time came, not destroyed. By the time that evidence box had aged out of existence, Mick Thorne was a detective and a name known to all in the Department. He had enough clout to make sure it stayed with the active evidence, even if it was shoved into a dusty corner and generally forgotten. Over the years, he'd managed to get down to check on it from time to time, just to make sure it was still there. He knew exactly when he would come for it and now was that time.

Mick pulled the gray sedan into the underground parking. His parking permit was still good for another two months. Even though he was retired, he knew no one would question it.

He locked the car and stashed his keys in his pocket. He walked past the elevators because where he was headed was down here in the bowels of the building.

He went through an unmarked glass door and walked down a short, unadorned hall with beige tile flooring that would have looked more at home in someone's kitchen. At the end of the hall was a closed metal door that bore a sign: "*Evidence.*"

He opened the door and faced a stocky police sergeant sitting behind a metal countertop and behind inch-thick Plexiglas. He looked around 40, balding, and was studying some papers in front of him. The nametag on his shirt read, *Hawes.* He didn't seem to notice Mick had entered.

He was absently dunking a half-eaten cake donut in a coffee cup and slurping a bite every few seconds. Mick dismissed his thoughts of obvious cliché and instead envied the man his snack.

There was an indent in the countertop in front of him and the Plexiglas ended about 2 inches above the indent. This would permit someone to pass an object or document in to the sergeant.

To Mick's left was another metal door, which he knew led into the evidence vault. He also knew the sergeant at the desk very well. He knocked on the countertop and the sergeant looked up.

"Mick Thorne! What are you doing down here in the dark?" he asked affably. "It's good to see you! I thought you were retired now. Aren't you?"

Mick chuckled. "It's good to see you too, Leroy. Yes, I'm retired. Just since last month, but it seems longer." He smiled. "I'm down here in the basement because I would like to check something out."

Leroy's cheerful demeanor faded just a little. He

rubbed his chin. "Oh, I don't know, Mick. You got a written request?" He looked worried, probably guessing that he was about to be asked to do something that was not altogether on the up-and-up.

"Yes, of a sort," said Mick. He pulled a slip of paper from the pocket of his wool coat and passed it through the indented tray in the countertop.

Leroy picked it up and scrutinized the little piece of paper with a squint. "This looks pretty old," he said. "I don't think I've ever seen a file number that short and I know this form hasn't been used in at least 20 years." He looked at Mick and back down at the paper in his hand. "Is this legit?"

Mick nodded. "It's legit. I've been carrying that slip of paper around for forty years, Leroy. Now that I'm retired, I'd like to have another look at the evidence in the box so labeled. I can tell you where to find it if you like," he offered.

Leroy got a little serious at that and set the last bite of the donut down. He turned toward the computer on his desk and typed rapidly for a few seconds. He scanned the computer screen with the same intense squint as he had the slip. He looked flustered as he turned back to Mick.

"Do you mean to tell me that there is a box of evidence from a forty-year-old, closed accidental death in here?"

"That's exactly what I'm telling you. And I have authority to take possession of it, which is what I am here to do. Leroy, if you would be so kind as to get it for me. You can find it in the far south corner, behind the last row of shelves, next to the printer."

Leroy got out of his chair with some effort and headed back into the evidence vault behind a short wall. He was out of sight in an instant and was gone for a full ten minutes.

Mick heard muffled voices but couldn't make out what

they were saying. Leroy was sharing his bewildering tale with a co-worker, no doubt. After a few minutes, Mick sat in one of the two chairs that leaned against one wall just in front of the counter. The space was little more than a vestibule and it seemed silly that they would have guest chairs there, but as Mick sat down, he was grateful to take a load off.

He wondered if, by some twist of fate, the box had finally gone to be destroyed. Without the physical evidence as a starting place, Mick knew his progress on following his hunch would be slow indeed. After 40 years, he did not want to contemplate such a setback.

Finally, Sergeant Hawes returned carrying two worn and very dusty banker's boxes with taped-down lids and looking as though they weighed a combined ton. It seemed unlikely that the boxes contained anything all that heavy and Mick hadn't considered that he might not be able to carry them. He'd forgotten that there were two.

Hawes set the boxes on his side of the counter, opened the door, and holding the door with his foot, hefted the boxes again and brought them out into the vestibule. Breathing hard, he set them on the ground at Mick's feet.

"You're gonna have to sign for it," he panted.

Mick produced a pen from his shirt pocket, but Hawes waved him away. "It's an e-signature. You can do it on this box with your finger." He produced a wireless device, not unlike those delivery drivers often use to have customers sign for packages.

Familiar with the procedure, Mick scrawled a signature with his index finger. He marveled at the accuracy of the signature and the technology that permitted it. It was similarly advanced technology that he hoped would help him prove his theory about this case.

He handed the device back to Hawes, thanked him, and fished his car keys from his pocket before bending to lift the boxes. They were heavy, but not so heavy that he couldn't manage them. He decided that Sergeant Hawes needed to get more exercise.

He took the boxes back to his car, set them in the trunk, and closed the lid. Mick wanted nothing more than to rip each of them open and look again at the evidence collected that long-ago night, but it would have to wait until he got home. He had waited this long, the twenty-minute trip home wasn't going to make a big difference.

He drove carefully, somehow wanting to avoid jostling the contents of the two boxes. It's not as though he was transporting a body, but he felt responsible for his cargo nonetheless. Someone had died all those years ago, and he wanted to find out who it had been. Then he wanted to find out where Ricky Harris had managed to end up.

Mick decided to make two trips from the garage into the den. The boxes were not terribly heavy, but they were unwieldy enough to make progress on the stairs a little dodgy.

He set the second one down and turned to open the drapes. He had the overhead light on as well as the lamp by his desk. He wanted to be able to see every detail. Turning to the heavy wooden desk, he opened the top drawer and withdrew a box of disposable surgical gloves. While the evidence inside these boxes was long since compromised, he did not wish to add to the problem.

Both boxes had copious handwriting on their respective lids. Most of that was illegible at this point. It was just notes from the few investigators that had handled the evidence when the case was still open.

Mick took an X-acto® blade from the penholder on the desk and cut the tape holding each lid to its box. He returned the blade and sat on the floor next to the boxes as he lifted the lid from the first one.

On top was a folded rich brown buckskin jacket. It was

dry, stiff, and crusty with age. Getting thoroughly soaked in ice water, then put in a plastic bag had certainly not helped the leather. There was a film of dusty mold over most of it, too.

Mick turned his head and took a breath. He really didn't want to breathe in that mold, but it was most likely harmless dust. The sun came in and warmed his back and he shifted to the other side of the boxes to get comfortable. The high leaded-glass window was original Victorian era as was the Queen Anne Hill home where he lived. That window and its fellows around the house let in plenty of warmth when the rare Seattle sun was out, but they also let in plenty of cold at other times.

The jacket was definitely vintage rock and roll attire. It was a dark brown buckskin with a long fringe across the shoulders in the back and down both arms. Mick remembered a time when he would have killed to own such a thing. He fished in the exterior pockets of the jacket. They were empty as expected, same with the interior breast pocket in the lining, nothing in there but a couple of long, light-colored hairs. He held one up and looked at it. He wondered then whether a forensic scientist could obtain any viable DNA from such a hair sample. He stripped off the gloves and went to his computer. Google is your friend, he thought.

After a quick search, Mick learned that there is not a lot of data to be found regarding forty-year-old DNA samples. He also learned that the likelihood of these hairs producing usable DNA was slim to none. Still, he put more gloves on and set the jacket aside. He would find out just how degraded that DNA was.

Beneath the jacket was a gallon-sized plastic bag containing the keys to the car, a wallet, the rental packet (now dried out), and a hotel room key that had to be for a room at the Edgewater Inn.

Mick removed the wallet. Like the jacket, its leather had seen better days and had not fared well underwater. He opened it and looked at the scant contents.

Inside there was an Illinois driver's license that had expired in 1976. It bore a photograph of a very young man with long blonde hair. He was grinning like a fool and clearly had not been taking the photographer seriously. There was also, oddly Mick thought, an expired Professional Musician's Union card. Mick hadn't known there was any such thing. He returned to the computer.

As it happens, there was and is such a thing, and Ricky Harris was a card-carrying member.

The rest of the wallet's contents consisted of a few credit cards. That was it. No cash had been found on the body, which fact even Harris's bandmates had found strange. Apparently, Ricky always carried cash.

"Well if you are going to kill someone, you might as well take their money," Mick said. "The dead don't need it." He put the wallet back in the bag.

The now-empty fifth of Jack Daniels was also in this evidence box. Its vintage label looked funny to Mick. Not that he would have been unfamiliar with it in the early seventies, but it was quite different nowadays.

He remembered that the paramedics mentioned that the body smelled of booze even after being in the water for so long. Some of the stains on the jacket were probably bourbon. *Which begs the question,* Mick thought. If I wanted to make something look like an accident, wouldn't I make sure the guy behind the wheel of the car appeared good and loaded? Why, yes, I would. It seemed fortuitous that Ricky just happened to have a bottle of booze on him at the time. Or was the guy in the car really drunk? Maybe when Ricky decided to fake his death, he killed a bum. Wouldn't a bum already be three sheets to the wind by that time of night? Of course. But the amount of alcohol readily available at the hotel put paid to that notion. Ricky had the liquor with him when he put the dead guy in the car. He planted that bottle, just as he planted his own wallet.

There were a few other things on the first box: the t-shirt and jeans of the dead man, his boots, and his underwear. None of that was of interest to Mick. He wanted the jacket for the slim hope of DNA—that was the only reason.

The second box had only paperwork: depositions from all of the band members and their technical people, agents, and hangers-on who traveled with the band. The reports from the officers on the scene that night were there too, including Mick's own.

He selected the files that held the depositions of Angela Gardiner, Rufus Priest, Don Ziemann, and Craig Wyman, the surviving members of Windy City. He took them to his desk and sat down. He put on his reading glasses and sat back, opening Angela's file first.

The detective who had questioned the band was thorough enough to speak to them individually, but he had no reason to suspect foul play, and he had kept the questions as routine as possible, it seemed.

His notes described Ms. Gardiner as "hysterical at times," "sobbing uncontrollably," "mumbling about forgiveness." The interviewer, a Detective Barrows, managed to coax from the grieving woman a story about how Ricky had caught her in bed with Priest and stormed out of the hotel in anger. She sounded as though she felt responsible for his death. Suicide? That was a possibility that had not occurred to Mick in all these years. There were times when he thought maybe, just maybe, he was wrong, and Harris died in a tragic drunken accident and that was that. But his gut feeling that things were otherwise never fully went away.

Was it possible that Ricky Harris had stumbled upon

the canal and deliberately driven over the edge? Was he so drunk that he just decided to end it all? Mick wondered.

But that still wouldn't explain why the body had been so badly abused before it went into the drink. Maybe Harris had found a late-night pub and managed to get himself into a fight. Problem is, there was no late-night pub anywhere near the canal in 1975. If Harris was that drunk, he would have never made it that far in his rental car. He'd have crashed or been pulled over first.

Suicide over a cheating woman, while plausible, just didn't answer enough of the other nagging questions. Mick promptly discarded that theory.

Rufus Priest had corroborated Angela's version nearly word for word. They were both spaced out on God-knows-what drugs that night, not to mention had been drinking, so it wasn't possible that they could have agreed on a version of the story beforehand. There wouldn't have been enough time.

Ziemann and Wyman had been in another room entirely and only barely recalled Ricky stopping in for a few minutes looking for Angela. He hadn't even sat down. They didn't see him again until they went to identify his body in the morgue.

Mick stopped reading and sat back in his old leather chair. He scratched his chin then rubbed absently at his temple, trying to imagine the scene in his mind.

Ricky walks into the room, exchanges a few words with Don, and then exits and makes for his own room down the hall. He walks in on the Angela-Rufus tryst and becomes enraged. He leaves the hotel and gets in his rental car and starts to drive.

Where's he going? No place, because he's emotionally wrecked and freaking out about his next move. What's he going to do now? His girl and his best friend have betrayed him, he's drunk and/or high and in an unfamiliar city in the middle of the night.

He winds up at the Fremont Bridge and…what? Sees a drunk transient and gets an idea? Maybe, although it was awfully cold that night. Transients, even drunken ones, would be holed up someplace trying to stay warm.

How did the dead man get beat up? Did Ricky find him already dead and decide then what to do, or did he kill the poor guy who was in the wrong place at the wrong time? So many questions yet to be answered.

Mick got up and poured himself a short drink. He'd been reading for hours and it was nearly four o'clock in the afternoon.

He went to the document box and rifled through the contents until he came to the medical examiner's report. He took it back to the desk with his drink and sat down to read.

The coroner's findings were not remarkable in that the blood work showed the deceased did have alcohol and traces of marijuana in his system. He had water in his lungs, sufficient to have drowned him.

The abrasions and contusions on his face and upper body were consistent with an automobile accident, according to the report. Mick wasn't so sure. But at least when he entered the water, the guy was still alive. He was just alive enough to have drowned. Was he unconscious? It seemed so. He was found behind the wheel, still clutching the bottle of booze. That doesn't sound like a struggle to free oneself from the sinking car.

The report made no mention of possible hypothermia. Mick supposed that drowning made the man dead, whether he'd been freezing somewhat beforehand was moot. He carefully repacked all of the reports, statements, and other paperwork. He'd read them all more than once over the years and had long since formed his own theories about what happened that night.

He looked at the clock again and saw that he'd been studying and cogitating for six more hours, not even stopping for dinner. He concluded the marathon. Nothing in either of the boxes was sufficient evidence to prove his theory wrong or right. He finished his fourth drink and took himself to bed.

ຂໆຂໆຂໆ

The next morning, after a hearty breakfast of eggs, sausage and hash browns washed down with copious amounts of strong, black coffee, Mick felt ready to continue his investigation.

He sat down at his old desk and pulled an ancient Rolodex to him. He began flipping through the hundreds of alphabetized business cards and handwritten address cards. He paused at the letter H and flipped through the cards individually until he found what he was looking for.

Cole, Susan J., Forensic Pathologist, the card read. He punched her office number into his cell phone. She didn't answer, and it went to voice mail.

"Sue, hi!" Mick said. "It's Mick Thorne. Remember at my retirement party, when I asked you to stand by because I might need your help with an old case? Well, guess what? I'm calling to get your help. It's just an old cold case I'm working on as a hobby now that I'm retired. It would be great if you could spare me a little time. Thanks. Give me a call when you have a minute. Bye." He hung up.

He thought about his recent retirement party. His partner of ten years, Chuck Wilson had given him a great send-off. He even got a little teary-eyed, which for someone like Chuck was a big deal.

Chuck was six feet two and fairly slender. He tried to stay fit, but at forty-five, he was finding that more and more difficult. Where Mick had gone largely bald, Chuck had a full head of graying brown hair which he kept neatly short. He had sported a trim beard for a number of years but recently had shaved it off.

The incongruity of their physical statures earned the two detective partners the nicknames Mutt and Jeff. It was good-natured though, and they enjoyed the jest.

Mick was always intensely serious about the work. Chuck took a more lighthearted approach, only really digging in like a terrier when they were getting close to a collar. The contrasting work styles made for a seamless partnership. Mick knew that Chuck was going to feel the void even more than he could admit.

Chuck raised his glass high. "To my partner of ten years, my friend and my mentor, Mick Thorne. Happy retirement, buddy! We'll all miss you, but me most of all." Mick was deeply touched.

"You can't get rid of me that easily," he said with a smile. "We'll still take those annual August fishing trips to Twin Lakes, right?" he asked hopefully.

"Oh, hell yeah!" Chuck agreed. Much laughter and applause followed the exchange and Chuck was able to pull himself together. He talked on for a while about some of the cases they'd cracked, risks they had taken, and adventures they had shared over the years in what may have been the longest toast ever. Most people gave up and drank before he was finished. It was a great sendoff, indeed.

Mick got up and opened the drapes to let in the gray morning light. He scarcely had time to fetch a last cup of coffee when his phone rang. It was Sue.

"Mick! It's so good to hear from you," she said. "I remember our talk. I'm ready to help out with anything you like, as long as you know I'm doing it in my spare time, off the clock, right?"

"Absolutely. I wouldn't have it any other way," he said.

"I'm taking another look at that case from seventy-five,

where the rock star drove his rental car into the canal. You know the one I'm talking about?"

Sue was easily twenty years younger than Mick, but she'd been at the state Pathology Lab for the past 17 years and she'd heard all the stories. She knew what he meant.

"Of course! Everyone's heard that story. The Ricky Harris death story is Seattle rock and roll legend at this point. There's even an exhibit at the EMP about it."

"Yes, I've heard about that. I was a fan," he said. "So, I have the old evidence boxes here and I found some hairs on the deceased's leather jacket. I'm wondering if you could try to get some DNA from them."

"Well I can try," Sue said. "But it's a long shot."

"Oh I know," Mick told her. "And I don't have any DNA to compare it with since the case is so old, but I thought it would be the right place to start anyway."

"Sure, Mick. It will be fun to play a small part in a modern-day forensic investigation of history," Sue told him.

Chapter 8

Mory Taglio was an old man. He'd run a good business in Seattle for many years, and he was a respected member of the Italian-American community in the region. He'd been in the state of Washington long enough to have seen a Rosellini in the governor's mansion, for chrissakes.

His right-hand man, Tony D had been with him for much of that time. Tony had risen up through the ranks of Mory's company and had been a true and loyal employee for decades. Now the two of them sat in Mory's home office, enjoying an early afternoon cordial.

Mory was old, but he was also wealthy. His early days in abandoned warehouses and closet-sized office spaces were long behind him. His home on Mercer Island was only a few minutes from the Gates estate. He belonged to the same country clubs as many of the Microsoft millionaires he called neighbors.

Mory's home office was unabashedly modern with high ceilings and expensive lighting. A brightly-colored Dale Chihuly glass sculpture filled a recess in the wall specially built to show it off.

Tony D sat in a lavish, leather guest chair, opposite Mory's imported Swedish-built mahogany desk. He sipped at the cognac Mory had supplied. Long since Tony D had become accustomed to such luxuries.

"Tony," Mory began. "It has come to my attention that our good friend, Rocco, has been having some sort of senile episodes."

Tony looked up. "Episodes?" he asked.

"It seems," Mory went on, "that Rocco has been bragging about a certain hit. A hit from many years ago that ended clean as a whistle," Mory said. "Tony, do you remember such a hit from long ago?"

"I can't say that I do," Tony said tentatively.

"Sure, you do," said Mory. "Thor the Viking, remember?"

Tony's face went pale. He took a good slug of the cognac. He paused while it seeped, burning, down his throat. The calming effect he expected did not occur. The thought of that long hair pulling Thor's body from the water, then putting it in a car and sending it back into the water, made him cringe. It hadn't been until the next day when they saw the headlines that Tony D and Rocco had figured out who the long hair was that night. It was Ricky Harris of Windy City, faking his own death. Oh, how they had laughed at that! Ricky never knew that his every move had been witnessed by a couple of guys whose only interest was in ending a certain Thor the Viking.

"Why the f-f-fuck would he bring that shit up now?" Tony stammered.

"Why the fuck, indeed. I submit that our old friend Rocco has begun to lose it in his dotage," Mory said. "It is very important to me that this, shall we say, ancient indiscretion, remain buried in the past. Do you understand where I am coming from, Tony?"

"Yes sir!" Tony said, straightening in his chair. "I take it you would like me to disabuse Rocco of his reminiscing?" he asked.

"Precisely," Mory replied.

"I understand. Consider it done, Boss."

Tony D got up to leave, and as he approached the handsome, heavy, paneled oak door, Mory said, "And Tony, please make sure our old friend does not suffer. That would not be right."

"You can count on me, Boss," Tony said. He left the room and Mory knew the issue was now resolved.

෧෨෧෨

About an hour later, Tony was driving across the Snohomish River bridge on Highway 522, heading east. The spring weather was clear and bright, and the view was spectacular. As he sped along the bridge, he could see bald eagles in the trees above the river, fishing or hunting for the small animals that came down to the river to drink. Not far in the distance, the Cascade Range rose above the river in all its rugged, snow-covered glory.

Tony thought Rocco was lucky to have ended up in Twin Rivers Correctional instead of Walla Walla State Penitentiary in the opposite corner of the state. Here in Monroe, he was close enough that Tony had been able to visit him over the years. Rocco was doing a life stretch, even though none of the hits he was credited with had ever been legally pinned on him. No, Rocco was sent away for life for breaking and entering. Washington has a "three strikes and you're out" law, and Rocco struck out some ten years back.

At first, Tony had made time to visit every week. They had been friends and business partners for decades, having started working for Mory right out of high school back in Brooklyn.

Over the years though, the visits became fewer until now Tony could barely remember the last time he'd come. Rocco's phone calls had dwindled, too and the unintentional fading out of each other's lives appeared mutual.

The entrance to the prison was less than a block from the bottom of the off-ramp and Tony arrived a few minutes after crossing the picturesque Snohomish River bridge. He went through the security procedures, enduring a half-hearted pat-down, security wanding, and a quick trip through the metal detector. He thought it ironic that he had received more stringent security checks at the airport.

He signed in and followed the guard to the visitors' area. Tony had come unarmed. He had every intention of carrying out his boss's orders, but for old times' sake, he could not and would not dirty his own hands. There were plenty of acquaintances inside that would be happy to take the job for a small deposit into their accounts. Tony had decided in the car that he would have Dean Reynolds take care of business for him. Dean was an old friend and would have no trouble taking Rocco aside when the opportunity arose.

Tony sat in one of the empty plastic chairs on the visitor's side of a long Plexiglas divider. Each side had an old-fashioned telephone receiver to allow conversation. He didn't wait long before a guard escorted Rocco into the room on the other side of the divider. Rocco was smiling at this unexpected visit.

He and Tony were the same age, 67, but Tony felt that he had weathered the transition from youth to old age much better than Rocco. Maybe because Rocco had been in the joint for a while, he was showing his age more, who knows? Rocco's once thick black hair was thin to the point that the top of his head was shiny beneath the few wisps of gray that were failing in their attempt to cover it. His face was haggard with obvious jowls drawing it southward and his once-chiseled features were now crisscrossed with deep lines.

He sat down and picked up the phone on his side. "Tony, what a pleasant surprise!" he said. Tony returned the smile.

"Well, I hadn't been up here for quite a while and I was wondering how you are getting along. They treating you OK up here, Rocco?"

"Can't complain," said Rocco. "Most of the young guys, they leave us 'old school' types alone. That's what they call us, you know, 'old school.'"

Tony nodded. "I guess we are. So, Rocco, Mory heard that you have been reminiscing about the old days, is that right? You been telling the stories from back in the day when we were out there tearing up the town?" His smile was gone and had been replaced with a questioning frown.

Rocco must have noticed the change in tone because his own smile evaporated as fast as a drop of water in a hot iron skillet. He cleared his throat and looked down. "I may have, you know, when somebody asks," he offered.

It was enough and really, Tony thought, not necessary. What had to be done, had to be done and no admission or confession from Rocco would change that. He nodded again.

"I can see how spending time up here, day after day, might get you thinking about the old days. You want to share. I get it, Rocco. I just want to let you know that Mory would prefer if we let sleeping dogs lie. No point in dredging up the past now, is there?"

Rocco looked encouraged. "No, there sure isn't!" he said with enthusiasm and apparent relief.

Tony exhaled. Poor bastard thought the verbal admonition was the end of it. Maybe it was just as well.

"I can't stay, Rocco. I just wanted to see how you are doing and deliver Mory's message. You take care now, my old friend." He held his free hand out as if to shake Rocco's, and Rocco pretended to return the shake from his side of the glass.

"Thanks, Tony. And thanks for coming. I will be

mindful about this, and I appreciate it."

He rose from the chair on his side of the divider and a guard appeared to escort him back to his cell. Tony rose too, but only until Rocco was out of sight. Then he sat down again.

A few minutes later the guard returned, escorting a second prisoner to the chair Rocco had just vacated. A slight, fortyish man with fine brown hair and wire-rimmed glasses sat down. He appeared nervous and twitchy, just as Tony remembered him. He was breathing hard as though he'd just run a few blocks, but Tony knew it was his usual state. Dean Reynolds seemed perpetually on a coke trip. He was wired and on edge all of the time. He just was.

"How come you want to see me?" he asked, that nervous edge in his voice coming through the phone just fine.

"I got a job for you, Dean," Tony said. "It won't take long, and you will be well compensated—half now and the other half after.

"Do tell."

The two men talked through the phones for a few more minutes, then Tony hung up the receiver and turned to leave. He took another deep breath. It was as good as done. He felt a faint pang of sadness, but it was brief and by the time he got back out to his car, it was almost gone.

Chapter 9

In an upscale condo in Chicago's Lincoln Park, a gray-haired couple sat sipping tea and enjoying a light breakfast. They spoke little and barely looked at each other as they ate.

Rufus and Angela had been married for more than 35 years and they had become almost a single unit, as long-married couples often do. The silence between them wasn't awkward, far from it. It was the companionable lack of need to speak to fill the empty spaces.

When they were both nearly finished with breakfast, Angie got up to refill her teacup. "Want some more?" she asked.

Rufe held out his cup. "There's something I need to tell you," he said as she poured. Angie didn't reply and put the teapot back on the gas burner, turned off though it was.

The morning light came in, reflecting off the lake, and bathed them in its golden glow. Angie sat down again, her long hair silver now instead of black. She took a sip from her freshened tea, then reached across the marble table and took Rufe's hand. "Whatever it is, we'll face it together," she said, smiling.

In the years since the band broke up, Rufus had lost most of his frizzy, curly white-guy 'fro, and gained not a few pounds. His beer gut preceded him into a room and his sagging jowls did nothing for his already rugged features.

He'd wondered more than once over the years why a beauty like Angie had chosen him, of all people.

The night Ricky died in Seattle was little more than a hazy, half-forgotten dream anymore. Rufe had given Angie some acid and dropped a dot himself when they realized that Ricky wasn't coming back from the venue any time soon that night.

They never intended to end up in bed, and neither of them had any recollection of sex. In the morning, it had all been about Ricky.

Rufe looked across the table at the woman he loved, still holding his hand this random morning in December. Their home was beautifully and tastefully appointed, and not without its finer points. It gave the appearance of wealth although Rufus knew better. The years had been kind to them financially. Even after the band broke up, the royalties had come steadily in for many years.

Ricky had left Angela a substantial insurance payout, and they had invested the proceeds from that to their benefit. It was that money, that margin that they lived on for decades after Windy City was no more. And now it was mostly gone.

"What do you want to tell me, love?" Angie asked.

Rufe had been mulling over how to broach the subject with her for many weeks. He'd rehearsed the conversation in his head more times than he could count. In his imagination, her response was never positive. He decided that the best course of action was simply to spit it out.

"We're out of money," he said.

Angie threw her head back and laughed. Her musical laugh always sent a thrill straight to Rufe's heart and today was no different.

She composed herself but couldn't hide her mirth even so. She sipped at her tea. "I know," was all she said.

"You know?"

She set her cup down and pushed her chair back, regarding him seriously. "Of course, I know. Just because I've let you handle the finances all these years doesn't mean I haven't kept track of things.

"I know the royalty checks stopped coming years ago. After 9/11 when the market tanked, we took some big hits. I know all of that."

Rufus was taken aback. "Why didn't you say anything?" he asked.

Angie frowned. "What was there to say? We're not getting any younger, we are old news on the music front, and neither of us has any other way of earning a living. What would you have me say?"'

Rufus looked out the dining room window at their expansive view. They owned the condo outright and in the present market, it would fetch a pretty penny. That would be a start, but it would hardly be enough to sustain them in the coming years as they began to require assistance and medical bills started to pile up. He sighed.

"I've been thinking about our next move," he said. Angie cocked her head and looked at him quizzically.

"Move? You don't mean selling this place?"

"I won't say it hasn't occurred to me. We could live off of the profit for quite a while."

"I know," she said quietly. She looked down into her teacup and sighed.

"But that's not what I've got in mind," Rufe went on. "I spoke to Ray last week. He liked my idea, and he's going to contact Don and Craig."

Angie looked up. "Oh, you can't be serious?" she said. "Get the band back together? That's your grand plan?" She rose from the table and put her cup and saucer in the sink. "Jesus Christ, Rufe! I don't think I could so much as carry a tune in a bucket at this point! Who's going to sing lead? Hell, *play* lead? We never found a replacement for Ricky because he was irreplaceable! How do you expect to do it now?" She looked at him and seemed to be waiting for a response. Her eyes held unshed tears.

Rufe wished he'd never brought it up, but there was no turning back now. He knew that she'd never stopped loving Ricky. If Ricky walked through that door right now, she'd run to him without hesitation. He knew it. He'd always known it. Angie had been kind enough over the many years of their marriage to never once utter Ricky's name, until right now. But the fact of the matter was that she was correct. The band broke up because without Ricky, there really was no Windy City. He was the voice, he was the guitar, he was the band. Don wrote most of the songs, but Ricky gave them life. In his darkest thoughts, Rufus felt somehow responsible for Ricky's death. He knew it had been a horrible accident but had Ricky not caught them giving in to their high, which is really all it had been, he would never have left the hotel that night and ended up driving his car into the water.

"Ray thinks we should have a contest," he offered lamely. "A nationwide contest to find a new lead singer. He said the publicity from that alone will generate CD sales again."

Angie shook her head. She was crying. "I don't want to go into some old folk's home relying on our Social Security," she said. "Is this really the only way out?" She looked up and wiped fiercely at her tears.

"It may not be the only way out," Rufe said, "but it's the fastest way for sure. The landline rang, and Angie went into the living room to answer it.

She spoke into the phone quietly, then held it out to Rufe. "It's Ray."

Rufe took the phone. "Hey, Ray." He listened for a few minutes, mumbling uh-huh from time to time. He saw that Angie watched him, unmoving. Her expression was unreadable, but he noticed she no longer appeared to be crying.

Rufe stared at the bookcases, the Steinway grand piano in the corner, and the gold records on the wall. The leaded glass French doors that opened onto a small terrace over-looking the lake were ajar. He felt the breeze coming in and shivered.

"They're all in, both of them," Ray was saying. Ray Adler had been Windy City's manager from day one. He had met Ricky in a bar so long ago now, that the band members no longer remembered who had first approached whom.

"Cool," said Rufe.

"I'm in talks with the record company now. It looks like they are intrigued by the contest idea. We'll get it out to all the classic rock stations. You and the rest of the band will do a tour of the major cities for the auditions. You, Angie, Don, and Craig will be the only judges.

"It's going to be huge, Rufe!" Ray said. "You guys will be a household name again pretty soon. The company is even thinking about a reality show surrounding the con-test. How cool is that?" Ray's excitement was barely con-tained.

Angie shook her head and went back into the kitchen.

"Sounds fantastic!" Rufe said. "Keep me posted." He hung up and followed Angie.

"You overheard?" he asked.

"Most of it," Angie replied.

"A contest? In this day and age? Who are we kidding, Rufe?"

"I think the contestants will likely be our age," he said. "But what's wrong with that? If Ricky were alive, he'd be no spring chicken now either."

She seemed to give that some thought. "I guess you're right. I never really picture him as anyway, but how we last saw him," she said.

Rufe sat down. "I know. I do the same."

They left it there and spent most of the rest of the morning lost in their own thoughts.

Chapter 10

The bright sunlight that found its way into the room through the slightest crack in the curtains failed to wake him, but Tim's insistent head butts to the face did the trick.

Thor rolled over and looked at the clock on the table beside the bed. It read 12:00 PM. Shit. It wasn't a school day of course, and he'd been out quite late, but that still meant he'd slept for nine hours. Nine hours and he hadn't even been drinking. Wow.

He got out of bed and went straight to the kitchen to get the cat food breakfast that old, fat Tim had worked so hard to obtain. The cat hopped up on the granite-topped island, purring his loud roaring purr and swishing his tail impatiently. That leap was no mean feat for a cat of Tim's girth and it spoke to his addiction to dry cat food. Thor set the bowl down and gave Tim an affectionate rub before heading back upstairs to take a shower.

When he got out of the shower a few minutes later he realized someone was ringing the doorbell. "I'm coming!" he yelled and dressed quickly.

He opened the door and was only mildly surprised to see Eric standing there. "Did I wake you?" he asked.

"No, the cat beat you to it by a couple of minutes. Come on in." He shut the door behind Eric and went to the kitchen. "I was just going to get some coffee, would you like some?"

Eric smiled. "Uh, yeah, it's not really morning anymore for me. I'm all good on the coffee front, thanks."

Neither man spoke as Thor went about preparing his coffee. Thor was pretty sure he knew why Eric was there, he had walked away after the gig without so much as a by-your-leave. He went over the already prepared excuse in his head as he poured his first cup.

Eric had seated himself at the table and waited patiently until Thor joined him. He was looking out the window at Tim, who had finished eating and popped out through the cat door cut into the side door of the house, just off the kitchen. The cat was already getting busy stalking a crow that was strutting around the trash cans at the end of the driveway. Thor followed Eric's gaze and laughed.

"I don't think the crow has anything to worry about. Tim's so fat he couldn't catch a cold," he said.

Never one to beat around the bush, Eric blurted out, "So where'd you go last night?"

Thor had practiced his response, but he was still a little startled by the abruptness of the question. He took a sip of coffee and sighed.

"I don't know. I finally called a cab, not sure where I ended up. On the Aurora Bridge, I think."

Eric raised an appreciative eyebrow. "That's a long walk from Parker's!"

"Yes, it was. And it was cold and foggy, and I got turned around pretty quick." He took another sip of coffee, starting to feel more awake.

"Look, Thor," Eric began. "I guess it's none of my business, but it was kind of weird the way you just walked out of there. We packed up your stuff and I made sure your car was locked, but that was all we could do."

Thor sighed again. "Yeah, I'm really sorry about that. I appreciate what you guys did. And, for the record, it is your business. I can't just play a gig with you and then leave you to do all the packing up at the end." He stared down into the blackness of the cup.

"It was the encore, *Phoenix*, that did it. Well, that man at the end, thanking me for singing it. It just hit me all of a sudden, flew all over me as my grandmother would have said. This man was thanking me, *me*, for singing that song and bringing back memories for him and his wife. And all I could think of was that it should have been Larry up there getting the accolades, not me. I just…I wasn't sure at that moment if I wanted to keep doing this.

"I'm a teacher, Eric. It's what I do, what I love. I enjoy playing and singing and hanging with the band, I really do, but it is and will always be an avocation for me, nothing more. That man made me feel like a star for just a moment. That moment belonged to Larry, not to me. And to the rest of you guys, too."

Nothing Thor was saying was untrue, he was simply leaving out the important part of why that particular song should so easily cut him to the quick.

Eric looked straight at him, brown eyes meeting blue. "Wow. I guess I never realized how hard you took Larry's death. You have to remember we didn't even know you existed until he died. I didn't really take into account that you lost a good friend, too."

Thor nodded. Eric was buying it and that was enough.

"For what it's worth, I did a lot of soul searching on my long walk last night and I realized that I was making much too big a deal out of it. This is supposed to be fun, right? So, someone enjoyed my singing, so what? How can I feel anything but good about that, you know? This morning I have a whole different outlook. I needed to take that walk, but I do apologize for leaving the rest of you in the lurch. It was pretty fucked up."

It was Eric's turn to laugh. "Water under the bridge, my

friend. Now, I want to tell you the real reason I came by unannounced today." He adjusted himself in the hardwooden kitchen chair and leaned across the table conspiratorially.

"I have a surprise for you," Eric said. "Guess what? It dovetails very nicely with my admission that I didn't know just how close you were with Larry. It relates to the disposition of his will. I admit I felt a pang of jealousy when Barbara told me, but I talked about it with Tom and the other guys and we all agree it is quite appropriate."

"He had a will?" Thor asked. Eric laughed again.

"That's all you got out of what I just said?"

Thor shook his head. "Uh, you mean he left something to me?" He was truly puzzled.

"He did," Eric affirmed. "Let's go, Barb's waiting for us."

"When we're finished there, do you mind taking me to retrieve my car?" Thor asked.

"Not at all."

Thor called Tim in and secured the cat door, so he couldn't go outside again. They got in Eric's car and headed east. Parker's was only twenty minutes from Thor's house in Richmond Beach, and they made it easily with the light Saturday traffic.

Barbara and Larry Malone lived in Shoreline, just north of the Seattle city limit and only a few miles from Thor's Richmond Beach home. With the light Saturday afternoon traffic, they made it there in less than twenty minutes.

Thor looked appreciatively at the sprawling rambler in the upscale neighborhood. The yard was beautifully maintained, and a lawn worthy of a putting green was surrounded by large rhododendrons and azaleas. There were Christmas decorations worthy of such a backdrop and the home seemed much more welcoming than he remembered. *This place must be spectacular in the spring and summer*, he thought.

It seemed odd to Thor that though his friendship with Larry had grown, he had never once met Barbara until the day of the funeral. Larry had talked about her constantly.

Barbara was a teacher too, but not at Chinook. An adjunct professor of astronomy at Seattle University, she was highly intelligent and well-liked by her peers.

Months had passed, and Thor realized the day of the funeral had been a blur, so he never really took in his surroundings at that time. That seemed to be the story of his life of late. He was just existing but never actually seeing. Going through the motions but not really living.

Barbara Malone met them at the door with a radiant and welcoming smile. "Come in, come in!" she said. She ushered them into the living room.

"Have you gentlemen eaten?" she asked. On the coffee table were small sandwiches and a pitcher of iced tea.

"I haven't, and I'm hungry," Thor said. Eric nodded agreement and they said down and helped themselves.

They chatted while they ate. "Please call me Barb," she told Thor. "I feel like I know you even though we've only met twice." She still had that lovely smile, and Thor noticed for the first time what a pretty woman she was.

Passing the 60 mark had taken a toll on her appearance, as it had for all of them, but she was still attractive. She was slender and her once golden-brown hair was now a pleasing silver-white. It complimented her hazel eyes, which held an amused twinkle. It was good to see her so cheerful after what must have been an awful few months.

She was wearing jeans and a black t-shirt with no slogans or embellishments. Her feet were bare in keeping with the cheerful sign at the front door requesting guests remove their shoes upon entering. Thor and Eric had dutifully complied.

Around her neck was a silver chain from which

depended a small silver peace symbol. It had a minute diamond in the center. She had small matching diamond studs in her pierced earlobes. They could almost keep up with the sparkle in her eyes.

"Larry talked about you all the time," Thor told her. "I feel as though I know you well too." He returned her smile and they shared a look that clearly excluded Eric.

"Yeah, Lare was a regular gabfest most of the time, that's why his secret with you took us all by surprise!" Eric said.

Thor and Barb both laughed. "Yeah, he was terribly strict about that," Thor said. "Every time I saw him, he was reminding me to keep it quiet. I didn't even know anyone I could tell had I wanted to."

He looked at the last bite of the finger sandwich in his hand and then popped it into his mouth.

"Well! I suppose this brings us to why we are here, yes?" Barb asked. She looked excited. "Thor, Eric tells me that you didn't know you were in Larry's will, is that correct?" She seemed eager to spill the beans.

"I had no idea," Thor said. "I don't know what to say."

Barb got up and motioned for them to follow. She took them to a door just off the foyer and when she opened it, they saw a staircase leading down. She led the way.

At the bottom of the stairs, Barb flipped a light switch and the basement was brightly illuminated. The basement was fully finished with drywall, white carpet (you could tell they didn't have kids or pets living there), and a sitting area around a big screen TV in one corner. But it was the center of the room that got Thor's immediate attention.

Arranged on the carpet, each on its own stand, were at least a dozen electric and acoustic guitars. They were all shapes, sizes, and colors. He recognized the classic Ovation Hollow Body and the Martin D41 Acoustic 12-string. There were a couple of Fender Strats and a Gibson Les

Paul that had to be 50 years old.

Barb stood to one side and indicated the collection with a flourish of her hand worthy of Vanna White turning letters on Wheel of Fortune. "Larry left them to you, Thor," she said.

"All of them?" It was all he could think to say.

She laughed her musical laugh and assured him that yes, they were all his, the entire collection. Eric had started to wander among them, there turned out to be fourteen in all, and stopped by the old Les Paul.

"Shit!" he exclaimed. "Thor, come here!" He was pointing at a faded signature on the body of the guitar. BB King, it read.

"Wow!" Thor said, reverently picking up the old guitar. He hadn't finished admiring it when Eric yelled again.

"This one is signed by Eric Clapton!"

"No shit?" said Thor. He refrained from mentioning that as Ricky Harris he had known Eric Clapton back in the day. But it did get him wondering. Something in the back of his mind was struggling to come to the front. What was it, Larry had told him so long ago? He had known about the guitar collection, it was Larry's pride and joy, and he knew some of them were signed by various artists, too, but there was something else. Something Larry had told him a couple of years before that was now buried in his subconscious. It was about the guitars though, of that Thor was certain.

"He mentioned he had a collection," he said. "I never dreamed in a million years he would leave it to me." He looked at Barb. "This is really…I'm overwhelmed. Thank you, and thanks to Larry, God rest him." And that was when he remembered what Larry had gushed about so long ago.

Larry told Thor that he and Barb had been out garage sale shopping on the weekend, something they enjoyed doing in the summer months when the weather was pleasant and there were many sales to be visited. Larry had scored the find of his life at one sale, so near to their home, he could scarcely believe it.

Larry had seen it, sitting on a stand, hardly clearing the dew-laden grass: a mint condition 1971 Gibson Flying V Medallion in the traditional red and white. "I about came in my pants!" Larry said at the time. But there was more.

Thor's heart began to beat a little faster. He wound in and out of the guitar stands, looking at each until he found the Flying V. This was definitely the one and he remembered Larry's story now all too well. He picked up the instrument and carefully turned it over to look on the back. There in permanent ink was a signature, *Ricky Harris*.

He had signed that guitar for a Seattle fan the night he died. He had used it on stage that night and without foreknowledge of the right angle turn his life was about to take, magnanimously signed it and handed it off the stage to the all-but-drooling kid.

Carefully, he replaced the guitar on the stand. He stood back and looked at Barbara. "You know collectively these are worth a small fortune, don't you?" he asked.

She nodded, the little smile still playing on- her lips. "I do. He wanted you to have them. I have no financial worries, so they are just a collection to me. I don't play, so they would sit here and gather dust. I think they need to go to someone who really appreciates them." She cocked her head to one side as if to say, "Don't you want them?"

"Thank you again. I'm beyond flattered. I will cherish them."

Barb walked over to a closet and took out a hard-shell guitar case. She set it on the floor and opened it. There was no guitar inside but there was an envelope. It was sealed and had Thor's name on it. She handed it to him.

"Believe it or not, I didn't know about this, but he was

very specific in his will that upon delivering the guitar collection to you, I was to give you this envelope. After the
reading last week, I came down here and looked in that
case as instructed and sure enough, there was the envelope.
I didn't open it, and I don't want or need to know what it
says. It was from Larry to you and I respect that." She
handed Thor the business-letter-sized envelope and
stepped back.

She and Eric were looking at him as if they wanted him
to read its contents then and there, but Thor hesitated. He
couldn't begin to guess what it might say inside, but he felt
a gut certainty that he did not want to share it with anyone.
Something was too weird about that posthumous commu-
nication. He put the envelope into the inside pocket of his
jacket to read at his leisure.

That seemed to satisfy Barb, and Eric frowned but
didn't protest. They made arrangements to come back later
in the week to carefully pack up the guitars to transport to
Thor's house. Each one had its own case and stand, and
Thor thought he had a great place to display them in his
own study.

They said their goodbyes and thanks again to Barb.
Thor asked her if she would like to get dinner one night
later in the week and she said she would love that. Both
men gave her a hug before they left.

They didn't talk much on the way to get Thor's car from
Parker's parking lot, which was not far at all from the
Malone house.

Thor took his keys out and prepared to get in his car but
paused. "Thank you for putting up with my eccentricities,"
he said.

Eric dismissed this with a wave of his hand. "As I said,
it's water under the bridge. I do have to ask though, are
you going to use any of those guitars on stage now?" He
looked hopeful.

"Yeah, probably, why not?" Thor shrugged. "I love that Flying V, I have to tell you." Well, that was true at least.

"Cool!" said Eric. "Later, man!" He rolled up the window on his BMW 320i and sped away.

Thor got in the car and started it. He put on his seatbelt and then, unable to stop himself, reached into his pocket and removed the envelope. He had planned to wait until he got home to read it, but curiosity was irresistible.

He slid a finger under the sealed flap and tore it open. The note on the tri-folded paper inside was printed in a neat hand.

Dear Thor,

If you are reading this, then I am dead. I don't know how long it's been from the time I wrote this to you reading it now, but I hope it finds you well and that my demise (hard to contemplate I must say!) wasn't too hard on anyone. Please keep an eye on Barb for me, I can't imagine what she's feeling.

Also, if you are reading this, then she's already given you the guitar collection. That brings me to my point. I want to thank you for the lessons and the friendship. I hope I realized my dream of becoming a musician full time, but if not, then you should know that every minute you patiently spent with me was treasured. Passing my "treasures" on to you is the least I can do. But there is something else I want you to know: I know who you are. I've always known. I saw it in your face the day I told you about finding the signed Flying V at the garage sale. I don't know how you faked your death and kept it secret for so long. But I do know that you kept my secret as well, and I appreciate that more than I can express. Your secret dies with me.

I'm glad I got to know you, Ricky. I wish I'd had the courage to discuss this with you when I was still alive. I don't know why you did what you did, and I guess I never will, but I want you to know that if you ever decide to "come back to life" you'll have more fans than you realize who would be rejoicing.

Much love to you, bro,

Larry

Silent tears rolled down Thor's face. He refolded the letter and put it back in the envelope. He shut off the car's engine and sat staring at the side of the building for half an hour.

When he got home much later than planned, he let Tim outside and put the letter in the sink. He fished around in the junk drawer until he found a matchbook. He lit the letter, envelope and all and made sure it was entirely burnt to ash. He turned on the faucet and watched as the last of the ash went down the drain.

Chapter 11

About four months after Christmas, Mick took a rare day off to watch his grandsons play baseball. The day was warm, and the baseball diamond was freshly groomed as the Little Leaguers took the field. Mick sat in the bleachers with Stephen and his daughter-in-law, Emily. The twins were adorable in their little uniforms with what seemed like too-large baseball gloves on their hands. Trevor played 3rd base, and Tristan was in the outfield. They were so small and gave it their best. It was a joy to watch. They seemed to get a kick out of it when Grampa would toss the ball to them to practice between games.

Trevor struck out his first time at bat, but Tristan managed to send a grounder between second and third and ran all the way to second, safe. Mick and Stephen jumped to their feet cheering and exchanged a high five. The next two kids struck out, and poor little Tristan was left stranded.

The second inning found Tristan squatting in the grass in the outfield, picking clover. As he did, the ball whizzed over his distracted little head and the kid on the other team ran home, with two RBIs in front of him.

Mick's cell began to ring, and he felt the vibration in his pocket. He pulled it out and saw that it was Sue Cole calling.

"Mick, I have to tell you something. It's important!"

"Oh? Do tell." Mick rose from the bleachers and walked toward the parking lot and away from the cheering, chatting crowd of parents. He put a finger in the ear that wasn't up to the phone.

Sue took a long breath and paused before speaking. She paused so long that for a moment, Mick thought his cell might have dropped the call.

"OK, so you know I can't tell you much about an open case that I'm currently working on, right?"

"Goes without saying, Sue. Just share what you can."

She paused again, perhaps gathering her thoughts before getting too specific about an open case.

"A body came in a few days ago from Three Rivers up in Monroe. An old prisoner got himself killed in a fight in the yard. Shiv through the heart, I'm told. The coroner took blood during the autopsy and that's what I've got here to take a look at. But that's not the interesting part.

"Let's just say the deceased was a good fella," she went on with an implied wink in her voice. "And suppose he had been talking with some other inmates just before his unfortunate run-in with the shiv."

"Where'd you get even that much?" Mick asked.

"The coroner got it from the white coats who delivered the body," she said. "The story is that this deceased old guy had been claiming that he killed the person in the car and that he knew Ricky Harris is alive and well because he saw him walk away that night."

Mick felt as though he'd been hit with a major league bat. His breath got shallow and he felt lightheaded. After all these years, really? Was this a dream?

He shook his head. "Sue, I know you can't give me the name of the dead prisoner, but I've got Twin Rivers, can you at least give me initials? Something to go on?

"Mick, I'll give you a name, but I swear to God, if it

goes any further, I'll deny I've ever met you!"

"It ends with me, Sue. You know you can trust me," Mick said. The thrill in his chest brought on by a break so soon after delving into the case again was almost more than he could stand.

"Rocco Fortunato and you didn't hear it from me!" She hung up.

Ricky Harris walked away from the scene of the accident. There was a witness. And if he was interpreting her cryptic description correctly, the late Rocco was a mobster. It was possible, hell, even likely that Rocco wasn't the only one to witness Ricky Harris walking away. But the thread of the story was thin, and while it seemed logical that it was this very tale that had resulted in Mr. Fortunato's demise, Mick couldn't be sure of that. Inmates get themselves in trouble all the time in prison. Bragging about old crimes and the like is hardly solid proof of anything, but it rarely will get one killed in the joint.

On the contrary, killing is a sport in prison. Inmates certainly have little enough of sport and entertainment. No, if Mr. Fortunato was terminated because he was telling this tale, then someone didn't want it known that Ricky Harris is still alive. Or, more likely, someone didn't want anyone to know that the dead guy in the car that night was killed by a certain Mr. Rocco Fortunato. Either way, Mick had to plan a short trip up north to the Twin Rivers Correctional Center. He had an old snitch who just happened to be doing a stretch up there.

He searched the contacts list in his phone and selected Chuck Wilson. He called Chuck's cell phone and it rang a few times, but no answer. He left a quick message. "Chuck, it's Mick. You know I've been playing with my pet case since retiring, right? Well, I've stumbled onto some new evidence that I think you need to hear. Give me a call when you get this, OK?" He put the cell phone back in his pocket and headed for the car, not bothering to let the family know he was leaving.

Where the hell did you go, Ricky?

❦❦❦

Nothing Mick did could quell the excitement in his gut. He was almost shaking with anticipation as he got into the car to make the drive up to Monroe. He stopped at the bank in his neighborhood and transferred $200.00 into a prison account with which he was very familiar. He decided to get that out of the way ahead of time. Snitches don't chirp for free, even when imprisoned.

He thought about Lester Tuttle and about their last meeting. It had been a few years ago and Lester's tip had been a good one. Mick tracked down a child killer who had an unfortunate crack habit which is what brought him into Lester's 'hood in the first place. It was Mick's last major bust before he retired, and he was proud of it. Lester had pocketed a substantial reward from the Department, although that part had been kept out of the press. A small-time dope dealer and confidential informant was not the sort of person who wanted fame and hero worship. He was in it for the money.

Lester was a tall drink of water. He stood an imposing six foot seven and had played basketball in college before blowing out his knee senior year and ending any chance at a professional career. Even with a college education, Lester had found it difficult to get work. Basketball was all he ever knew. Dunking is what got a poor kid from the projects a full-ride scholarship to the U-Dub.

Upon returning home from school, Lester fell into a depression and found himself tangled up in the drug trade in short order. Mick arrested him more than once in those early days and they formed a strange sort of friendship.

Eventually, Mick began to turn a blind eye to the dealing in exchange for credible local information. Some part of Lester that still had a conscience bubbled back to the surface of his psyche and he jumped into the role of snitch eagerly. Mick paid well, and no one ever suspected where the information was coming from. It was a good partnership.

The problem with being a confidential informant for a cop is that often other cops know nothing about the arrangement. So, Lester still got arrested from time to time. His most recent transgression, possession with intent to distribute, is what had landed him in the slam this time.

Mick enjoyed the trip up Highway 522 to the prison. He knew that with the body so recently delivered for autopsy, the late Mr. Fortunato hadn't been dead long and may have had a visitor in the not too distant past. Mick intended to check the sign-in book for just such a possibility.

He pulled into the visitor's parking lot, locked his car upon exit, and was whistling as he entered the prison. His bald pate felt the warmth of the early spring sun but there was little warmth inside the drab, gray building.

He checked his weapon at the security office and went through the metal detector, pat-down, and security wanding. He knew a few of the guards and they welcomed him back after a long absence.

Mick signed and dated the visitor sign-in, and then took a little time to page back in time to two weeks prior. He scanned the names and flipped forward to the next page, still scanning. Nothing jumped out at him until he got to three days ago. Mr. Anthony DiThomasso had come to visit and from the departure time, had spent almost ninety minutes visiting. That seemed odd to Mick, as most prison visits were kept to an hour. Then he saw why: Mr. DiThomasso indicated in the book that he was visiting

Rocco Fortunato and another prisoner, Dean Reynolds.

"What's so interesting there, Mick?" Reece Cummings asked. Reece was a former cop and a friend who had become a corrections officer in an attempt to slow the pace of his life a little. Mick wondered how that was working out for him.

Mick knew that he had no legal right to be snooping in the log and he would not be able to go back to earlier dates to see if and when Mr. DiThomasso may have visited on previous occasions. Still, what he had gleaned was helpful. He wanted to ask if Reynolds was the owner of the shiv that killed Fortunato, but that would let them know he had a lot more information on certain subjects than he was entitled to. Best to let it go for now.

"Sorry, Reece. Curiosity got the better of me. I was just wondering when the last time I came out here was. Must have been over a year ago, so I'm not finding any dates in this book with my signature!" He hoped he was keeping it light. This was not a conversation he cared to have.

"Yeah, I think it's been a while, Mick. You go on in now and enjoy your stay," he said with a wink.

Mick followed another guard to the consultation room and took a seat. He waited to pick up the phone until another guard escorted Lester in on the other side of the Plexiglas.

Lester was cuffed, and the guard unlocked the left cuff and locked it to a ring in the table on Lester's side. The chairs on the prisoners' side were bolted to the floor, lest someone get a notion to pick one up and crack a guard over the head with it.

"Long time no see, Mick," said Lester into the phone when he was properly settled. "To what do I owe the honor?"

Mick smiled. "Nice to see you too, Les. How's it going?"

"It's going, that's about it. Keeping out of trouble, laying as low as I possibly can until I get out of here. I've got six months to go, you know."

Mick knew. "Yeah, I'm sorry I can't run interference for you anymore. I would have kept you out of here if I could have, you know that.

"I'll get straight to the point, Les. I need some information and you are in the right place at the right time to get it for me. Can you help?"

"I'll need a little help from you first," Lester replied.

"Indeed, my friend. That's already taken care of. Check your balance when you get the chance.

"Are you keeping your ear to the ground in here as always?" Mick asked.

"You know it. People talk to me. I guess I have one of those honest faces." He laughed and there was genuine mirth in it.

"Yeah? Did you ever talk to a guy called Rocco?"

"Old School? Shit, yeah, I talked to him all the time. That old guy wouldn't shut up. I figure that's why somebody popped him the other day, just to get him to shut the fuck up. Did you know about that, him getting offed in here?"

"Yes," said Mick. "It's why I'm here. I'm interested to know what he was talking about that got him talked right into his grave."

"Everybody called him Old School because he was old, but also because he gave off that gangsta vibe. You know, like he was one of those old-time guys who walked around with a Tommy gun in a violin case."

Mick smiled.

"He was always telling stories of back in the day when him and his partner, Tony D did this or that job. He was pretty proud of the fact that they were hitmen, and he made no secret of it either.

"He even claimed that he was the one who killed the guy they found in the canal back in the seventies. You know, that rock star guy? Only Old School said it wasn't the rock star, it was some small-time numbers guy who was in over his head."

Mick straightened in his chair. "Is that all he said about it?" He tried not to sound too eager, but he was fairly certain he was not succeeding.

"Oh no! He had quite the story to tell. It seems Old School and his partner took the guy out and then tossed him over the bridge into the canal. Then they watched as this long hair comes along and fishes the dead guy out of the water, stashes him in the car, and pushes the car back into the water! Hell of a story if it's true." Lester shook his head.

"Did he say what happened to the long hair?" Mick asked.

Lester rubbed his strong brown jaw with his untethered hand. "I don't know that he did. You know Mick, I didn't pay much attention to him, he was always yakking about something, bragging and probably exaggerating about most of it. I don't think anyone paid him much mind."

"But you remember that story."

"Well yeah, that one. He was taking credit for helping a famous guy fake his death. It's kinda memorable."

"I suppose so," Mick said. "Did Old School happen to mention who the small-time numbers guy was? Did he give a name?"

Lester thought for a moment. "Yeah, he did. I remember because it was funny. It was one of those things that made him sound like he shoulda been in Chicago in the twenties."

Mick lifted a bushy red-gray eyebrow.

"The guy he killed was called Thor the Viking. That's kind of hard to forget if you ask me. The story never changed, including that guy's name, but he must've told it a thousand times."

"I appreciate your time, Les. I think that's all I need to ask today," Mick said.

"Any time, my brother! Glad I could be of service." Lester winked and sat patiently as Mick got up to go.

Once back outside and in his car, Mick sat for a moment wondering what his next step should be. His decades-long suspicions were confirmed. This brought him to a fork in the road.

First, he had to find out the identity of the deceased man in the car. He had a name, even if it was a nickname. Surely the first name, Thor, was correct. Rocco had indicated the guy was running a petty numbers racket and had run afoul of his financial backer. The financial backer was Rocco's boss. Mick could always go through old missing person's records to see if a local young man fitting Ricky Harris's description had disappeared in January of 1975.

The other fork, and probably the more important one, was tracking down Ricky Harris. While it looked as though Harris was innocent in the murder of his replacement, any other crimes that he might be charged with, tampering with a crime scene, hiding evidence, criminal desecration of a corpse, were all well past their statutory expiration dates. But at the very least, he was a material witness to a murder and that made it extremely desirable to find him.

"Find out who the dead guy was, you find Ricky Harris," Mick said to himself. Time to call in a few more markers at the department.

As if reading his mind, the phone rang. It was Chuck.

"What's this exciting new evidence you have for me?" Chuck asked.

"I came up to Twin Rivers to visit Lester," he said. "You are not going to believe what he told me!

"I guess some old guy up here got shivved recently. Les says the guy was telling stories from back in the day about having killed a dude and tossing him in the canal. It seems some long-hair happened along at that very moment and pulls the dead guy out of the drink, places him in the car, and pushes the car into the canal with the dead guy in it. What do you think of that?"

"I think if it's true, you are the luckiest son of a bitch that ever walked the earth!" Chuck laughed. "How can I help you with this info?"

"I need you to look for a criminal record from the early to mid-'70s for someone named Thor. I don't have a last name, but he might have an alias of Thor the Viking. Can you do that?"

"On my own time, sure. I'll take a crack at it. Don't you think it would be easier if I just gave you access?"

"Would you do that, Chuck? That would be fantastic!" Mick said.

"I don't think our IT guys are looking for hackers who have permissions. I'll give you my credentials, so you can log in and do the search yourself. That work?"

"Absolutely! Thank you, my friend. I'll keep you posted."

"See that you do," Chuck said and hung up.

Chapter 12

Dead Salmon was near the end of their first set of the evening at the Tractor Tavern in Seattle's old fishing and Norwegian immigrant-centric neighborhood, Ballard. The Tractor was known for showcasing the best local live music and had been that showcase for decades.

The old brick building with its concrete dance floor didn't seem as though it would offer up much in the way of acoustic glory for a live band, but it did. The high open ceiling, dearth of windows, and heavy brick walls contained the sound in perfect euphony.

The band was just finishing David Bowie's *TVC 15* when Thor saw Barbara sitting at a table with some other people he didn't know, sipping a glass of red wine.

She smiled when she realized he'd spotted her and he returned the smile with a nod. They finished the set and he carefully placed the Flying V in its stand before joining Barb at her table. Her seatmates had gone to the bar or the restrooms or both, because she was now alone.

Thor caught the eye of one of the bartenders as he sat and motioned for a beer. The bartender gave him a quick two-finger salute in acknowledgment and he turned to Barb.

"Hey there, lady! You came to see us play!" It was a statement, not a question.

"What choice did I have?" she said. "You promised me two weeks ago that we would do dinner, and yet I haven't heard a peep out of you!" Her mischievous smirk told him she wasn't really scolding.

He hoped the dim lighting prevented her from seeing him blush. He had thought about calling her numerous times, but each time something stopped him, and he would put the phone down.

Thor sighed. "No excuses. Primarily because I can't come up with one on the fly."

"It's OK. I really wanted to hear you play with the guys, and until recently, it's just been too hard for me to think about watching the band without Larry."

"Oh, of course. I think that's why I am a little surprised you are here tonight," Thor told her.

"I hope it isn't speaking ill of the deceased to say this," she began, "but you sing a lot better than Larry did. And I don't think he would mind me saying so. He really valued your friendship."

Thor laughed. "It was mutual. He was a good friend." He thought of the letter and how Larry spoke to him from the grave. He wondered if Larry's dying declaration of keeping his secret included his wife of thirty years. Sharing juicy pillow talk with one's spouse implies confidentiality that Larry may not have considered as letting the cat out of the bag.

Thor searched Barb's eyes for some sign of recognition, of a kept secret, but he saw nothing. She was just a friend and had no reason to think of him as anyone but Thor Swenson, Professor of Mathematics.

"I noticed you brought one of the guitars from the collection," she said.

"Yes, that has always been one of my favorites to play. I used to have one just like it." He watched her for a moment to gauge her reaction to that admission. She simply sipped her wine, oblivious to any subtext.

"Are you going to stay for the next set?" he asked.

"Yes! I'm having a great time. I wouldn't mind dancing, but all the guys I know are in the band, what to do?" She smiled.

"Dance by yourself, of course!" His beer arrived, and they talked a while longer before he had to excuse himself to go back up on stage.

Barb took Thor's advice and got up to dance as soon as they began to play. Eric waved at her and Tom leaned into the mike over his keyboard and said, "Welcome to the lovely Barbara!"

At the end of their second set, the band played Blues Travelers' *Run Around.* Thor set his guitar down and hopped off the stage to join Barb, on the dance floor, while Eric played and sang. Roger had donned a harmonica holder and was doing his usual credible job of playing the harp while he still managed his bass. He was no John Popper, but he did all right.

Thor whisked Barb around the floor in a sort of slow samba, never taking his arm from her waist. She followed gracefully and in a few moments, the floor cleared and left them in an impromptu spotlight.

After the song, Thor bowed, and then they both applauded the band.

Barb and Thor went back to her table and the remaining band members joined them. They ordered beers all around, except for Barb who had another glass of wine.

As the men prepared to return to the stage for their final set of the night, Barb got ready to go.

"You can't stay until the end?" Thor asked.

"No, two's my limit if I'm driving," she said. "Call me tomorrow, and we'll have that dinner you promised me." She kissed him on the cheek.

"Will do," he said and gave her a quick hug. He

watched her leave as he strapped on his guitar.

☙❧☙

The following evening found them at John Howie Steak House in Bellevue. It was one of Thor's favorite places and he was pleased that he'd been able to get a same day reservation.

They shared a bottle of Chateau Ste. Michelle Cabernet and talked, mostly it seemed, about Larry. Eventually, the conversation turned to more personal histories and Thor found himself at ease with her more than he had been with any woman in all his years of being single. A tiny voice in the back of his head was trying to sound a warning of some kind, but he silenced that warning every time it came up.

"You know, Larry and I had a good marriage, a good life. But really, for the past fifteen years or so, we were just platonic. We haven't slept together in all those years. Most of the time, I hardly knew he was there. He would go to the basement and play his guitars, park in front of the TV, or whatever. We barely spoke," Barbara said.

Thor was taken aback. "I'm very surprised to hear that," he said.

"Really? Did he talk about me much when he was with you?" she asked.

"Well, no. But most of the time we talked about music, the band, school, that stuff," Thor said.

"Right. You talked about all aspects of his life except one: me." She cut a bit of her steak and brought the fork to her mouth with her left hand like Europeans do. Thor found that charming.

He sipped his wine and waited for Barbara to speak again.

"Please don't get the wrong idea, Thor," she said between bites. "I'm not saying we hated each other or anything like that. It's just that we were entirely platonic. We didn't have any children as you know. So, I think the habit of each other is what kept us together. I loved him in my way and I'm certain it was mutual. But we just haven't been a couple for a long time. We were just two room-mates, really." She dabbed at the corner of her mouth with a napkin.

"You've rendered me speechless," Thor said. He grasped his wine glass and held it aloft. "To friendship," he said. Barb picked up her glass and returned the toast.

"To friendship!" They both drank.

After that, the conversation turned to lighter topics and they laughed and joked. Barbara asked about the band's schedule for the rest of the summer.

Thor, Eric, Roger, Burt, and Tom all left summer quarter classes to their various assistants and other teachers, so that they could devote the summer to performing. The University seemed to encourage this.

Thor knew his presence in Dead Salmon was the main factor in their increased popularity and demand. He had managed to raise the quality of the performances of each of the other individual members of the band and it showed. They didn't do it for the money—they did it for the love of the music.

"I am so glad I came to watch you guys last night," Barb said. "I am also glad I waited. I would have felt self-conscious tagging along without Larry there. It's not something I would have done when he was alive. I think the guys might have found it odd. But I did have fun!" she said.

"I want to come watch you, more often."

"Yeah, the other guys' wives come now and then," said Thor. "It would be really nice to have you there." He smiled and reached across the table and put his hand over hers. She smiled too and didn't object. The tiny voice chimed in again, and he mentally slapped it back into submission.

They finished their after-dinner coffee and Thor paid the check. As he was driving her home, she turned to him suddenly and said, "I know I promised not to ask, but frankly it's killing me. I have to know what was in that letter from Larry!"

Thor's heart sped up and he stared straight ahead at the road wondering how to respond. His capacity for lying on the spur of the moment was not a thing he was proud of, but it was one of his many talents.

He took a deep breath and was determined not to look at her as he spoke.

"It wasn't anything earth-shattering," he began. "It was mostly heartfelt thanks for the time we spent together, things he had learned from me, stuff like that. He can't have known he was going to die, so I'm not sure what prompted him to write it, but it means a lot to me and I'm glad he did."

"I know exactly when he wrote it, even though I didn't know of its existence until the reading of his will," she said. "I'm sure he wrote it when he decided to leave you the guitar collection." She smiled, and a tear threatened at the corner of her eye. "I think he would be thrilled to know you are using some of them when you perform."

"I hope so," Thor said.

He pulled into her driveway, got out, and opened the passenger door for her. He walked her up to the porch and quickly gave her a chaste goodnight kiss.

"Would you like to come in for a minute?" she asked.

The tiny voice was no longer so tiny, and she must have noticed his hesitation. She smiled a knowing smile.

"When I was much younger, I used to think of old people having sex as possibly the grossest thing I could imagine. You know how when you were a kid, even though you knew the facts of life, your parents doing it was somehow not a thought you could ever entertain?"

Thor laughed in spite of his growing anxiety. "Yeah."

"Well I no longer find the concept gross at all," she said. She unlocked the front door and he followed her in.

e⁄ɔe⁄ɔ

Thor woke to the sound of someone softly snoring. He thought at first it was Tim. The fat cat had a prodigious purr to go with his formidable girth, but snoring was not one of his customary noises. He remembered all at once where he was. Shit. No really, *shit*. The tiny voice of last night was now a piercing scream at the forefront of his consciousness. What the hell was he doing?

He got out of bed as quietly as he could and found his clothes in a pile on the floor. *Oh jeez, I didn't have that much to drink. What was I thinking?*

The events of the night replayed in his head and he couldn't deny he was attracted to Barb—had been ever since he first met her. The sex had been welcome and ter- rific if he had to rate it, and it sucked that he should regret it so much, but there you go.

"I take it you're not planning to stay for breakfast?" Barb asked behind him as he zipped up the fly of his jeans.

He turned around to see that she was propped up on one elbow, the sheet discreetly pulled up to her throat. That she was naked beneath, he knew and felt the first stirrings of arousal.

"Yeah Barb, that was probably not the best idea." Well, that was lame.

"I'm not surprised to hear you say that. You've been bouncing back and forth between having fun and running from me since Friday night at the Tractor. Why the ping pong game?"

He ran a hand through his gray hair and looked down at his bare feet. "Because it has occurred to me more than once that I am quite successfully taking over Larry's life, and I hate it!" He blurted out.

Barb remained calm. "In what way? He wanted you to have those guitars. I doubt he ever thought that you would end up playing with the band, but I know for certain he would have loved the idea. And as for me, well don't you think your position sort of invalidates anything that I may be feeling?" She stopped and let that thought hang in the air for a bit.

"I'm not looking to replace Larry," she said after a moment. I just happen to like you, Thor. What can I say? I've always been a sucker for the lead guitarist. When all the other little ten-year-olds were drooling over John and Paul, I had a huge poster of George on my wall!"

"You're right, and I'm sorry. It was unfair not to ask how you are feeling about all of this." *You just can't know that this isn't the first time I've taken over someone else's life*, he finished silently. But he relaxed a little and sat on the edge of the bed.

"While I'm sure my cat can live off of his stored fat for quite some time, I do think I need to get home to feed him. That aside, I would dearly love some coffee."

"You got it," she said and rose from the bed. When she did, Thor knew that the coffee was going to have to wait a little longer, as was Tim's breakfast. Yes, Barb was right. There was nothing gross about old people sex at all.

Chapter 13

Mick enjoyed the ride home from the prison. In fact, he had not felt this good in years. Ricky Harris was alive and possibly well. He would be old now, probably at least as old as Mick. 65? 67? He couldn't remember how old Harris had been when he supposedly died. He would look it up some other time. Now he was going to find out whose identity it was that Harris had stolen.

He drove straight home and fired up the old desktop. He had not been retired long and this may or may not be his last case, but Mick decided that he would not ask for any more help from still active-duty friends if he could avoid it at all. Favors owed are a currency best spent sparingly. He was not surprised to find that Chuck had already sent him an email with the sign in information. Sweet!

He began with missing persons reports that were filed on or within three days of January 14, 1975. It had been his experience that people who were truly missing were usually missed well within the somewhat arbitrary 24-hour requirement. This did not necessarily hold true for juveniles who often ran away, but adults who went missing unexpectedly were usually missed early on.

Mick pored through old records for over an hour before he came to the conclusion that Thor, no-last-name, the Viking had no family or friends interested enough in his sudden disappearance to call the police about it.

Next item to check then was a criminal record. That was going to take some time. Even though the records were old and publicly available, with only a first name and a span of a few years to go on, there could be hundreds of records.

Mick looked at his watch and saw that it was after five p.m. He wanted his mind clear for this research, which promised to take some time, but he felt the need to celebrate the con's story that vindicated his decades-old suspicions. Being right never felt so good.

He rose from his old leather desk chair and went to the sideboard there in his den to pour a small Scotch. He took a bottle of ten-year-old single malt and poured two fingers' worth into a rocks glass. God forbid there were rocks in it though. A fine Scotch needs to be enjoyed neat. Whiskey was an Irishman's drink, and while he usually preferred vodka, this was a special little toast.

"To you, my dearest Rosie," he said, raising the glass high. "You never doubted me, and you always supported me in my quest to solve this case. My love, I'm almost there." He sipped the rich brown liquid and savored the taste on the back of his tongue as it warmed its way down his throat.

Rosie had been gone, going on five years now, and Mick still missed her every minute of every day. Stephen had come around much more when she was alive and eager to play with the grandkids.

Mick had almost retired when she died after losing her long and miserable battle with cancer. It was a battle that you wouldn't wish on your worst enemy. He watched it eat her up little by little, day after day. The doctors never held out much hope. By the time she was diagnosed, she was in stage four and had little time left.

She tried radiation, but it made her sicker and did next to nothing to stop the progression of the disease. After that the doctors wanted to try chemo, but she refused. "I want my last days to be good days. I don't want to be sick as a dog in some hospital bed. Take me home, Mick," she had said. And he did.

It was killing him too, watching her die. But he did his best to stay strong for her. When she got to the point where she could no longer rise from the bed, he had the hospice nurses come and visit several times a day. One night she was especially bad and in so much pain Mick could almost feel it.

She writhed and moaned in agony, for three hours, before finally she just sort of wound down and stopped. Mick sat with her for a long time before he got up the courage to admit she was gone. He called the hospice nurses and they came right away. They took care of everything.

Mick sighed and walked to the window. He looked out at the old neighborhood and sipped his Scotch. Rosie's passing had been unimaginably hard but now, with the buffer of time, he could think of her with love and humor and most times not cry. She was his rock and his reason for living and without her all he had left with this case. He wondered if at the end of the investigation, he would be able to content himself with occasional visits from Stephen and the grandkids. He doubted it.

He finished his drink and returned to the desk. Criminal records it was. He decided to start in 1970. If Thor had a record, he may have done time. If he had done time, he was most certainly not incarcerated in January of '75. He would work his way forward in time and if he found nothing, he would go a little farther back.

Mick knew he was taking a big leap and an even bigger chance by assuming that Thor had been approximately the same age as Ricky Harris when he died. He may have been somewhat older if he was a small-time hood with ties to organized crime.

The autopsy report mentioned a male between the ages of 20 and 35. That would have been more or less accurate to apply to Harris, so once again no one had questioned the finding. Because the victim had been positively identified by his friends, no further investigation was needed. As a matter of course, the pathologist had taken fingerprints. The original fingerprint cards were still in with the autopsy report. None of that had any bearing on whether or not Thor was in his thirties when he died. If he was, then it was conceivable that he had a criminal record going back well prior to 1970. Mick sighed again at the enormity of his task.

Were he still on active duty, he could hand this bit of research off to someone else, and they, in turn, would have a computer application that would zip through the thousands of records in mere minutes. But he was retired, and he had no such program. He went to the records archive that Chuck had so graciously granted him access to. It was something he had used many times before and it felt familiar to put in the search parameters.

At first, he tried *Thor*, but that brought back much more information than he bargained for. Next, he put in Thor* which indicated that Thor was the first name. Mick knew that Thor the Viking might well be a nickname that no one else used besides Rocco, but as it was all he had to go on at the moment, he would stick with it.

The search results were pared down, but there was still a daunting amount. "I don't suppose your last name might be Anderson or something, so I can find you right off," he said. He opened the first file. Mick found it incredible that there were so many guys named Thor in Seattle who just happened to have criminal records.

Out of curiosity, he pulled open the bottom desk drawer. There resided in this drawer a very large and heavy anachronism, a phone book. Even without the

Yellow Pages, the old Seattle phone book was a heavy tome indeed. Mick opened the White Pages at A and began to rapidly scan the first names in each column. He didn't find any at first, so he skipped forward twenty pages and began again. After a few minutes, he realized that Thor is an extremely common name among Seattle locals of Norwegian extraction. Who knew?

He put the phone book back in its resting place and went back to the computer screen. He minimized the page he was looking at and opened a new tab in the browser. He went to Google and typed "images Ricky Harris" in the search bar.

Many pictures came up and he eventually chose a close-up headshot and left that one on the screen. Then he went back and opened the first criminal record of a man named Thor. This guy bore no resemblance to Harris at all, so he skipped on. Most of the records he could eliminate without seeing the mug shot because the DOB indicated that the individual was too old in 1970.

Whenever he came upon a record that indicated non-violent crime and the individual was around the right age, he would stop and compare the mug shot side-by-side with the headshot of Harris. A lot of them were blonde, some were tall, some were short, some fat, some thin, but none of them could have been easily mistaken for Ricky Harris.

Nineteen seventy produced no likely suspects, so Mick forged ahead to '71 and began the laborious process anew. He was neither surprised nor unhappy when '71 bore no more fruit than '70 had. He pressed on.

By 8 o'clock, Mick realized that he was hungry, so he stopped to make a sandwich before going back to his research. At times he wanted to throw the goddamned computer through the window it was so bloody slow, but he would take a deep breath and persevere. He washed the sandwich down with another dram of Scotch which had the added bonus of making the search a little more fun.

When he was near the end of the S last names, Mick came upon the record of one Thor Ragnar Swenson, age 27. Mr. Swenson had been arrested in 1972 on suspicion of running numbers. Bingo. He sat up in the chair and hesitated before bringing up the mug shot. Could this be the guy? At long last, could it be?

He pulled up the picture of Harris and reduced it in size to half what it had been. He dragged it to the right side of the screen. He clicked on the arrow by the virtual criminal record that would turn the page to the mug shot. He tried not to look too closely at it until he had reduced it to the size of the Harris photo.

He dragged it across the screen until the two pictures were side by side. He studied the picture of Swenson. He was a nice-looking kid with long blonde hair, blue eyes, and an "I don't give a shit" air to his visage. Then Mick's heart nearly stopped. In the publicity photo, Ricky Harris was wearing a leather jacket. The picture was of his face, there was enough of his shoulders showing to display the leather jacket.

Very deliberately, Mick got up from the desk without looking at the Harris picture for the ten-thousandth time that night. He pulled the lid off of the first evidence box and removed the buckskin jacket. Without thinking, he put it on and went to the hall mirror. He looked at himself, noticing how the shoulders looked in the reflection.

Then he took it off and put it back in the box. He went back to his desk and looked again at the Ricky Harris photo. It was the same jacket, he was sure. The fact that the fringe wasn't visible made no difference. Thor Swenson had been wearing Ricky Harris's jacket the night he died.

Slowly, Mick shifted his eyes to the right and looked at the picture of Swenson. He studied the handsome young face for several minutes. He looked back at Harris. The two young men were not identical twins, but that they could have passed as brothers was clear. The resemblance was uncanny.

In his mind's eye, Mick added some swelling, bruising, and two black eyes to Swenson. He was confident that damage of that sort, not to mention an hours-long submersion in exceedingly cold water, would have been enough to convince even close friends of Harris to identify the wrong body. Mick had found Thor the Viking at last.

The very best part, the part that Mick couldn't have hoped for in his wildest dreams, was that right below the picture, digitally enshrined on the page, were a beautiful, perfect set of the original Thor Swenson's fingerprints. Mick could scarcely believe his good luck.

He rose from his desk and went to the corner of the study where he'd stashed the evidence boxes from the Ricky Harris case. He took the fingerprint cards the attending pathologist had made during the course of the routine autopsy.

Then Mick went back to the computer and printed off a copy of Thor's fingerprints from the criminal record. He held them side by side and thought they looked the same, but he was no expert and he wanted no holes in his case.

Mick was positively gleeful as he rifled through his ancient Rolodex. There was more than one fingerprint expert's card in there and he would start with the first one he came to. Mick Thorne had plenty of friends in the forensics field. Surely someone owed him a favor after all these years.

Ah, there it was. Dennis Stern, Fingerprint Analyst, King County Sheriff's Office. Dennis didn't owe him any favors, but he was a friend and Mick felt confident that he would be willing to compare the two samples.

Oh Ricky, I'm coming for you, he thought as he went upstairs to bed.

ℰↃℰↃ

A few days after Mick learned how the death of the original Thor Swenson really went down, he realized it could be beneficial to know what happened to Rocco's partner after that night.

According to Rocco, the two had finished off Thor once they realized he was not going to pay up. It had been their real reason for taking him to the bridge in the first place. But they did offer him one last opportunity to make good on his debt, so Rocco's narrative went.

Mick sat at his computer and began searching for the criminal records of Rocco Fortunato. He now knew Tony's last name, thanks to the visitor's log at the prison. It was possible that DiThomasso was a common Italian surname. He had to hope it wasn't.

He started with the prison records. If Tony was also incarcerated, it may have been him who decided Rocco had talked enough. Also, it might just lead him to the headman who had ordered Thor Swenson's death to begin with. That was a name Mick could really use.

If Thor Swenson was a common local name, Rocco Fortunato was just the opposite. In the local records at least, he was the one and only. It was fairly easy to find his rap sheet and after that Mick dug up all of the court proceedings and appeals that had led to Rocco's life stretch at Twin Rivers.

Bingo! Rocco was no rat, but he did frequently mention his good friend, Tony D in his testimony. Tony was providing an alibi for the most recent crimes. The jury didn't buy it, nor the judge and Rocco went literally up the river for the rest of his days. The transcripts gave Tony's full name: Anthony Carlo DiThomasso. Mick smiled. That also, was likely to be a unicorn-rare name in these parts, not that there wasn't a small Italian-American community in the Northwest, but it was definitely small.

Tony's rap sheet was not as long as Rocco's and he'd had very few serious charges. Back in the eighties, the FBI investigated Tony D for racketeering and interstate transportation of stolen goods, but they couldn't make anything stick. It looked like Tony was the leader of the pair and Rocco ended up taking the rap more often than not.

One name that come up only once, was Mory Taglio, a friend of Tony D's. That name was quite well known to Mick and anyone else in Seattle who kept up with the business scene. Mr. Taglio was very wealthy and influential with many businesses and social connections in the area. Was he the money man who wanted Thor killed? Oh, that would be too good to be true. Now, in the 21st Century, Taglio was well respected and had friends in high places, going all the way to the governor's office. It was unlikely that any forty-year-old cold case could scratch that angelic veneer. Mick decided to forget it for now and track down DiThomasso.

It didn't take much more digging to find out that Tony D was currently the CEO of Italia Meats, one of Taglio's many legitimate businesses. *Holy shit!* Mick thought. This may have been a mob hit and Ricky Harris had undoubtedly witnessed it.

Mick could scarcely believe his luck. He felt an excitement he hadn't felt in years. He brought up the word processing app on his pc and began to type. His office looked like a tornado had blown through it, but all the newspaper clippings, scraps of paper and evidence boxes made perfect sense to him.

He began to catalog and document his findings. He now had the identity of the deceased, knew that Ricky Harris was alive and well when his car went swimming, and the identity of the real murderers, one of whom was still living and working right in town. If he could tie Taglio to the rest of the story, the shock waves that would go through Seattle would rival the aftermath of the Trump election.

Mick could hardly hold his eagerness in check when he called Chuck to tell him the good news. Chuck answered on the first ring.

"Already? Really, you got something?" he asked without so much as a hello first.

"I do and it's thanks to you for letting me in the database!" Mick said. "I have conclusive proof that the dead man in the car that night was not Ricky Harris. It was a man by the name of Thor Swenson."

"You're sure?"

"Positive. But I'm having a second pair of eyes look at both sets of prints just to dot all the i's and cross all the t's."

"That's great, Mick! But before you get too far ahead of yourself, don't you need to find out what happened to Harris? What if he's not alive anymore? He'd be as old as you are by now, so…maybe he died that night. Didn't you say he was a witness, and the killer knew he was a witness? Sounds like they might have taken him out that night, don't you think?"

Mick was quiet for a moment. The thought had crossed his mind, but with the near certainty that Ricky Harris walked away that night, he didn't give the idea much scrutiny.

"I think there's a certain logic to that, yes. But my CI didn't mention anything of the sort and he stressed that the story never changed in the retelling by Fortunato. I'm pretty sure if he and Tony D had tracked Harris down and killed him, that would have come up in Fortunato's stories, don't you?"

"Well, I think you've made some real progress, Mick. I don't think I'm comfortable going to the DA to ask them to reopen the case yet, though."

"No! No, of course not. I'll keep building my case. I've got some leads to go after still. When I bring you a case it will be rock solid, I guarantee!" He ended the call with a promise to buy the drinks when that time came.

ɛ⁄ɔɛ⁄ɔ

Chuck Wilson sat back in his chair and looked up at the drab acoustic-tiled ceiling of the homicide squad room. He folded his arms behind his head and put his feet on the desk.

His desk was positioned in a corner near the windows on the south side of the building. It was pressed up against a wide pillar that he supposed was part of the load-bearing construction of the building. He had a terrific view of the building across the street, not much more. On the average rainy Seattle day like today, he could barely even make out that much. It was some view.

There were pictures of his granddaughter as an infant taped haphazardly to the pillar. There were a few other pictures and tchotchkes scattered around and the other usual useless detritus of decades at the same desk.

Mick had always been careful to keep his obsession about the Ricky Harris case to himself most of the time. Chuck was pretty sure everyone else in the department had entirely forgotten about it if they were even old enough to have remembered in the first place.

In the past few years as his retirement approached, Mick had been likely to talk about it more and more. Even then, he only talked about it with Chuck.

So, learning that he was spending what sounded like all of his time on this closed case didn't come as much of a surprise. But it was astounding that Mick seemed to have actually made some progress toward proving his theory.

Chuck sighed and put his feet back on the floor. He looked around the room to make sure no one had overheard his brief conversation with Mick. It didn't appear as though anyone had.

For the first time since Mick's retirement, Chuck found himself wondering just how much of a case Mick was going to be able to build. Could he go to the DA's office with this? And if he did, would they really reopen a forty-year-old suicide? He supposed they would, given sufficient evidence to make it a homicide.

Mick said he could prove, with fingerprints, that the body in the car was not that of Ricky Harris. That was a huge break in his case. Not to mention a jailbird hitman claiming to have killed the guy who ended up in Ricky Harris's car. Chuck's mind was gearing up for some real whodunit contemplation then.

He got up and went to get his customary cup of 2 pm coffee. It would be little better than oil pan sludge and have the same heartburn-inducing properties, but it would keep him alert for the rest of the afternoon.

He returned to his desk, took a deep breath, and opened the file on top of the growing stack on his desk. He had plenty of already open cases to worry about without doing Mick's sleuthing for him. Chuck contented himself to wait until Mick came back with more than just a suspicious set of prints and a mouthy, and probably senile hitman's imaginings. He sipped at the sludge.

Chapter 14

O h, my freakin' God! If I hear *Phoenix* one more
time, I swear I'll scream!" Angie dropped heavily
into a well-cushioned theater seat. "This is the first
leg of the contest. We have nine more cities to go to. I
don't think I can stand it!"

Angie, Rufus, Don, and Craig sat front row center in
the Symphony Hall in Chicago. The ten-city tryouts tour
began where it all started for Windy City. Not only were
they originally from Chicago, but their first real gig had
been to open for Yes in this very venue. Their manager,
Ray Adler, sat a few rows back, letting the band make all
the decisions.

The term theater in the round had to have come from
this beautiful, acoustically perfect hall. It was well lit and
decorated with golden hues that harkened back to another
era. Angie thought it was a weird place to stage rock concerts, but it did. She had to admit, regardless of her annoy-
ance at the repetitive nature of the auditions, this was a
wonderful place to hear a concert.

Ray had arranged an "American Idol" style contest but
without the audience. The band would hear two numbers
from each wannabe and choose the top three acts in each
city to return in ten weeks to this very theatre to compete
against the other Ricky Harris stand-in hopefuls.

The auditions began in Chicago where the band started

out and would culminate in Seattle where the band met its end. Angie made no secret of her distaste for the whole affair, but Rufe loved the idea, and they did need the money. Ray was talking about making a live reunion album during the tour that would follow once they chose Ricky's successor.

The contest entrants numbered in the hundreds in Chicago alone. It was going to be a really long tour.

"It was our biggest hit," Rufe said mildly. We are going to hear it a lot more, and we are probably going to hear it done much worse than that last guy."

"Oh, Jesus save me," she said and buried her face in her hands.

Some of the contestants brought backup bands—others came solo and brought cheap guitars and amps. They ranged in age from late teens to mid to late sixties. A number of the older guys may have been pretty good singers, way back when, but now age had done its number on the ol' pipes and most of them didn't stand a chance.

By the end of the day, the group was worn out. They went for dinner and drinks to discuss the results.

"You have to admit, we saw some pretty great guitar work from a couple of those guys," Don said between mouthfuls. He was enthusiastically digging into his pasta. The years had been kind to Don and he looked much the same as he had when Angie and Rufe last saw him. He was still tall and thin, and his shoulder-length brown had faded to a pleasing gray. Angie thought his teeth were a bit too perfect and concluded he must have replaced them with dentures somewhere along the way.

Of the four of them, Craig had changed the most. He was still packing more than a few extra pounds and nowadays was almost entirely bald. He was attacking his lasagna with gusto and chasing it with copious amounts of wine.

"Yeah," said Rufe. "I thought that really young guy had a great voice, you know which one I'm talking about?"

Angie rifled through the pile of photos in front of her, occasionally picking at her chicken Caesar salad. "Here, this kid?" She handed the picture to Rufe.

"Yeah, that's him!" He showed the picture around the table. "You guys remember this guy?" Don and Craig nodded, and Ray picked up the picture.

"His name is Brent Caplan," Ray said. He made some notes in the tablet he had on the table before him. Apparently, his dinner was going to be the martini at his left hand.

"Good, we're finally getting somewhere. You have two more to go. Pick 'em, and let's get out of here." He sipped the martini.

"You're the company man," Rufe said. "Don't you have any input?"

"Nope. It's your band, I'm just here to listen and record." He smiled and winked at Angie.

She groaned in response. "I am trying my best not to totally freak out. I don't think I can make an objective choice."

"Oh, come on. They weren't all that bad. Most of them, yeah, but some of them obviously have talent. What about that big heavy-set fellow, what was his name?" Don asked.

"Oh yeah," said Pat. "I liked that one. We could play with him."

Angie started digging through the pictures again until she found the shot of the gentleman they referred to. They all agreed he would be the number two choice. One more to go and they could all go to bed.

During the audition tour, the four remaining band members had to practice along with their judging duties. They hadn't played together as a group, not even for a joke, in well over twenty years. Rufe and Don took turns on vocals when Angie wasn't singing, and they found that they could still sound pretty good without Ricky's lead guitar.

It was their practice jams that kept Angie in the game. She enjoyed working with the guys again and it was fun to play rock star once more after what was literally a lifetime. She knew this little bit of fun might just get her through the rest of what promised to be a tedious audition tour.

Finished with the Chicago tryouts, they were heading on to New York. After that, Philadelphia, Memphis, St. Louis, Salt Lake City, Denver, Los Angeles, San Francisco, and finally, Seattle.

Chapter 15

The fresh air, redolent with the aromas of pine, fir, and hemlock, swirled around them as Thor and Barb made their way to the trailhead at Wallace Falls State Park.

"I can't believe you talked me into this," Thor said with a laugh. He hadn't been on a hike in, well, ever actually. He felt like for a guy his age, he was in pretty good shape and according to Barb and the literature at the ranger station, this was an easy day hike.

The parking lot was packed and even though it was mid-morning on a Friday, the trail already had plenty of hikers. Some looked like old hippy types like Thor and Barb, but there were young folks too, and families with kids. Thor decided that he probably hadn't overestimated his fitness level, and he was eager to get to the trail.

"You'll do fine," Barb replied as she caught up with him. "Just pace yourself.

"I used to love to come up here, but as you well know, Larry wasn't much of an outdoors kinda guy." She smiled to let him know she wasn't getting sad about Larry again. She looked positively radiant in her cargo shorts, hiking boots, and t-shirt. Her long gray hair trailed down her back in a thick braid, and she had a sturdy walking stick to finish the ensemble.

"I see a bunch of little kids. Look, that woman has a

baby in a backpack!" Thor pointed to a young couple in front of them. The baby had turned around and was watching them curiously.

The weather was perfect for this enterprise; low 70s with a light cloud cover. No danger of rain, but they would be in deep forest for most of the hike anyway, so rain wouldn't be a big issue.

They soon came to the real entrance to the trail. It bore a sign with a quote from Wordsworth, "Come forth into the light of things, let nature be your teacher." Here the woods got heavy and darker, the old-growth evergreens were covered with moss and the rush of the Wallace River was audible to their right.

They settled into a slow, steady pace and after half a mile of broad, flat trail, came to a fork. To the left, the trail continued on into the distance, staying wide and flat. To the right, there was a wooden gate that made it clear that foot traffic only could go beyond this point.

"Which way, my dear?" Thor asked.

"To the right. We want to see the falls. This is the lower falls, then in another mile or so, up that is, we get to the mid falls. That is the most spectacular view, but I want you to make it to the top today! You in?"

"In for a penny, in for a pound I guess," he said. "Just as long as there is room for the helicopter to come airlift me to Harborview up there, you know after I have a heart attack from all this exertion!" He'd made the joke before he realized that might be a bit unkind based on the relative newness of Larry's death, but she laughed and assured him he would survive the climb.

They hiked on in silence for some time and Thor was getting winded. He found a great deadfall at the top of a hill that ran quite steeply down to a whitewater bend in the river below. He signaled Barb to stop and sat on the log, taking a sip from the water bottle slung over his shoulder.

She joined him on the log and he gave her a quick kiss.

"Yer killin' me here," he said. Barb just smiled. "Hey, did we talk about lunch?" he asked, only slightly more serious.

"You'll work up an appetite. We can stop at a café in Sultan on the way back, OK?"

"I was kind of thinking right about now sounds good for some food," he teased.

"Rest break over!" she declared and hopped to her feet. "Let's go!"

They continued up the trail and Thor had to admit that while they were steadily climbing higher, it wasn't altogether difficult. They must have been keeping a slower pace than most because soon they were virtually alone in the woods and the remoteness felt familiar and good.

He looked around as they walked. The river came in and out of view but was never out of earshot. The rest of the mountains too came in quick glimpses through the trees. The air was incomparably fresh, and it was incredibly soothing. He understood why Barb would bring him here.

"I do believe this is where my soul dwells," he said after a while. She stopped and looked at him, clearly thrilled.

"I feel the same way! I love it up here. I'm so glad you are enjoying it!" She hugged him and then hiked on.

They stopped a few more times, for Thor mostly, before they finally arrived at what Barb called the mid falls. There was a picnic table and a built-out overlook. They walked out onto the overlook and could feel the spray from the rushing, cold glacial runoff. The falls were beautiful and they both took a lot of pictures.

Several people had passed them going the other way and Thor thought those people were probably considering this the end of the hike. It was not yet noon however, and he knew Barb wanted to go all the way to the top, which he understood was another mile, the remaining leg not so easy a hike.

Barb was still taking pictures when Thor decided to take a rest break at the picnic table. There was the young couple with the baby, having lunch. The baby was working on a bottle and stared at Thor intently.

He offered his hand to the young man and said, "Thor Swenson." The young man shook it and said "Bjorn Andreasson. This is my wife, Anna." He had a thick Norwegian accent.

"Pleased to meet you," Thor said.

"You are Norwegian?" Bjorn asked.

Thor laughed. "Well, in name only. American as apple pie, I'm afraid."

He looked at the young man. "Microsoft?"

Bjorn smiled. "Novo Nordisk," he said. "Pharmaceuticals."

"Ah." Thor nodded. "And who is this fine fellow?" Thor asked, gently brushing the baby's plump cheek with his finger.

"This is Ander," Bjorn said with a proud smile.

By this time Barbara had joined them at the table and introduced herself. She asked if she could hold the baby and they were happy to oblige. Thor watched her and thought it sad that she didn't have grandchildren to enjoy. She was a natural.

After a few minutes, she put the cheerful Ander back into his backpack resting place and returned his bottle. "Are you going to the top?" she asked Anna.

"No. Ander is getting tired. We just wanted to get him out and get him used to hiking. This is one of our favorite outings and we are excited to share it with our son." She smiled a beautiful, bright smile as Bjorn looked on with obvious adoration.

"It was great to meet you guys! Have a safe trek back

down the hill," Thor said. He and Barb stowed their water bottles and prepared to get back to their hike. Thor was pretty sure he and little Ander were feeling the same right about now, but he didn't want to rain on what was turning out to be an otherwise perfect day. He tried not to think about the evening's gig that he would have to play later. All this physical exercise was not going to leave much left-over for performing.

The change in difficulty was immediate and after only a few minutes Thor found himself breathing much harder and really struggling to keep up.

After another half hour, the trail was quite steep, and they had to use the built-in log steps and handrails that switched back and forth across the mountain. Even now, in summer, there were occasional patches of old snow on the ground, dotting the loam beneath the trees. It was clear those were snow patches that would never melt all year round. Perhaps they were the birth of a glacier-to-be, some million years in the future. The temperature was cooler, another indication of increasing elevation.

The distance between them grew. Thor figured Barb didn't want to stop in case she might not want to get going again. *I know the feeling,* he thought.

He did stop, though. She was completely out of sight, and he thought she must be at the top by now. *Dear God, this can't go* that *much higher can it?* After a few minutes he was breathing a little more normally and he felt like he could probably make it to the top. He gave it his all and before long stepped into a small clearing. Barb was on the much humbler overlook that was built out near the very top of the falls. No picnic table up here. Screw you if you made it this far you should have eaten beforehand, was the message that was sent to Thor. Barb waved.

"I wasn't sure you were going to finish, so I decided to come on up without you," she said, still a little out of breath.

"This is a glaring anticlimax after the mid falls, you know," he responded between great gulps of air.

"I told you! The view is better at the halfway point. The thrill is making it to the top." She grinned. "And you did it! I'm so proud."

"Yeah, well check your phone for a signal. You may still need to call in that helicopter any minute," he panted.

He came to her and leaned against the rail, putting his right arm around her waist. "I'm glad I came, but I have to wonder about something. You do remember I have a gig with the guys tonight, right?"

"Sure."

"And are you planning to join us?"

"Oh, hell no! I'll be way too tired. I'm going to have a nice dinner and go to bed early. This is hard on a woman my age!" She laughed.

"Really? You think I'm going to let you live to get to the bottom?" He laughed too and hugged her.

As soon as they were breathing normally again, they started down. It was downhill all the way and they made very good time. By the time they reached the parking area, it was going on 2 o'clock and there were many people just beginning their hikes.

As Barb suggested, they did stop at a little café in Sultan and had a terrific lunch of homestyle meatloaf, mashed potatoes with gravy, and green beans. It tasted like a feast fit for a king after that hike and Thor cleaned his plate.

When they got back to Barb's house it was approaching 5 o'clock and they fell into bed, exhausted. Thor woke after 7 and headed home to shower and get ready to meet the band at the Liquid Lounge in Seattle. Their first set began at 9, so he had plenty of time to prepare. He carefully did not wake Barb when he left, taking her at her word that she wasn't planning to attend the show.

Showered, shaved, and only partially rested, Thor pulled his car into the parking area at Experience Music Project. He had his signature Les Paul with him, but the amps and his other guitars would have come with the band van.

He wasn't late, but he wasn't exactly early either, and he hoped Eric wouldn't be pissed that he was not going to be much good at setting up. He just concentrated on saving what little energy he had left for the performance. When he walked in carrying the guitar case, Eric nodded in his direction, Tom clapped him on the shoulder and Roger smiled. Nobody was mad.

"You look like refried shit, man," said Eric. "What's up with that?"

"Barb took me on a hike today. We went to the top of Wallace Falls. I feel like refried shit if you must know. Jesus Christ, I'm tired. Needless to say, she's at home sleeping," he finished.

Eric cracked up. "Oh my, have you got this relationship sewn up! I guess it's good if you both had fun. Did she forget you were playing tonight?"

"Nope. She was highly cognizant of my schedule the entire time. I think it was her plan to break up the band. You may as well start calling her Yoko."

Tom was already midway through his soundcheck, and Thor felt the need to catch up. He was shocked when Barbara came through the door and grabbed a table near the front. He finished his preparations and went down to meet her.

"I thought you were going to pass on this gig," he said.

She smiled. "Of course not! I just said that to get you back for pretending to be so exhausted!"

"Pretending?" He shook his head and returned to the stage.

Dead Salmon had spent the summer changing up their

playlist. For one thing, at Thor's insistence, they added more Emerson, Lake, and Palmer to their repertoire so that Tom could really shine on keyboards. Thor always stepped down from the stage to dance with Barb during *Runaround*, and they had taken *Phoenix* entirely out of the lineup.

During the break between the second and third sets, Bert took Thor aside.

"Have you seen that old guy sitting with what must be his son in the front row, Thor?" he asked.

"No, why?"

"He's been staring at you for the entire show. He looks like he wants to throttle you or something!" Bert was generally a man of few words and he was showing grave concern to be bringing this up, Thor knew.

"Do you think it's someone you know?" he asked.

"I don't know. I'll look for him. I can't think of anyone who might be angry at me," Thor said.

They both took a last sip of beer and returned to the stage. Bert settled behind his drum kit and then gestured toward the front row with a jut of his chin. Thor looked and saw a man about his own age sitting with a younger fellow who looked to be in his 30s. They both had drinks in front of them and were in fact staring rather intently at Thor. He saw that they noticed him returning their stare, so he smiled and turned away to pick up his guitar.

Throughout the band's third and final set of the evening, the older man in the front row did seem to be staring. Thor would glance at him from time to time, then run his gaze over the rest of the crowd as he sang and moved about the stage.

During the performance, the man finished two more drinks, while his companion appeared to have been nursing the same drink all night. They finished with the last song of the evening, an acoustic ballad that Thor had written just for Barb. He sat on the edge of the stage, the lights came down and the waning crowd leaned in as he began to sing. The rest of the band set their instruments down and left the stage. There was a single spotlight on Thor.

He sang of love and loss and finding love again. Barbara started to cry when she heard her name and realized the song was about her. It was the first she'd heard it. Thor had been keeping it a secret until he was ready to roll it out. That is why he was so glad that she had come to the show after all.

When he finished, the applause was booming, and Barb ran up to give him a hug. She pulled him clean off the stage and he laughed and spun her around.

"No one ever wrote a song for me before," she cried. "That was so lovely!" She hugged him again.

The crowd was filing out and the band began to pack up for the slow trip home. Thor looked around for the two staring men, but they were nowhere to be seen. They were not familiar to him in any way and he wondered what the deal was. He shrugged and turned his attention to his instruments.

Chapter 16

D ad, I'm not going to take no for an answer!" Stephen was saying. "You have been cooped up in here for months and frankly, I'm worried about you!"

He went to the window and threw open the drapes. "Look how dark it is in here! Are you depressed or something? I swear your obsession with this old case is eating you alive. You need to get out, Dad. Have you even left the house since the boys' Little League game? You know, the one you ran out in the middle of?"

"Yes, I did," said Mick. "I took a drive up to Monroe just the other day."

"That was two months ago, Dad! And you went to interview an inmate at the prison, don't think I don't know that.

"You didn't go fishing at the lake this summer with Chuck like you always do. I know because I asked him! You blew him off. He's worried about you too! He knows you are working on that old case and told me he thinks you need to let it go. He's right. So, you found some fingerprints, so what? You have a whole lot of nothing according to Chuck.

"Admit it. You are obsessed with this old case and you're getting weird about it. You need to drop it!"

Mick took a deep breath. "You're right, I know. I've

sort of hit a dead-end, and I'm not sure what else I can do. If it were an open case, I'd get an order from a judge to exhume Ricky Harris's body, so that I could prove that body belonged to Thor Swenson. Only I can't get an order, because it's a closed case and I'm no longer on active duty.

I think I have may have solved it partially, because I have a set of fingerprints that came from Harris's body and also a set of fingerprints of Thor Swenson, the person whose identity I believe Harris stole that night. They will show that the body in the car and Thor Swenson are the same person, but I don't know what happened to Harris.

It's only because I've waited so long to chase down my theories that it's hard to let go. I've learned things that lead me to believe this was a small part in a much bigger case." He sat down in his favorite armchair.

Stephen relaxed a bit. "I know. I'm sorry that you made a little progress only to hit a wall. It must be frustrating. But tonight, I want to take you out. There's a band playing at the Liquid Lounge tonight that does classic rock—it's right up your alley. You'll have fun, come on!"

"Ha! Give up my rock and roll obsession to go listen to rock and roll. Well, why not? It's not as though I have other plans," Mick said.

"Is Emily coming?" he asked.

"No, we couldn't get a sitter, but she insisted I come drag you out of the house kicking and screaming if that's what it took."

"I won't kick and scream. Can we get a bite to eat first?" Mick asked.

"You bet! The Pop Kitchen is awesome, we've been there a few times and it's right around the corner." Stephen said.

Mick grabbed a light jacket because he knew they would be out after dark. Once the sun goes down in Seattle, the temperature quickly drops.

They managed to get the last table for two in Pop
Kitchen and ordered sandwiches that came with home-
made potato chips and local beer. It was fantastic, and
Mick felt like he had awakened from a long, intense
dream. Things seemed so weird outside his insular world
of the 70s Seattle rock scene, following up on leads so old
they had died from boredom decades past.

He started to realize just how deeply he'd embedded
himself in what had started out as a fun project. His dis-
covery of a young man who happened to go missing on the
very night Ricky Harris died had so bolstered his certainty,
that his theory was correct, that he'd forgotten to keep on
living while he researched.

It had been so long since Mick had eaten something that
didn't come out of a can, that the sandwich tasted just that
much better. The beer was delicious and cold and the perfect complement to the grilled ham and Havarti sandwich.

"The boys would like to see their Granddad soon too,
you know," Stephen was saying. "And Emily misses you.
She really wanted to come tonight but as I mentioned, she
was determined that I get you out of the house. She's the
one who went through the Entertainment section of the
Times to find a band we thought you would like."

"Cool," said Mick between mouthfuls. "I'm looking
forward to it!"

"When I spoke with Chuck, he also mentioned that it's
not too late to take that fishing trip this year. Maybe you
should give him a call. You know, take advantage of this
warm weather while you still can."

Mick swallowed a bite and took a sip of his beer. "I
think that sounds like a great idea." He didn't add that it
would be a good opportunity to straighten Chuck out about
how serious the fingerprint evidence was once Denny confirmed it.

They finished their dinner while talking about the

twins, how Stephen was doing at work with his narcissistic boss, and other more mundane things. The one thing Stephen refused to discuss and went to great lengths to change the subject when it appeared that the conversation might head that way, was Mick's old case.

They finished dinner and walked around the corner toward the Museum of Pop Culture, wherein could be found the Liquid Lounge. They bought tickets at the door and Stephen refused to let Mick pay. They enjoyed the MoPOP for about an hour before they headed into the Lounge. Mick lingered at the Jimi Hendrix display. It was pretty cool, he had to admit. Like many locals, Mick had never been to MoPOP before. It was a Seattle icon and not having been there previously was like saying you'd never been up in the Space Needle or seen the Ballard Locks. He felt remiss.

They rounded one corner and found the exhibit commemorating Ricky Harris's death on the night of the Windy City concert in 1975. It was little more than a plaque with a brief blurb about the accident, accompanied by a black and white photo of the rental car being pulled from the canal.

Stephen shook his head and laughed. "I might have known they would have something in here to remind you. I should have thought of that before deciding to take you on the tour," he said.

"Nah, it's OK, son," Mick replied. "We're here to have fun. Let's go." He clapped Stephen on the back and they headed out of the MoPOP.

There was a short line going into the Lounge and as they shuffled along the wall, waiting their turn to pay the cover charge and get hand stamps, Mick noticed a lit marquee with a poster that proclaimed, "Tonight! Dead Salmon! Classic rock for the ages!" Also on the poster were portraits of five men, all about Mick's age and looking very serious. Each one had a name printed below it. Front and center was a tall man with long gray hair. The name below this photo read, "Thor Swenson." Mick's stomach dropped into his shoes. He felt dizzy. He took a deep breath and rubbed his temples. He tried looking away and then checked again. The name was the same. It was not his imagination. It could not possibly be a coincidence, could it? Could Stephen have known in any way that this man would be in this particular band? He didn't think so. He thought it had to be a lucky accident.

But was it? Mick had learned if nothing else, that Thor Swenson is a very common name in the Seattle area. He started to point out the poster to Stephen, who was ahead of him and paying the cover charge by this time but decided against it. That Stephen was making a sincere effort to see that he forgot about the case was apparent. There was no reason to show him what he would certainly write off as coincidence.

They had arrived early enough to get seated well before the band began to play, so they were fortunate to get a table at the front. Mick ordered his favorite vodka rocks and Stephen ordered an Old Fashioned, which he planned to make last for the rest of the evening.

"I'm designated driver tonight, Dad," he said. "You drink whatever you like. I'll just have one and then switch to water or something."

Mick looked around at the dimly lit venue and saw there were framed works of art along the walls, backlit alcoves housing what had to be Chihuly glass pieces, and Art Deco style barstools along the perimeter of the bar.

He wondered why he'd never heard of Dead Salmon, a local band when this rapidly filling lounge proved they had quite a following. Just playing at this place was a big deal for a local band, considering that the Lounge often hosted nationally known acts, too.

By nine when the band took the stage and the house lights went down, there was standing room only and a line out the door of the place. They started with *Don't Fear the Reaper* by Blue Oyster Cult and then played an eclectic series of popular classic rock songs, one after the other.

Mick had to admit that Swenson was a good singer and great on the guitar, but he didn't see anything right off the bat that shouted Ricky Harris. He also found it interesting that they played a lot of ELP and Yes in the first two sets, but no Windy City, who were of the same ilk.

He thought surely, they would play *Phoenix*, a rock anthem if ever there was one, but they did not. He couldn't take his eyes from Swenson the entire night. The sound was too loud for Stephen to try to make much conversation and Mick contented himself with absorbing as much of the performance as possible.

It wasn't until the end of the final set, the last song of the night that Mick knew he'd found his man. Swenson sat on the edge of the stage, his long gray hair in a ponytail behind him.

He wore a t-shirt and jeans and had picked up an acoustic 12-string. He began to play a lilting melody and soon his voice joined the guitar. If Mick closed his eyes, he could pretend it was 1975 and this was a Ricky Harris solo at a Windy City concert. The man's voice was identical, if slightly more mature.

But he didn't close his eyes. Instead, he looked around at the slightly thinned crowd and saw a bunch of people intently enjoying the song. It must have been an original. Mick wasn't familiar with it and he saw that no one in the audience was singing along, so it seemed as if no one else recognized it either.

He began to get nervous again. This was Ricky Harris, calling himself Thor Swenson. He'd found his missing piece. But how to prove it? That was going to take some doing.

Mick looked over at Stephen and felt a brief pang of regret. In his effort to get Mick to give up the case, Stephen had inadvertently helped him solve it.

The song ended and a woman at the next table jumped up and gave Swenson a hug. Mick took that as his cue to exit and he pulled Stephen along with him.

When they got back to Stephen's car, Mick leaned against it while Stephen unlocked the doors. He'd had more than a few drinks and the booze was starting to hit him, hearty dinner notwithstanding.

"Looks like I'd best get you home," Stephen said, and he helped Mick into the car.

"Yeah, I think I was tossing back the vodka at a quicker pace than I realized."

"It's OK, Dad. I'm just glad you had a good time. You did, didn't you? Those guys were pretty good, don't you think?"

"Oh yes," said Mick. "Very good. Quite professional."

Stephen drove carefully and eventually got Mick home. He helped his father up the stairs and into bed. Mick was still awake when Stephen left, locking the front door behind him.

He lay awake for some time, serious buzz notwithstanding. He wanted more than anything to get up and start looking for Thor Swenson, aging garage band artist. But he knew from his previous search for Thor the Viking that the name was common, and his search would be tedious. As he drifted off to sleep, he thought about confronting the man in the band. How sweet would that be?

When he awoke, Mick saw that he'd slept for over nine hours, a new record. He couldn't remember his dreams, but he knew they had to do with chasing down this latest lead. He tried to remember if he'd mentioned anything to Stephen last night but didn't think so.

He fetched some coffee and sat down at his desk, to once again sift through his people finder online. He searched for hours but could not come up with anyone in his mid-sixties who might be in a band. He searched on Dead Salmon too and found a Facebook page that hadn't been updated in some time. Thor Swenson wasn't even mentioned on it. Some guy named Larry Malone was fronting the band when that page was created. There was no corresponding website and no mention anywhere of a new band member. Mick decided to take a new tack.

The boys in the band were certainly old enough for at least some of them to be retired, but it was possible that one or more of them had day jobs. He couldn't remember the names of the other band members, so he went back to the Facebook page. He started with founding member, Eric Jensen. Common enough name, but he might still be easier to find.

The first Google hit was an Eric Jensen, Head Coach of the Chinook University Cohos football team. Well, that can't be him, can it? But it was. Jensen was a coach at the "Little U" as it was known locally. Unbelievable. He wondered how the band members knew each other. Were they all academics? He went to the university's website. There was a faculty directory, and while he thought it highly unlikely that Ricky Harris somehow ended up a university prof, it might be a good place to start for the rest of the bunch. He went back to the Facebook page and wrote down the names of the other four guys. There were quite a number of Thor Swenson on Facebook when he did a search, but none of them were the right guy. Larry Malone notwithstanding, that certainly is the same band, no question.

Now back to the Chinook University faculty directory. He started at the top of the alphabetical list and the next name he came to was Roger Collins. Roger is a Professor of English Literature. *And a pretty good bass player to boot*, Mick thought. Then he found Larry Malone, the lead guitar and vocals according to the Facebook page, but the big man had not been in evidence last night.

Next to his bio in the directory, it said *(Deceased)*. Ah, the plot thickens. So, no more Larry. They needed a new frontman for their little band. How the hell do they find the one and only Ricky Harris? Because by now, let's face it, Mick is convinced that is who the Thor Swenson he saw playing last night really is.

After the late, lamented Larry, Mick found Tom Morrison. He was in the History Department. He looked to be a studious sort and the very talented keyboard player from last night seemed to fit the part of a historian.

Last but not least, Dr. Bertrand Scott, Professor of Physics (and part-time drummer) rounded out the roster. Mick couldn't help himself and he scrolled down the page just a bit further. There it was, unbelievably, right in the middle of the page, bold as brass and big as life. Thor Swenson, Ph.D. Chair of the Mathematics Department.

"Are you serious?" Mick said aloud. Was it really possible that Ricky Harris, the twenty-something rock legend who came from a humble background with no education, had become the head of the math department at Chinook University?

A lifetime had passed since that fateful night at the Fremont Bridge, so anything was possible. But how had an intoxicated, likely freezing kid who assumed the identity of a small-time thug, built himself into an educated, respectable, member of the community? The only way to find out would be to get it from the horse's mouth. If Mick approached Swenson with everything he knew, he might spook him and never get to the bottom of the case. It would be best to take his time, stake out Swenson and get as much information as possible first. Then, when he can no longer deny who he is, confront him.

He read the rest of the bio, short though it was. Swenson had never married and had no children. He was a Chinook University alum, having done his post-graduate work at the UW.

"Well I'll be damned. You never left Seattle. That's absolutely astounding."

Mick went back to Google to find a calendar that would show when and where Dead Salmon w playing next. It was almost September and they would be heading back to school soon. He wondered if they performed during the school year. Of course, the football coach would have his team practicing well before the fall term, so it seemed as though they did play when school was in session—good.

He found that they were scheduled to play the Edison Inn that very Sunday night. *Where the hell is Edison?* Mick wondered. He mapped it. Edison, it turns out, was halfway between Mt. Vernon and Bellingham, hell and gone to the northwest. Mick was impressed that they would drive all the way up there to play in some podunk tavern when they clearly had enough of a following to pack a venue as popular (and national act attracting) as The Liquid Lounge. He figured they knew the owner or something.

Whatever it was that had them going way out there, Mick decided he was going to go too. It would be a nice Sunday drive, in this the very best weather of the year. He'd get a good view of Mt. Baker as the sun was setting to the west over the north Sound. It would be fun. He thought for a moment he should see if Stephen and Emily wanted to come along, but then he decided that his planned fandom was more than he wanted to share with the kids just yet.

There was no such thing as a music video back in the seventies, but Mick was pretty sure there must be some concert footage of Windy City available on YouTube. He did some searching and indeed, he found several examples of Ricky Harris performing live. He tried to remember some of the mannerisms and guitar licks the guy from the previous night had evidenced, but it was age or the vodka or a combination of both that kept him from getting a clear picture in his mind. That was all the more reason to make the trek out to the boonies to see the band again. *It's just got to be him*, Mick thought.

Mick's cell phone rang. He picked it up. It was Dennis Stern.

"Hey Denny! I could use some good news about now. What do you have for me?" Mick asked.

"You're in luck, Mick. The two sets of prints you provided are a match. They both came from the same person. The set that came from the dead body was a little wider, but I remembered that you told me the guy drowned. That would explain the discrepancy. Regardless, they are from the same person. Absolutely no question in my mind."

"Oh, Denny you have no idea! You've just made my day! I can't thank you enough. Now, if I should be so lucky as to get someplace with this evidence, would you be willing to testify to that in a court of law?"

"Sure, why not? You obtained these prints legally, didn't you?" He sounded concerned.

"Definitely. They are all on the up and up. Now I just need one more set and I'm there. Thanks for this and stand by. I may need you to look at some more in the near future."

"You got it," Denny said.

Chapter 17

The drive up to Edison was always fun for Thor and Barb. Once they left I-5, the scenery became much more rural and the view of the mountains was spectacular this time of year. They had a good view of Mt. Baker for most of the trip, and the Sound was occasionally visible off to the left. The tulip fields in Mt. Vernon were empty now in the late summer, but in springtime, they were alive with brilliant tulips of every hue. They passed dairies and cornfields and the occasional alpaca farm.

Conversation was at a comfortable minimum. They were happy in each other's company and often no words were needed. They both enjoyed the natural beauty of the journey and that was enough.

Early on, Thor had strongly objected to making such a long trip to play at a very small pub, especially on those occasions when he had school starting the following morning. But Barbara had been able to talk him into giving it a try, just for her. She knew the owners and had been going up there with Larry for twenty years.

Once he'd made the trip, Thor saw the appeal. The Edison Inn was a small, earthy, very Northwest-style tavern. It had a tiny stage and even smaller dance floor, but the locals packed the house to standing room only on Sunday nights when the live music was there.

Some weekends, the Edison hosted classic rock bands,

other weekends country and western acts packed the house. The clientele ranged in age from late thirties to late seventies, but no customers hesitated to hit that dance floor just as soon as the band began to play.

The bar was long and fronted the kitchen. Delicious American standard pub food could be had until closing time. They offered burgers and fries, grilled cheese, fried chicken, meatloaf, macaroni, and cheese, and because they were just close enough to the Canadian border, they sometimes offered poutine for their visitors from the north.

The hardwood floor was worn and warped, but the little dance floor was kept level and smooth. There was a large mirror behind the bar, a row of taps that all sported some Northwest micro brew's logo, and a wine rack to one side as something of an afterthought. It was dark and dank and smelled of beer and grease. The local crowd was a friendly, loud bunch who all knew each other. Dairy farmers and fishermen mostly, they came here to escape the labors of the day.

Because the trip was long and some of the guys did have Monday morning classes most of the time, the band started their first set at 7:00 and wound up at 10:00. That still made for an exhausting hour-long drive back to Seattle, but the performance high usually carried them all the way home.

Thor and Barb arrived just after 5:00 and hurried to unload Thor's gear from the car and stash it on stage. They wanted time to get dinner. The poutine was Barb's guilty pleasure and it was on the menu this night. French fries and cheese curds with gravy might not sound like dinner to most, but to Barb it was heaven.

Thor watched her chow down with relish and he had to laugh. He'd tried the concoction and judged it nasty. "To each her own," he said with a grimace. "Next, you'll be putting tomato juice in perfectly good beer," he teased.

"Try and stop me!" she said, laughing.

"Yeah, well don't try that when you're out with me. I'll have to leave you to find your own way home. I think I'll try the chicken fried steak as long as we're throwing healthy dietary choices to the wind."

The rest of the band trickled in and by 7:00 they were heading to the stage preparing to play. They kept to the same song list that they had used Friday night at the Liquid Lounge. Thor would again play *Barbara's Song* solo as the finale. He figured it would never be quite as special for her as the first time, but he was proud of the first thing he'd written in over forty years and it showed.

Thor picked up the Les Paul and strummed the opening notes, A^m, G, F, G, A^m, of *Don't Fear the Reaper*. He was really feeling good and for some reason couldn't wait to get into his office on campus in the morning. Fall quarter classes for him didn't start for another week, but he had plenty of preparation to do, a new teacher to welcome to the department, and a wide-eyed crop of freshmen to look forward to. Playing with the band was fun and had really brought him back to life in a way he didn't expect. But teaching was his first love and his love of math was easy to share.

True to form, folks got up to dance almost immediately and the crowd had swelled to a number that would have made the local Fire Marshall nervous. Fortunately, the Fire Marshall was not in attendance.

Thor and Eric were jamming on the Allman Brothers' *One Way Out* when Thor turned to glance at the crowd. There, at the very first table past the dance floor, sat the old guy from Friday night. He was alone this time and drinking a beer instead of a hard drink, but Thor was sure it was the same guy. He was staring with that intent look and following every move. Thor quickly turned back to Eric lest he forget what he was doing.

He continued to play and did his level best to not look at the guy, but he could still feel those eyes burning into him. The dude had to be some kind of mental case, not a fan. There was something just weird about the whole thing. For him to drive all the way up here, well that was beyond weird, it was eerie.

They finished the first set and Thor sat with Barb for the break. She had a cold beer waiting for him. They never paid for drinks when they were playing the Edison. Dead Salmon in the house meant plenty of customers for owners Jim and Judy Wood, and they gladly supported the guys in the band. Judy and Barb were old schoolmates, and they did their best to chat and catch up, even over the music and crowd noise.

They were laughing about something when Thor sat down. Barb gave him a peck on his sweaty cheek. "Yuk," she said, wiping her mouth.

He chuckled. "Well, gee, thanks."

"I didn't mean it like that," she said. "You're sweaty."

"Oh," he said distracted. He reached across the little round pub table and grabbed a napkin to wipe away the sweat. He set it on the empty seat beside him and acknowledged Judy. "Good to see you, Judy."

"Back at ya, Thor," Judy said.

"You look all serious, Babe," said Barb. "What's going on? Is Eric's guitar out of tune again?"

Thor shook his head. "No." He turned around and looked at the lone fan sitting at the front table. There were three other people seated around the same table, but it was obvious the guy was not with them. For once, he wasn't looking at Thor. He seemed to be staring into his beer instead.

Thor turned back to the ladies. "See that guy up there in front? He's wearing a navy-blue sweatshirt and jeans. I don't think he's with those other people at that table." He pointed as discreetly as he could in the direction of his ardent fan.

Both women nodded. "Do you recognize him, Barb?" he asked.

"Yeah. Isn't that the guy Bert pointed out to you Friday night?"

"Yes! It's the same guy. What the hell is he doing up here in Edison on a Sunday night, staring at me?"

"I don't know. I guess maybe he likes your music?" Barb offered.

"Who would follow us all the way up here unless they were someone we know or had invited? It's weird and it's not a coincidence. I'm pretty creeped out if you want to know the truth."

"I'm sure he's harmless," Judy said. "Maybe he just enjoys your music."

"You know, I might buy that explanation if he danced or tapped his foot or talked to anyone else, but he doesn't. He just sits there and stares at me. It's disturbing, I tell you!"

Judy laughed, but Barb knew better and patted his arm. "I hear you, Thor, but I think it really is just a coincidence. Let it go. If it happens again, then we can talk about it."

He sighed and took a long drink of his beer. "OK. Yeah. Twice isn't that big a deal. But still…"

Judy motioned for Jim to join them and they moved on to other topics, with much laughter and joking. Thor finished his beer feeling much better, took a quick bathroom break, and rejoined the band on stage.

At the end of the evening, he played *Barbara's Song* and sang it as though they were the only two people in attendance. Barb had told Judy it was coming, but the heads-up did not lessen her emotion. Judy cried as Thor sang. It brought the house down and had people shouting for an encore. That is something Dead Salmon never did, but just this once, for their friends, they capitulated.

For the first time in months, they played *Phoenix* as the encore number. Every patron in the joint was on their feet and tables and chairs bumped and slid as people made room to dance. It was a really great ending to their summer season. Going into fall, football season and school was Dead Salmon's call to cut back on the performing, and concentrate on the real world. They only had one more gig before the long winter hiatus. Thor and Barb enjoyed the drive home that night more than ever before.

❧❧❧

On Monday, Thor was feeling proud of a super productive day in the office. Late in the afternoon as he was preparing to head out, Eric popped in. That was a first.

"Afternoon, Coach. What brings you to the smarter side of campus?" Thor asked with a grin. "Are you here to beg me to turn a blind eye to the fact that your star wide receiver, Mr. Ty Wiggins, is failing Advanced Calculus?"

"Wait, what?" said Eric, alarmed. "He is?"

Thor was still grinning. "He was until recently. He came to see me last week. He pleaded with me not to tell you. He knows the repercussions and I know you can't spare him if you hope to keep winning. I assigned a tutor to him. My understanding is that he's working hard. Fear not."

"Yeah, like you would know we've been winning," Eric said.

"I confess Mr. Wiggins had to explain what a wide receiver does and how he is a key part of your offense. I'm afraid I don't know much about football, as you know. But because of this, I've decided just for you I'm going to become a football fan. I'll even start coming to the games on Saturdays."

"That would be terrific!" Eric said. "But none of that is why I'm here. I wanted to tell you this last night, but there just wasn't time and it was so damned noisy in there, as usual."

"No shit. Hey! Did you see that old guy up front? You know, the same one that was staring at me Friday night? He went all the way up to Edison to stare at me again. What the hell?"

"Yeah, as a matter of fact, I did notice. We all did. Tom saw him first and mentioned it to the rest of us, but Bert said absolutely not to point him out to you because it would freak you out."

"Well it did freak me out! Barb said once was no big deal, twice was a coincidence and I should just forget about it unless it happens again." He fiddled with a pen on the desk and didn't meet Eric's eyes.

"I think that's good advice," Eric said. "I mean, it was kind of weird, I won't argue, but who knows? Maybe he's an old queen and he's got a crush on you. Stranger things have happened. I wouldn't lose sleep over it."

"Yeah, you're right. Barb's right. I guess I'm getting paranoid in my old age," Thor conceded.

"That's not why I'm here either, though," said Eric. "I have a surprise for you. You're not going to believe it. I already told the other guys and they're all for it. Good thing you're sitting down. You ready?"

"Ready as I'll ever be," Thor said.

"Windy City is doing a reunion tour!"

"Really?" Thor was genuinely surprised. "When? Are they coming to Seattle?"

"Yes, but that's not the good part. Right now, they are doing a nationwide search for the next Ricky Harris. It's a contest. Seattle is the last stop on the search."

Thor thought he might puke. His heart started to beat so wildly that he was sure he would have a coronary that would dwarf what killed poor Larry.

"Wow," he managed to get out. "That's pretty cool."

"No, it isn't!" said Eric. "This is: I signed you up for the auditions! It's going to be on October 10th at the Paramount. Dude, you are a shoo-in! Nobody wields that axe like you do! And your voice? Come on! Everybody knows you do the best Ricky Harris impression in the world! You can't lose!"

Thor tried to speak, but no words came out. He really didn't know if he was going to be able to avoid puking. How could Eric do such a thing without asking him first?

He put his face in his hands and tried to take deep breaths. Eric said nothing. He tried to rationalize that Eric had no idea what he'd done. To him it was something fun, a game. He couldn't have known the depth of the pain it would cause. Thor took another deep breath and looked up.

"I can't do it," he said flatly.

"What? Why not? Hey man, I laid down a $500 entry fee! You can't back out. You're bound to win this thing! Don't you think it would be fun?" He was obviously not expecting a negative response.

"I said I can't. Maybe I won't would be more accurate. I can't believe you would do that without asking me first! What were you thinking?" He got to his feet and stared across the desk at Eric.

"What was I thinking? I was thinking that maybe my friend would want to share his immense talent with the world! Is that too much to ask? What's wrong with you? Why wouldn't you want to give this a try?" Eric looked really hurt, but considering his feelings was not something Thor was prepared to do.

"I'm not doing it and that's final," Thor said. "See you later." He slammed his laptop shut and grabbing it, stormed out. "Lock the door when you leave," he said. He felt Eric's eyes on him as he walked down the hall.

He was supposed to go straight over to Barb's for dinner, but as he sat in his car, he wasn't sure he wanted to see her now. He wondered if she knew about this. He started the car.

He wanted to think about why his reaction was so strong. Why were those old, old feelings still so near the surface? After all this time, why would he get nauseated at the very mention of Windy City? He thought about Dead Salmon's upcoming gig Friday night. It would be the last weekend gig for a while, as Saturday football games were taking up all of Eric's time and focus. Dead Salmon would go on a break for the rest of the fall and pick up performing again sometime after the new year.

He wondered if Eric had thought about whether he could take the time to go back him up at this supposed audition. Who was doing the auditions? Would Angie be there? Rufus? How was it possible that he hadn't heard about this before now? Surely there would have been some mention of it on the radio?

But in the car, he mostly listened to NPR these days, not music stations. If any mention of the contest had been on the local news, he'd missed that too.

Shit. He found himself pulling into Barb's driveway in spite of his unwillingness to see her. He mentally kicked himself for that habit. *Jesus, what an idiot I am!* he thought.

He locked the car and walked up the steps and rang the bell. She met him at the door and handed him a glass of merlot. He gladly took it and flopped onto the couch.

"Rough day?" she asked.

"Not until just a little bit ago. Eric came to see me."

She grinned. "He told you?"

"You know about this too?" he asked.

"Of course! He came over to my table last night and

told me all about it, but he was very determined that I not mention it to you. He wanted to be the one to tell you." She was still smiling.

"What possesses any of you to think this is a good idea?" he shouted.

Her smile faded. "Why wouldn't it be?"

Thor set the wine on the coffee table. "Because I...can't," he said.

Why indeed? He realized that short of the truth, there was no earthly reason why not. There was no explaining why he wouldn't be flattered and thrilled to get such an opportunity. He'd made a good show of performing and playing rock star on the weekends, and they all knew he enjoyed it. How could he conceivably explain to Barb or Eric or any of them that Angie Gardiner had been the love of his life? That she had betrayed him so long ago. That he could never face her again.

When he thought about it that way, it sounded so stupid. Even to him. He was 64 years old for Christ's sake! Wasn't it time, he got over Angie? He hadn't seen her in forty years. God, was he so emotionally fucked up that he would let something so ancient, so really trivial when he thought about it, completely overshadow his life all these years later? He was a respected member of the community. He had a brilliant and successful career. He was in love with a wonderful woman. Why was he reacting to this as though it had all happened last week?

Barb just watched him. She could probably see the wheels turning in his head, and she gave him the space, to process whatever he needed to process. She picked up his half-empty wine glass and went to refill it.

When she came back, he accepted the glass from her and took a long drink. At that moment, he decided to tell her everything. It was a knee-jerk reaction to be sure, and he knew that if he thought about it too long, he might change his mind. He also knew that if he didn't tell her now, the whole long sordid story, he would never be able to explain his behavior and she would always know he had a secret.

"Babe, sit down," he said. He took her hand and led her around the coffee table to sit next to him. "It's kind of a long story, but it's time I told you." He proceeded to say out loud what had only ever been in his own thoughts for four decades.

When he finished, there were tears in her eyes and his. He sipped at the last of the wine.

Barbara dabbed at her face and stood up. "I'll get more." She reached for his glass. Her own was long since empty. She drank it while he spoke, and she sat rapt, hanging on every word.

When she returned, she sat next to him again and he hugged her.

"You're the first person I've ever told that to," he said. "It's such an enormous relief, you can't begin to know."

"If I heard that story from anyone else, I'd think they were the biggest fucking liar on the planet," she said without inflection. "But you're telling the truth, aren't you? You really are Ricky Harris." She sounded awestruck, and he thought it best not to reply.

"How did you do it? Where did you go after you left the car in the water?"

He took a deep breath and began talking again. "It was indescribably freezing. I'm sure I was in the early stages of hypothermia. I found a phone booth that still had a phonebook and that had a street map in it. Thor's address was on his driver's license, so I found his apartment, it wasn't very far. I'd taken his keys too, so I let myself in.

"I knew his clothes would fit me. I took a hot shower, changed, and went to bed. I slept for most of the next day. When I got up, I ate, and then I sat there and wondered what to do next.

"I turned on the TV and watched the news stories of my own death. I watched them pull the car from the canal. I listened to all the tearful interviews. I was hurt that no one seemed to interview Angie, although I later learned that she had refused to speak to the media.

"I had a lot of time to reflect on my life. It took me a few days to make a hard and fast decision on what I was going to do with the rest of my life. I knew I needed to lay low for some time until the big news of my death blew over.

"I ended up pursuing my other dream—my real, my first dream. I decided to go back to school. I found out that Thor didn't finish high school. I had, so it wasn't hard to get a GED as Thor. Then I applied for student loans, got a job at a little deli there in Fremont, and went back to school.

"I'd always been good at math and I decided that would be my major. I was accepted at the UW and that's where I did my undergraduate and post-graduate work. I supplemented my meager part-time wages by giving guitar lessons on the side."

"Didn't anyone ever recognize you?"

"No. Not really. That first night after the shower, I cut my hair off and then shaved my head completely. When it grew back in, I dyed it brown for the longest time. When it began to turn gray, I let it go back to blonde. Once in a great while, someone would mention that I bore a resemblance to Ricky Harris, but as the years went by, that became less frequent and eventually stopped." He looked at her.

"So, you understand why I'm so freaked out, right? I am Thor Swenson. I have been for most of my life—much longer than I was Ricky Harris. I just don't think in terms of Ricky Harris anymore."

"No wonder you were so angry at Eric!"

"I wasn't angry. I just couldn't accept what he was telling me. You see why I can't do it, right?" he asked again. He was imploring her.

"I see why you think you can't do it, yes. I'm not sure I agree with you, though," she said.

"Seriously? You think I want to see those people after all this time? After what I did to them? I can't!"

"Why not? I think you owe it to them," Barb said. "You owe it to yourself, too. Shit, you owe it to me at this point! All of you need closure. If you didn't, you wouldn't be so upset by the thought of coming clean with them.

"Thor, I get it," she went on. "Angie and Rufus did an incredibly shitty thing to you. No argument from me there. But what you did to them was orders of magnitude worse! You said you'd been drinking and smoking dope, I get that too. You were young and impetuous and probably not in the best decision-making frame of mind. But Jesus Thor, you faked your death! You were famous! Oh my god, I was one of the millions of fans who cried when I read the news!" She said it as though it was finally sinking in that she was actually sitting in the presence of the one and only Ricky Harris. She took a good slug of the wine and then just sat there looking at him.

"I don't know if I can," he said quietly.

"I want you to at least consider it. You have made a great life for yourself. You have absolutely nothing to lose by going to that audition. What are the chances that they won't even recognize you? You don't exactly look 23 anymore, know what I mean?" She smiled again, and he began to feel a little better. The weight of his secret was lifted a small amount and that was a pretty damned good feeling too.

He thought about what she said. What if they didn't recognize him? He was just some old guy with a good voice and a talent for the guitar. Another fan in a long line of fans who thought they could step into Ricky Harris's shoes for a while.

"You really didn't know the content of the letter Larry left for me, did you?"

"No. I told you I never read it. I wanted to, but I never did."

"The letter was to tell me that he knew somehow. He guessed that I was Ricky. In all of our time together, he never once gave me any hint that he knew. I was stunned when I read that letter. He kept my secret for me and now I'm asking you to do the same."

"You know I will."

"OK, I'll do the audition. But if it all blows up in my face, I'm blaming you." He was only partially kidding.

She kissed him. "I'll take that chance. Now call Eric and tell him you are sorry for being an ass. What you just shared with me goes no further than this room. I'm glad you told me, but you don't have to tell anyone else. You are Thor and you always will be."

He sighed. "OK. I'll call him right now."

Chapter 18

Dead Salmon's last gig of the summer was at Parker's in Shoreline. Of all the venues they played, this was Thor's favorite. It had the biggest dance floor by far and all the middle-aged and older folks came out to dance to the oldies.

Thor was feeling so much lighter after having unburdened himself to Barb, that he was much freer on stage than he had been in a long time. He had not realized how much emotional baggage he'd been carrying around all these years. Now that seemed like another lifetime, as though it had all happened to someone else. He was Thor Ragnar Swenson and he was proud of the successful person he'd become. He was starting to think about retiring and spending the rest of his days with Barb. That was a really great mental path to go down.

Autumn was a good place to take some time off from performing. School really picked up in the fall and all five of Dead Salmon's musicians had busy schedules. Eric's Cohos were scheduled to play their first away game of the season, the following week at Gonzaga, so Eric was going to be scarce for the next several months while he was consumed with football.

The entire band was stoked by the concept that Thor was going to try out for the Windy City contest. They all loved that Barb had talked, a very reluctant, Thor into going along with the audition and he said he would only do it if they were there to back him up. The whole band agreed, except Eric who would be at a game and unable to make the audition. "Somebody has to get video, so I can see this later!" he said.

In their practices, along with the usual late-summer song list, they began to rehearse some Windy City tunes. Thor was adamant that he would under no circumstances perform *Phoenix* at the audition.

"Seattle is the last stop on their audition tour," he said. "That means they will have heard good, bad, and awful renditions of *Phoenix* over a hundred times by the time they get here. It means that whatever acts come before us at the Seattle audition, they will hear it a few more times. We are not going to play *Phoenix* and that's final!"

"So, what do you suggest?" Roger asked.

"I'll want to showcase my guitar skills, but also be able to do some singing. I was thinking of *Last Time Over the Ocean*. It's got that funky break in the middle that really gives me a chance to improvise. I like the lyrics, too."

"That's a little-known one of their songs," Tom opined. "We haven't played it before. We'll have to rehearse as much as we can before the audition."

"Agreed. I know it, I've played it before," Thor said. He was trying hard not to smile. *As a matter of fact, I wrote it*, he thought.

"Well, you get to do two songs," Eric added. "What are you thinking of for the second one?"

"I'm going to do *Barbara's Song*. I think performing an original will really impress them." There was general agreement with that idea and Thor produced some sheet music for Tom, and then called up *Last Time Over the Ocean* on his MP3 player, so they could re-familiarize themselves with this more obscure cut from Windy City's first album.

The five of them with Barbara and a couple of the guys'
wives following along arrived at Parker's and began setting up for the gig. They had eaten dinner as a group at the
Southampton Arms which was just a few blocks up the
road.

As they had for most of the summer, they opened the
first set with *Don't Fear the Reaper* and played with such
feeling that the crowd didn't hesitate to get up and dance
right from the start.

Halfway through that first set, Thor saw the stalker-fan
come in. All of the tables near the dance floor were occu-
pied, so the guy was forced to take a seat at the bar. He
ordered his drink and true to form, began to stare at Thor
and ignore the rest of the band. He didn't seem to enjoy
the music at all, just sat there staring.

Thor decided he was going to confront the man, right
then and there. He would go straight to him, after the first
set, and find out what was going on. At the same time, his
enthusiasm for the performance began to fade.

They finished the set with David Bowie's *Fame* and as
he finished the number, Thor wasted no time setting his
guitar in the stand and jumping down from the stage.

Barb met him midway across the room and handed him
a schooner of beer. He took it and said, "thanks, but I have
something I have to do," he said.

Stalker-guy had managed to find a seat at a table for
two and was sitting a little closer to the stage than before.
He was watching Thor's approach intently. He did not
seem to be surprised or even concerned that the object of
his obsession was approaching as fast as the crowd would
permit.

When he reached the table, the guy didn't get up, but
Thor was still taken aback by how short he was.

Everything about him was weird and his vibe did not improve with proximity.

Thor took the unoccupied chair and turned it to face him. He straddled it and set his beer on the table. He reached out with his right hand.

"I don't believe we've met. I'm Thor Swenson. Thanks for coming to the show."

The little man took the offered hand and shook it. He had a firm grip. His eyes never left Thor's.

"Mick Thorne," he said.

Thor dropped his hand and returned to his beer. "Well you'll have to forgive me, Mick, but I'm more than a little creeped out by your presence here tonight.

"This makes three shows in a row, including last Sunday up in Edison. I thought it was odd that you would travel way the hell up there, but everyone else assured me that you're just a fan. Is that correct, Mick? You a big Dead Salmon fan?"

Mick didn't mince any words.

"I know who you are, Ricky," he said matter-of-factly.

A week ago, that statement might have sent Thor into a panic attack of epic proportion, but now that he'd come out the other side of sharing his secret, it had a considerably lighter effect.

"You must have misunderstood. I said my name is Thor," he said.

"Maybe you've gotten used to being called that, after all, I imagine it has been over forty years since anyone called you Ricky," Mick said. He took a sip of his drink. "But you are Ricky Harris and I can prove it."

"Dude, I think you are seriously tripping. You must have me confused with someone else."

"Are you going to tell me that you don't know who Ricky Harris was?"

"Of course not. Everybody knows who he was. We play

some Windy City tunes sometimes. But about halfway through the summer, we change up our song list. Keeps it fresh. If you were hoping to hear some of their music, I'm afraid you waited until too late in the year." Thor took a big gulp of his beer.

Mick's gaze never wavered. "Forty years ago, you witnessed a murder. Then, for reasons only you can explain, you took the dead man, swapped wallets, keys, and I think some clothes, and then put him in your rental car and pushed it into the canal."

Thor's felt a shot of adrenaline go through him. His heart started beating faster.

"You assumed his identity and never reported the murder. A lot of water has flowed under the old Fremont Bridge since then, but I think I could still arguably make a few charges stick. Tampering with evidence, desecration of a corpse, stuff like that."

"Are you a cop?" Thor asked it before thinking that the very act of posing the question might raise suspicion.

"Used to be," said Mick. "I was the cop on the beat the night Thor Swenson lost his life. Oops, I mean, Ricky Harris. I was first on the scene. I saw the car in the water and called for backup. I'm retired now, but I've never given up on the case. You see, I think someone got away with a serious crime that night, regardless of what the investigation uncovered. I intend to expose you." He calmly sipped at his vodka rocks.

"Let's say, for the sake of argument, that you're right," Thor said. "Why would I do that? Why would I throw away a great career, with nothing but greater potential and more of everything coming my way only to become a teacher? What would be the point?"

"You tell me," Mick answered. "That's a question that has kept me up many nights, let me tell you. I thought for the longest time that you killed Swenson. But recently,

I've learned that isn't the case. So, you dodged a very big bullet there, my friend."

"I'm not your friend. This is all ridiculous speculation. You have the wrong guy. Do you have the slightest idea how many people named Thor Swenson live in Seattle? It's a common name, believe me. You've got the wrong guy," he said again.

"I don't think I do. You're the right age, the right build, and coloring and you play a mean guitar, Ricky. It's a little hard to hide that, not to mention your voice. You sound like Ricky Harris. Just like him. I'm surprised that you don't make more of an effort to disguise those facts. Make the occasional sloppy mistake on a guitar solo, let your voice struggle with some of the higher notes, something. But you don't. You're right out there in front of everyone and no one questions it. Well, I do, and I'm going to expose you for who you really are."

"Why?" Thor's voice was strident, and people turned to look toward the previously quiet conversation.

"I told you. Crimes were committed that night," Mick said quietly. "There is no statute of limitations on murder, and you are a material witness. I can't prove a murder was committed unless I show that Ricky Harris is still alive, and the real Thor Swenson has been dead all these years." He finished his drink.

"You're out of your fucking mind!" Thor said. "If I ever see you at another one of my performances, I'll have you thrown out, do you understand? You can't prove jack shit, and no one will believe you!"

"Have you ever been fingerprinted?" Mick asked.

Thor smiled. Aha! Here was the way out. "Not that I recall, no. I've never been arrested." *So there, asshole.*

"I have Thor Swenson's fingerprints. He had quite the criminal record before you saw him die."

"Well good luck with getting any more for comparison," Thor said as he rose. He downed the rest of the beer and slammed the empty schooner down on the table. "Why don't you fuck *all* the way off!" He turned and stomped back toward the stage.

෧෮෧෮

"Jesus fella, haven't you ever watched an episode of CSI?" Mick asked as Thor made his way through the crowd. He carefully put his thumb and forefinger inside the recently emptied glass and spread them until he could lift it off of the table. He placed it in a plastic bag and sealed it, dropping the evidence into his oversized jacket pocket. He rose from the table and left.

෧෮෧෮

Thor was in a bad state when he returned to the stage. The whole gang had witnessed the confrontation, but none were aware of the nature of the apparently heated conversation. It had been heated on Thor's side, at least. Thor was still gritting his teeth as he picked up his guitar.

"OK, I'll ask since no one else will. What was that all about?" asked Tom.

"That dude! He's fucking stalking me and I told him to get lost. It's too weird, and I won't have it!"

"What did he say?"

"Oh, some bullshit about being a fan," he lied. "I told him we have lots of fans, and they don't come to every show and stare at me." He was beginning to calm down in spite of how weak he knew this explanation sounded.

"What makes you think he was lying?" Tom pressed.

"Because he knew a lot more about my personal life than he should have! He's stalking me, I swear!" He put the strap of his acoustic around his neck and began to play the opening chords of *Runaround*. That was not the next song on the playlist, but the band knew better than to argue and they all joined in.

Chapter 19

Tony D had been doing some serious research of his own. He had found that the termination of Rocco's life in the joint was not as depressing to him as he feared it might be. But he did have a little regret, and the whole thing got him thinking about that night in the distant past when they took out Thor the Viking. They had watched in fascination as the long-hair had fished Thor out of the drink, put him in a car, and then pushed him back in. It was one of the most amazing sights of his life, and he and Rocco had laughed about it often over the years.

Now, a short time after the unfortunate demise of Rocco, Tony was thinking about that night again. Forty years ago, the two of them had been young, full of themselves and neither ever gave a shit about what others thought of them. Maturity has a way of eroding that sort of hubris, and Tony was thinking more and more that they should have followed the rocker, taken him out too, and thrown him into the water behind Thor and the car.

But that might not have had the same wonderful effect that the long hair faking his death did, vis-a-vis the built-in alibi for Thor's murder. No one missed the petty thief, no one had questioned his absence. All eyes had been on the headline death of a famous person. Tony shook his head. He and Rocco had been so thrilled with the idea of Ricky Harris inadvertently taking the rap for them, that they never worried about the fact that he must have witnessed the killing.

But the truth was that Harris was a living witness and could have fingered them at any time. Of course, that would have outed his little subterfuge, and to be sure, that's why he never did it. But if Rocco's stories of Harris faking his death ever made it outside the prison walls, things could change.

Tony had been thinking these thoughts for several weeks after leaving Dean to dispense with Rocco. The realization that Ricky Harris should probably be eliminated now was slow to dawn on Tony, but when it did, he was certain it was the right thing to do. He did not share his musings with Mory. That could cause more trouble than ever it was worth. No, that was one sleeping dog that should continue to lie. For good.

Tony knew that the odds of Harris ever hearing of Rocco's death, or even that Tony and Rocco had witnessed the identity switch, were all but nil. Harris could not possibly know who had thrown Thor the Viking over the bridge. But Tony didn't get to this point in his life by being sloppy. Harris was a loose end, however harmless. And loose ends always need to be dealt with eventually.

The question then became how to track down the person who had become Thor Swenson. Tony took off his jacket and went into his study, which wasn't as lush and lavish as Mory's, but it was pretty fancy in its own right. He poured himself a drink and sat down at the desk. He opened his laptop and logged in. He decided to start with fairly broad searches and go from there. This wasn't something he was accustomed to doing, so he felt very much like a fish out of water. But he was committed now to finding the new Thor Swenson and taking him out.

Tony began by searching on the name and trying to go as far back as possible. What would Harris have done that night when he was all wet and freezing? Most likely he would have sought shelter and maybe dry clothes.

He tried to remember watching Harris walk into the shadows as he left the scene. Which way had he gone? He and Rocco had been laughing their asses off, due partly to the joint they had shared as they watched the unexpected show. He did remember that during the switching coats portion of the entertainment, he had seen Harris both re-move and then put something back in Thor's pocket.

So, it was possible that he had taken Thor's keys and been able to get into his apartment for someplace to stay. But that old apartment building had long since been torn down and replaced with expensive new condos. He didn't know how to go far enough back in public records to try to trace the new Thor's steps forward. He thought about that for a minute or two.

Tony decided to see if the new Thor had committed any crimes. The newfangled background check apps were pretty darned thorough as it turned out. Tony was able to find the real Thor's rap sheet, along with a couple of traffic tickets on his driver's license that had occurred many years after the real Thor was dead.

Well that was interesting since dead men don't drive cars. It seemed as though Harris had stayed around Seattle for quite some time after assuming his new identity. Tony wondered if Harris ever knew how lucky he was to get pulled over using Thor's identity and skating with just a ticket and without having any warrants served on him. Lucky indeed.

Nothing more came up on the criminal side, so Tony switched to a people search. He found it hard to believe that there could be so many people in the Seattle area with such a stupid name.

Their ages were also given, so it was easy to whittle the list down to a more agreeable size. That done, he ended up with a manageable list of only five men. They were arranged alphabetically according to the middle initial. He clicked on the first name and was redirected to a site that wanted money for a search on the name.

"Well ain't that a bunch of shit." Tony wasn't bothered by spending the money, as much as he was the idea of giving a sketchy website his credit card information. But he sighed and pulled his wallet from a back pocket. He selected the card to use and with only a slight hesitation, entered in the numbers.

That action had the undesirable effect of causing a whole bunch of pop-up windows telling him for $9.95 more he could get birth and death records, family trees, and all sorts of useless and annoying information. He methodically closed them all and returned to the task at hand.

Thor A. Swenson was a plumber with a wife and three kids who lived in Lake City. Tony kept searching until he found a photo of the guy. He laughed out loud. There was no way this short, fat, unkempt old fart was the person he was looking for. For starters, he was nowhere near as tall as Harris had been.

He returned to the list and clicked on the second name. This was Thor C. Swenson. Tony discovered that the forty bucks he'd paid for the privilege of learning about the plumber was just that, for learning about the first guy. He was asked to reauthorize the credit card a second time for this next name. This was going to get expensive quickly.

He paused with his finger over the mouse, the pointer of which was poised over the Submit button on the screen, and mulled it over. Tony was a wealthy man thanks to his long association with successful businessman, Mory Taglio. A couple of hundred bucks was lunch money to him. He wasn't worried about the expense, as much as he wondered just how badly he wanted to find this Harris-now-Swenson guy.

What were the odds that some con who happened to overhear Rocco's old-geezer boasting would get out of prison and immediately go around blabbing that a rock star's death forty years ago was faked? *Slim to none would be my guess,* he thought.

If by some razor-thin happenstance that an ex-con found the topic gab worthy, who the fuck would believe him? How many Elvis sightings had there been in the years following The King's death? Nobody with brains put any stock into those either.

On a whim, Tony Googled, "Ricky Harris lives" just to see what would come up and sure enough, there had been plenty of fake death theories and Ricky Harris sightings circulating out there. They were all old, the most recent one appeared to have been updated last sometime in 1997. So that meant that it was a virtual certainty that Thor Swenson would never get wind of the fact that someone had seen him pull his little switcheroo all those years ago.

Still, once Tony got hold of a notion, he was like a terrier with a bone. He was not going to let Swenson live any longer than he had to. It was just something that needed to be done, as it should have been back in 1975. Tony D does not leave loose ends. Besides, it might give Rocco's death a little more meaning. He clicked on Submit.

Tony continued to pay to play, losing faith in success with each name he researched. By the time he got to the fifth name on the list, he was pretty sure it was a dead end, too. But he'd come this far, so may as well finish what he started. One of the Thors was already deceased. Plus, reading about his devout Christian faith and avoidance of drugs and alcohol, assured Tony that he was not the right guy. The other two had both joined the military prior to '75, which meant that neither one of them could be Harris who was busy making music, not serving his country prior to faking his death.

With resignation, Tony clicked on the Submit button a fifth and final time. Thor R. Swenson turned out to be a major hit on the search. The guy was a tenured professor at Chinook U. He had published papers, on mathematics no less, and received numerous awards for his work in the field. Tony sighed. No way was this upstanding man either a small-time thug or a drinking, drugging rocker.

He decided to get his money's worth though and finished looking through all of the information that came up. Toward the end, to his great surprise, was a blurb about a local classic rock band, fronted by none other than Thor Swenson, Ph.D.

"No shit? Seriously?" Tony said. He began typing furiously into the computer, looking for the education records of this Thor. He found way more than he bargained for, up to and including an address and phone number. So, he wouldn't have to track him down on the university campus. That could be a plus.

Tony went back and re-read the blurb about the band. It had appeared only the week prior in the Chinook U *Parr*, the student newspaper. Dr. Swenson's membership in this band with other professors was common knowledge around the school, apparently. The story mentioned that the band, Dead Salmon, would be auditioning for a chance to play with the real Windy City.

What the fuck? Tony couldn't believe what he was reading. Some record company was paying for this promotional stunt and they were having a nationwide competition to replace Ricky Harris. Wow. But why would Swenson do it? Wouldn't he be worried the exposure might let the cat out of the bag?

Those are some balls this guy has, Tony decided. He looked at the photo of the band that was prominent over the article. Thor was easy to pick out. It really was him. He hadn't changed much at all. His hair was gray, and his face certainly belonged to a man in his late sixties, but that was about it. Tony wondered how Thor could be so dumb as to think his old bandmates wouldn't recognize him. It was very weird.

On the other hand, the audition at the Paramount Theater could be just the place to take him out. There would be few witnesses and they'd all be down by the stage. Tony had attended enough concerts and plays at the Paramount over the years to know the layout quite well. He could slide into a back-row seat, take his aim and slide back out in the dark before they registered that a shot had been fired. Sweet.

"It's a date," he said to the picture.

Chapter 20

Mick found that he had started to enjoy the Dead Salmon concerts. It wasn't like going to see a big touring band perform. Bands like Dead Salmon played local taverns and bars and the experience was usually much more personal. It was nice to be able to have a drink while you listened to some good old tunes.

He thought the guys in the band were all pretty good, not just the ringer they had doing most of the singing. He had been wondering if the rest of the band knew who Thor was, but after Swenson's reaction to his accusation last night, he had to figure they didn't. If it was common knowledge among the band, and even the wife who seemed to always attend their gigs, Swenson might not have reacted as angrily as he did.

Mick wasn't surprised that he denied everything, or even that he was dumb enough to provide a full set of prints. But he would have been extremely surprised if Swenson had admitted who he was or taken the charge calmly.

He looked at the beer glass on the seat next to him, still in its plastic bag. He hoped it contained even one clear print that could be unequivocally differentiated from those of the real Thor Swenson. Maybe Mick couldn't prove that Thor Swenson was really Ricky Harris, but he could certainly prove that the body fished from the canal forty years ago was not.

Mick was on his way to Dennis Stern's lab. He wanted to be there when Denny lifted the prints from the glass and compared them to Thor's. He had called ahead and was eager to get this last piece of the puzzle in place. Then and only then could he go to Chuck and lay out the case against Ricky Harris.

Once he proved his theory that the body had been placed in the car that night way back when the case could be reopened as a homicide. Mick would be able to introduce the evidence of Tony DiThomasso's involvement, along with the now-dead Rocco Fortunato.

He knew that painting this murder as a mob hit was opening a much bigger can of worms than he'd fantasized about all these years, but what a way to end his career. He knew the case would be turned over to Homicide, who might then have to work with the Organized Crime unit to get any traction. But the connection to Mory Taglio's companies was too enticing to ignore.

He pulled the Taurus into the parking lot of the King County Courthouse building which housed the County Sheriff's headquarters. He took the elevator to the fourth floor and, carrying his prize carefully, headed down the hall toward the Forensics lab. Denny's office was in the back.

"Hi, Mick!" he said. "Welcome back. I didn't think I'd be seeing you again this soon after you said you were going to have another set of prints for me."

Mick went to shake hands, but Denny demurred. He was wearing latex gloves.

Denny was a few inches taller than Mick and more than a few decades younger. His mid-length dark brown hair was unkempt and at present was supporting a pair of thick, black-rimmed glasses. He was wearing a lab coat over a shirt and tie. He definitely looked like a lab rat. Mick handed him the bag with the schooner in it.

"Oh, I see," said Denny. "You didn't tell me I'd have to lift the prints from a glass. That's a departure. I don't work in the field much. Usually, by the time I get prints, they are fresh on cards or provided digitally so that I can compare them to what I find in AFIS."

"Can you do it?" Mick asked.

"Sure, no problem. Let me grab a dusting kit. I'll be right back." He trotted out into the open lab area and returned a moment later with the kit and a set of metal tongs.

He opened the bag and gingerly pulled the beer glass out of it. A few drops of stale beer dripped onto his desk.

"Oh God that smells awful," he said. He blotted the drops up with a tissue. With his left hand, Denny gently grasped the very bottom of the glass, ensuring that he didn't spill any more of the noxious liquid.

He took a soft brush and dipped it into an open jar of black powder. Turning the brush in a rotating motion, he dusted the black powder all over the glass. At least five fingerprints appeared. He held the glass up to the light.

"Looks like we may have something here," he told Mick.

He set the brush and glass down on the desk and removed his gloves. From a drawer in the desk, he produced a fresh set of latex gloves and put them on. Then, he took a dispenser of clear tape out of the dusting kit and drew a strip about two inches long. He carefully put the tape over one of the fingerprints and then removed the strip of tape from the glass.

He stuck the tape to a card he'd readied ahead of time, and a clear black fingerprint was now present on the card.

"That's a thumb," he said. Mick nodded.

"It's very clear, too. I probably don't need more than that since I have clear thumbs from the other two samples. Do you want me to take them all?"

"Will a single thumbprint be enough to stand up in a court of law as to whether or not it is from the same person?" Mick asked.

"Probably. But if you want, I can lift the rest of them. It never hurts to have more than you need."

"No, it certainly doesn't," Mick agreed.

"Fair enough," said Denny. He finished taking the rest of the prints from the glass. Two of them, the left index and middle fingers, were also very clear. The others were smeared and would be of no use. Denny removed the second set of gloves and typed into his keyboard. A screen came up that showed the side-by-side comparison he had shared with Mick previously.

"These are the two sets of prints you already gave me."

He held up the new prints and performed a visual comparison to the ones on the screen. "Well, I'll digitize these and do the computer analysis to be one hundred percent certain, but I can tell you without hesitation that the person who left the prints on this glass is not the person whose fingerprints are on my computer screen right now."

Mick was elated. "That's great!" he said. "How can you tell so easily?"

"It's pretty obvious, actually," Denny said. "See these areas on the first two fingers? They're callouses. Those are common on guitar players' left hands. If you look, Thor had no such callouses."

Mick looked, and the differences were clear to him, too. He also noticed that Thor's left thumbprint was a series of rings spreading out from the center; whereas Ricky's left thumbprint looked like a wave swirling across the thumb.

I'll send this set through AFIS, too and see what comes up," Denny said. "If your guy doesn't have a criminal record as you believe, then I should get no matches."

"Thank you, Denny! You have no idea how much this helps!" He gave Denny an uncharacteristic slap on the back.

"Call me when you have the definitive results, OK?" he called over his shoulder as he practically ran from the lab.

Chapter 21

The old Paramount Theater on the corner of 9th Avenue and Pine in Seattle smelled dank and musty. Originally built as a movie theater by Paramount studios in 1928, the lavish interior was decorated in the Beaux Arts style. Its 2,800 seats made for a relatively informal venue for a band that back in the late seventies had been able to fill sports arenas. For the purpose of the Windy City auditions, it was just the right size and the acoustics were perfection.

Angie and Rufus held hands as they walked onto the stage. They didn't talk, both lost in their own reverie, recalling a fateful concert night from decades past.

They stood there for a few minutes, looking around the theater, taking in the gaudy, gilded cornices and red velvet seats, before stepping down from the stage and taking seats in the center front row.

"I'd forgotten what this place is like," Angie said. She had softened on her annoyed and frustrated stance about the try-outs as their tour had progressed, and she was now looking forward to the day's performances by hopeful contestants.

"It really was a cool place to perform, wasn't it?" she asked.

"Yeah. It still is," Rufe answered. "It's kinda small compared to some of the places we've stopped on this trip, but I like that. Makes it intimate, you know?"

Angie nodded as Don, Craig, and Ray joined them in the front row. A middle-aged man who looked as though he may have had a love for good beer, or even bad beer, was plugging his guitar into the amp provided and starting to tune it.

He didn't have a backup group as so many did and was listed on their contestant roster as Brandon Biggs. Angie smirked as she read his name. *He's big all right,* she thought.

Old Brandon began to play *Phoenix* of course. He did a decent job with the guitar work, throwing in some nice and very appropriate improvisation throughout. His voice was another matter. He stayed on key, and it was obvious that this fellow may have had a halfway decent voice in his younger years. But time had not been kind to his voice, and he sounded as though there was a good supply of sand in his throat.

Maybe that's why he drinks a lot of beer, Angie thought again. Still, it wasn't the worst rendition they'd heard of the old hit by this point in the contest. And his performance didn't seem to suffer for lack of backup. So. all in all, it wasn't a terrible way to start the long day.

Angie read down the list in her lap. They were going to hear at least thirty acts today and there were more on a waiting list if time allowed. Each act was permitted two numbers of their own choosing. An unfortunate majority of them did choose to start with *Phoenix*, although after hearing it hundreds of times, Angie was inured to any more craziness brought on by frequent lack of talent and the numbing repetition. In fact, she had discovered that with so many of them doing the same song, it became just that much easier to decide between them. Some of the acts made it their own, with a unique and professional sound— some of them butchered it so badly that they were easy to eliminate. Others were playing it so close to what they heard on their old vinyl albums that they demonstrated a lack of live performance skills. A very few had actually been pretty good, and those were the ones who got selected for the finals.

Mr. Biggs finished his second piece, *Echoes of Emptiness*, another Windy City hit that the band had now listened to several dozen times in their trip across the country. Biggs didn't do that number any justice either, but he gave a good effort, and they thanked him as he left the stage.

Angie put a checkmark next to his name. She had developed a system to remind her at the end of the day's auditions, which ones she had liked and would want to see again. Her checkmark indicated a firm thumb's down. If she liked an act, she put a star next to the name. There always seemed to be far fewer stars than checks and on her personal list, and there had been no stars at all on her Memphis roster.

The guys told her she was imagining things, but in Memphis, she was sure she detected a country twang from every act and just did not feel good about putting anyone through to the finals. They proceeded with three of the acts that auditioned that day in spite of her dissenting vote and those three would be called to the finals in Chicago in October.

She glanced down her list for the next group. They were called "The Jake Vinge Band," and she assumed Jake was the one who wanted to take Ricky's place.

While those guys set up, she read on down the list. There were individual names and band names but the one second from the bottom caught her eye. "Dead Salmon." She smiled. That seemed like a strange name for a band, even though Seattle might be proud of its seafood heritage. The image of a dead fish did not conjure up feelings of joy and music and harmony for her.

That band would be something to look forward to just to see if they could rise above the name. She figured they were probably younger, grunge types. She was still smiling when Jake's band started to play *Phoenix*. Angie sighed.

ℰↄℰↄ

"Do we have everything?" Thor was asking as they finished loading the last of the band's equipment into the van. They were not scheduled to come on stage until 3:30 in the afternoon, but he wanted to get to the Paramount as early as possible. Even if they had to park some way off and then move the van closer as the time to unload approached.

He had to admit he was getting increasingly nervous. In the intervening weeks since Eric had first dropped the contest on him, and then after his emotional confession to Barb, Thor had come to a peace about things. He thought he had allowed the weight of forty years of pretty terrific living to push any old, dusty emotional baggage out of his mind for good. Several times, he actually considered telling his bandmates the truth, but he never did. He wanted to get this contest out of the way first.

Eric had called him a "shoe-in" when he first mentioned entering the contest, and he knew that was the case. He had not allowed himself to contemplate what the consequences of winning could be. Now he could think of nothing else.

In spite of Barb's insistence that they probably wouldn't recognize him since they would not be able to imagine a still-living Ricky, he was certain the converse was true. He knew Angie would not be able to look into his eyes and see anyone but Ricky Harris. He didn't know how such recognition could possibly end well.

But, as Barb kept saying, it has been a lifetime since the

events that made him Thor Swenson. Angie had married Rufe, not too long after Ricky's death, and the band had stayed together only for a short time after that.

Angie and Rufe had led a quiet life since then from what Thor had been able to read about them over the years. They still lived in Chicago and had two adult children. Craig and Don had gone on to other bands and studio work and done pretty well for themselves.

None of them would still be emotional about Ricky, would they? The surprise of learning that he didn't die that night would be huge, sure, but enough time had passed that they really couldn't be angry with him about it anymore, right?

These thoughts swirled round and round in Thor's head as they loaded the van. No one answered his question about making sure they had everything because he'd asked it five times already.

"I guess I'm not hiding my nerves very well, am I?" he asked.

All three men laughed as though he'd told an especially good joke.

"I'll take that as a no." Thor got in his car and brought up the rear of the four-vehicle procession leaving Eric's house.

Chapter 22

Mick went straight to Palomino, his and Chuck's favorite downtown watering hole. He called Chuck as soon as he left Denny's lab and felt fortunate that Chuck was available and ready for lunch. No discussion about location was needed.

Chuck's office was only a few blocks from the restaurant, so Mick knew he would get there first. True to expectation, Chuck had secured a table and waved Mick over as he walked in.

The smell of garlic wafted through the air. They shook hands and Mick sat down.

"I'm not going to forgive you for bailing on our annual fishing trip, you know," Chuck said.

Mick looked chagrinned. He really did feel bad about that.

"I know," he said. But when I tell you what I've got, you just may change your mind about that forgiveness." A waiter came over and took their drink orders. When he returned, Mick was grateful to have something besides water to sip as he shared his news. He waved the waiter off when asked about lunch orders. "Give us a minute, please."

"I've just come from the county crime lab," he began, then stopped. It might make more sense to explain how he had come by three sets of fingerprints.

"Yeah?" Chuck said.

"Sorry, I was thinking I'd better start a little closer to the beginning." Mick sipped at his vodka rocks.

"You know I had a set of autopsy fingerprints in the old evidence box from the Ricky Harris accidental death, right?"

"Right," said Chuck

"So, in the course of my investigation," Mick went on, "I got the identity of the person who I believed Harris killed and stashed in his rental car that night."

"I know," Chuck said. "You talked to your snitch up in Twin Rivers."

"That's right. So, I did a little digging and it turns out that kid had a record. Thor Swenson was his name."

Chuck snorted.

"Anyway, as you may recall, there were no fingerprints on file for Ricky Harris back then. So, the set that the coroner took during the autopsy just got filed into evidence and forgotten.

"I took those prints, plus the ones from Thor Swenson's criminal record to the crime lab for comparison. Guess what? They were an exact match! Thor Swenson was the dead man in Ricky Harris's rental car forty-two years ago." Mick paused to enjoy Chuck's reaction.

"I thought we already knew that. You told me that," Chuck said.

"Well yeah, but I didn't have confirmation from an expert then."

"Look Mick, I'm glad you got it definitively confirmed, but that still doesn't warrant opening an old case of accidental death, you know?"

"No, no! I know that! There's more!" Mick said excitedly.

"I found Ricky Harris," he said. "I can't prove it is him, and he won't admit it's him, but I can prove that he is not Thor Swenson."

"How do you know he won't admit it if you're so sure it's him?" Chuck asked.

"Because," said Mick, "I confronted him."

"You did what?" Chuck sounded alarmed. "Mick, you can't go around harassing people on a hunch! You have no legal authority to confront the guy. You know that!"

"Calm down," said Mick. "I didn't represent myself as anything other than what I am: a retired cop. He was perfectly willing to talk to me. In fact, it was him who approached me. That is how I obtained his fingerprints. He left his beer glass on my table. Aside from the fact that I effectively stole the glass from the bar, I think it was fair game."

"Let me get this straight," said Chuck. "You are telling me that this man is calling himself Thor Swenson?" Mick nodded.

"And you believe he's Ricky Harris?" Mick nodded again.

"I haven't told you the best part," Mick added.

"He's in a classic rock tavern band that's making the rounds all over town and almost to the Canadian border!

"Chuck, I've heard him play and sing. Believe me, when I tell you, it's Ricky Harris!" Mick paused to take a drink.

"The real kicker is that he's a tenured professor at Chinook University! He's got a Ph.D. for cryin' out loud! Can you believe it?"

Chuck leaned back in his chair. "A Ph.D., no shit?"

The waiter returned and they both ordered their usual choices without ever cracking a menu. Chuck had the Chicken Parmigiana, and Mick went with the Lasagna.

"I didn't recall you being such a Windy City fan," Chuck said.

"Oh, actually I was. It's why I was so excited and totally captivated by the case. I was the one who found that car in the water. That afforded me quite a bit of celebrity back then. Press from all over the world wanted to interview me.

"You know I wasn't allowed to say much. It was an active investigation for a little while, and then the Public Affairs Liaison did all the talking. But I enjoyed it while it lasted.

"The fact that I was so familiar with the band is one of the reasons that I am so positive I've got the right guy. I recognized him the first time I saw him."

"You've seen him more than once?" Chuck asked around a mouthful of chicken.

Mick grinned. "Yeah. I guess I've been kind of a stalker. I wanted to be absolutely certain before I confronted him." He took a bite.

"Like I said, the band plays all over the Puget Sound area. It was easy to follow them from one gig to another."

"And he agreed to have a beer with you?" Chuck asked.

"Not exactly. I was planning to talk to him that night anyway. Dead Salmon was playing at Parker's Ballroom which isn't too far from home for me, so I picked that place to talk to him.

"I know he had noticed me," Mick added. "Every time I went someplace to watch the band, he would stare at me with a less than cordial look on his face." Mick laughed.

"Then, before I could approach him, he came to me. He just walked over to my table and sat down. He introduced himself," he said.

"He introduced himself as Thor Swenson?"

"Yep."

"Interesting. So, he left the beer on the table and you took it for prints?"

"Right again," said Mick.

"And now you are just coming from the lab to tell me that his prints don't match the deceased, Thor Swenson's prints, is that it?" Chuck asked.

"Yes." Mick sat back in his chair and patted his stomach. "This stuff always fills me up too much, but it's so damned good I can't stop eating it!"

"I'm still not sure proving that the deceased was Thor Swenson is enough to reopen the case," Chuck said. "Mostly because it's so old. I think it would be different if this happened a few years back instead of over forty, you know?"

Mick sighed. "I suppose you're right. But how do I get Harris to admit who he is?"

"That is a tough one, Mick. It may take some time. You may not be able to at all. If you bug this guy enough, and you did say he was a bit hostile when you spoke to him, he may get a TRO to keep you away. Then what do you do?"

"I don't think we'll have to worry about that. Look, if we can get the DA to reopen the case, even just to look at it, we may have enough already to subpoena Swenson and force him to cooperate. We could promise to let him keep his identity. He has a lot to lose if you think about it. Stature in the academic community, tenure among other things. No, I don't think I'm going to have too much trouble convincing him that he needs to come clean. He's a material witness in a murder. That won't go away." Chuck seemed to consider this and nodded.

"But in the meantime, there's more to tell," Mick added.

Chuck raised his eyebrows. "More?"

Mick smiled again. "Oh, it gets really good from here," he said.

"You know I got the story of what really happened that night from my snitch who regaled me with tales of the late Rocco Fortunato."

"Yeah, I've been meaning to ask how you found out that Fortunato was dead," Chuck said.

"I would prefer to keep that source confidential. It really isn't germane to the facts of the case," Mick said diplomatically.

"This made me go back and do some digging into the unfortunate Mr. Fortunato's criminal past," he went on. "He was a lifer thanks to the three-strikes law. So, I looked up his final court appearance." Mick sipped his drink.

"He repeatedly referred to a friend by the name of Tony D," he said. "Mr. Anthony DiThomasso, to be precise, who testified as a character witness for Fortunato. I'd heard that name before, so I looked into DiThomasso's background. He runs one of Mory Taglio's companies here in town."

"Seriously?" Chuck leaned forward. He sounded much more interested in the story suddenly.

"Seriously," Mick said. "It seems Tony D has had his run-ins with the law from time to time, but not much has stuck. Most recently, the Feds brought him up on tax evasion, but the charges were eventually dropped for insufficient evidence.

"Taglio's name has never come up in any of Fortunato's or DiThomasso's dealings with the law, but they are all connected. It's beginning to sound a lot like the original Thor Swenson wasn't just a random murder—he was a mob hit."

Chuck whistled. "That's a big bite you're taking out of the old assumption apple, Mick," he said. "If you're right, that could get a DA to sit up and take notice. You think you can connect the dots enough?"

"Yeah," Mick answered. "I think if we go far enough back into DiThomasso's background, we might find all sorts of things that would hurt his squeaky-clean image. And he will lead us straight to Taglio."

Chuck appeared to think for a moment. Finally, he looked up at Mick. "Do it," he said. "I'll get in touch with my friend in the Prosecutor's office and get some wheels quietly turning. You bring me everything you possibly can on this mob connection, OK? I mean everything."

"You got it!" Mick said. He thought that lasagna never tasted so good.

❧❧❧

Mick couldn't wait to get home to begin his deep dive into the lives of Rocco Fortunato and Tony DiThomasso. He had a great feeling about this now that Chuck was on board.

He felt as though his entire life had been leading up to it. To have what started out as a sensational but relatively small case turn into a potential organized crime bust of epic proportions was so much more than he'd allowed himself to dream about over the years. It would be a fitting end to his career, indeed.

He turned on the radio to KZOK, his favorite oldies station. Steve Slaton was on the air and he was talking about Windy City. Mick increased the volume.

"Yes, Windy City fans and Ricky Harris wannabes, your dreams have come true," Slaton was saying. "The band will be at the Paramount Theater all day today hearing auditions for a new lead guitar and vocals. The winner will get to join the band for a reunion tour beginning in January! I'm sorry to report that they are not opening the auditions to an audience. But we have a new tour to look forward to and that is exciting news! I'll play you a Windy City lost classic after these messages."

Mick's mind raced. The surviving members of Windy City were in Seattle right now. He wondered if they would be in town until tomorrow. If he could get even one of them to see Thor Swenson in person, he could prove Swenson was really Ricky Harris. He had to try.

He turned the car around at the earliest opportunity and started the cross-town drive to the Paramount Theater. *This day just keeps getting better*, he thought.

Chapter 23

Thor tied his hair back to keep it out of the way. On impulse, he decided to leave the gray ponytail for the performance to help change his appearance in a small way. As the afternoon wore in, he'd become increasingly worried about anyone recognizing him. He considered wearing dark glasses, a hat.

He tried to tell himself it didn't matter after all of these years, as Barb had tried to convince him. But the fear of being exposed had been with him for so long, he was finding it much harder to let go of than he thought it should be.

The stage manager, a kid of maybe 19 or 20, poked his head out the backstage door and called for Dead Salmon. They picked up their gear and went in. Bert's drum kit was at home. He would be using drums provided by the contest organizers instead of having to schlep an enormous drum set all over town.

The four of them walked onto the stage and began setting up, plugging in guitars and tuning. Bert sat at the provided drums and played a few rattles and rolls. He worked on getting a feel for the bass pedal.

Thor busied himself with tuning his own guitar. He chose Larry's old Strat for this. The signed Flying V would have been fun to play again, but would have served as a big, bright neon sign saying, "I'm Ricky Harris! Look! I still have my old guitar! Remember me?" Yeah, that was not an option.

Barb followed them on stage, only to go down a set of side stairs and take a seat several rows back. She had been acting a little star-struck out in the alley behind the theater. Thor could only imagine how she would feel at the sight of the real Windy City sitting a few rows in front of her.

He gave her a hard time for it before they entered the theater. He reminded her that she's been sleeping with Ricky Harris this whole time. Meeting the rest of the band should be nothing. As she headed for the stairs, he caught her sleeve.

"You remembered the camera, right?"

She smiled and held up her cell phone. "Yes, for the thousandth time, I'm recording you guys. Relax. You'll do great!" She gave him a peck on the cheek and walked down into the darkness of the seats.

Thor felt like the band was a little thin without Eric and he hoped it wouldn't sound like that. The video was mostly so Eric could see how the audition went. He wondered how the game was going. *Go Cohos!* he thought, but he didn't feel it.

Thor allowed himself a very brief glance at the people sitting in the front row. Every one of them was looking directly at him.

"So, you guys are Dead Salmon?" Rufe asked.

"Yeah," said Thor, a little too quickly.

"All right," said Rufus. "Lay it on me, man."

Thor strummed the opening A^m of *Last Time Over the Ocean,* and the rest of the guys joined in. They had been practicing the piece like mad, with and without Eric. Thor realized that while he missed Eric's rhythm guitar, the song wasn't diminished much from his absence and he thought they sounded pretty good.

☙❧

All of Windy City and their manager, Ray, sat up a little straighter in their seats. This was the first time in hundreds of auditions that they had heard this particular song, and all of them were more than a little impressed.

Dead Salmon gave it their all and Thor sang with astounding heart for a man of his age. When the song got to the guitar solo, Thor all but lit that fretboard on fire.

"Jesus Christ," said Rufe. "This guy not only looks and sounds a lot like Ricky, but he plays like Ricky too!"

Murmurs of agreement from Ray, Don, and Craig. Angie stared at the man on the stage, taking no heed of the rest of his band. She'd been looking forward to Dead Salmon because she thought they had a funny name, but now she was not laughing.

When he began to sing again, she realized Rufe was right. The guy was a Ricky Harris clone. It was so eerie, and she felt a growing sense of sadness as she listened to what could only be the voice of her long-lost lover.

Rufe leaned in to talk to Ray and the guys. "I'm not kidding. Talk about saving the best for last! I'm inclined not to bother with the finals, Ray. This is our guy!" They all nodded in agreement but Ray said, "Let's talk about it later. Let them finish."

Dead Salmon finished the song and was treated to a round of applause from the little audience. Thor smiled and murmured a thank you into his mike.

He picked up an acoustic 12-string and donning the strap, proceeded to sit down on the edge of the stage. The other band members set their instruments down and Bert got up from his stool. The three of them walked off the stage. The light technician brought the lights down as pre-arranged, leaving a single spot on Thor.

He played some minor chords and started to sing a ballad. It was not a song any of them were familiar with.

Rufe looked at Angie. "Original?" he mouthed. She shrugged.

ୡେଓ

For the first few bars, Thor looked out into the seating past the judges trying to see Barb. The spotlight on him, combined with the darkened theater prevented him from finding her, but he knew she was recording.

He began to relax and tried to get into the song more. He decided to play it just as he had at several local venues. When he could help himself no longer, he glanced down at Angie. She was watching him intently and met his gaze.

He noticed that while she had obviously aged, her eyes were unchanged. The feeling that coursed through him then was stronger than he could bear, and he tried to look away. It was no use.

Without warning, Angie jumped to her feet and shouted, "Ricky!"

She turned and ran out of the theater through a right-side exit door. Thor stopped playing and watched her go. The rest of the band and Ray sat in stunned silence. The four of them wore astonished expressions.

Thor rose from his sitting position on the edge of the stage and set the guitar down. He couldn't think of a thing to say. Rufe looked up at him with a very puzzled expression.

"I'm so sorry, man," Rufe said. "You really do sound a lot like Ricky. I think it just got to her. Made her a little more emotional than she was prepared for." He sounded like he was trying to convince himself more than Thor.

Barb came up the steps and jogged over to Thor.

"She just recognized you, idiot. Go after her."

Thor nodded. He turned back toward the band in time to see Rufus heading for the door.

"Let me go," Thor said. Rufe stopped and looked at him.

"I'm the one who upset her," said Thor. Let me go."

Thor stood on the edge of a precipice then, not knowing whether to jump or turn around. He decided to jump.

"She's right about me. I have to be the one to tell her." He didn't wait for Rufus's response, just turned and ran out the door after Angie. When he got outside, he saw that she hadn't gone far. She was just outside the building and in her short sleeves appeared cold. Her back was to him, but he could tell she was crying.

"Ange," he began. At the sound of his voice, she whirled around to face him.

"It's really you, isn't it?" she asked incredulously. "It's really you."

He nodded, unable to find any words sufficient to communicate the depth of his nameless emotion.

"Why?" she asked.

He still couldn't think of how to respond, and she slapped him, hard. He rubbed at his cheek and nodded again.

"That was well deserved and a long time coming, I guess," he said at last.

"You ruined a lot of lives that night!" She sounded furious. "But Ricky, how? *Why*?" she asked again.

He took a deep breath. "I came back to the hotel to find you and Rufe together. You'll never know how deep that cut me, Ange. I left, as you know."

"But how did you survive? You died in your car that night!" She was crying again.

Thor closed his eyes, remembering like it was yesterday.

"I just got in the car and drove. It was super cold and foggy, I remember that. I was drinking, I was crying, and I was confused. I felt so betrayed."

Angie started to say something, but he put a finger to her lips. "Let me finish," he said. She pulled his hand away from her mouth and watched him as he continued.

"I came to this bridge and saw two men roughing up another guy. I pulled into the shadows and turned off the lights. I didn't want to get involved, and I didn't want anyone to see me in the state I was in, so I just watched.

"They beat him up pretty bad, and then just like that picked him up and dropped him into the canal."

Angie looked startled.

"The two guys ran back to their car and left. I didn't have time to think about it. I got out of the car and jumped into the water to see if I could save the poor guy.

"It was so incredibly cold, and it was pitch black. I had a hard time finding him, but I managed somehow.

"I pulled him up on the bank and noticed that he looked a lot like me. Angie, I swear I didn't plan it to turn out this way. It just happened!"

"You put him in the car and put your ID on him, so we'd think he was you?" she asked.

"Yes."

"Where did you go then?"

"I had his ID, so I found his apartment. I got dry and went to bed. When I saw the headlines the next morning, I really felt as though there was no turning back. You all thought I was dead and in my frame of mind at that time, I felt that was best for everyone." Thor stopped, drained. He had imagined this conversation a thousand times over the years and it was only slightly less emotional in reality because he had already confessed everything to Barbara.

"Do you really believe I ruined your life?" he asked.

"Of course, you did!" she said angrily.

"Did I? You and Rufus have done all right. You have a beautiful family, you are grandparents. It would appear I did you a favor."

"Is that how it looks to you? Why do you think we're doing this stupid contest and tour? Huh? Because we need the money, that's why! Without you, there was no Windy City. We didn't last. None of us ever enjoyed the success we would have if you hadn't...gone. What have you done with your life? You threw it all away that night." She wrapped her arms around herself to keep out the cold.

"We should go back in," Thor said.

"No! I want to know what you have been doing for forty fucking years that you couldn't have at least given us a hint that you were still alive!" Angie said.

"I got a job and went back to school. You know I always wanted to go to university and get a degree. There was never any time once the band took off, but it was always in the back of my mind.

"I supported myself with part-time jobs and giving some guitar lessons, in later years, when I was less likely to be recognized.

"By the time I was working on my post-graduate degrees, I had published some papers and was able to get scholarships. I have a Ph.D. in Mathematics," he finished.

Angie looked at him as though he was from Mars. "Why math?" she asked.

"I don't know," he said. "It came easy to me. It was sort of like the music, very structured and orderly. I guess I just like that." He shrugged.

"What does one do with a math doctorate?" she asked.

Thor smiled. "Teach," was all he said.

Angie watched him for a few moments. She didn't seem sure what to say next. Thor let her think. He didn't interrupt.

"Why did you decide to do this contest? Surely you knew we'd recognize you!" she said finally.

"I didn't think you would. I still don't think Rufe and the others did, although I told Rufe that you were right as

I was coming out here. If I hadn't, I think Rufe would have followed me. Barbara has probably filled the rest of them in by now. Can we please go back in? I'm freezing out here."

Angie came close and looked up at him. The sorrow in her eyes was almost more than he could stand. The regret of forty years crashed down on him like a wave.

"I'm so sorry Ange. I've never regretted my successes in life, but I've regretted what I did to you every day since. I don't expect you to forgive me, but please believe me when I tell you how truly sorry I am."

He tried to take her hand, but she jerked it from his grasp. "You were the love of my life," she said just above a whisper. "I'll never forgive you." She went back into the theater and left him standing alone in the cold.

Chapter 24

Tony spent the morning leisurely lingering over breakfast, enjoying a second cup of coffee. The weather wasn't too bad for this time of year, and as long as the rain held off, he could handle the cold dampness of the air.

He sat on the terrace enjoying his view of Lake Washington. His house had over 200 feet of lake frontage and in the summer, he kept a small speed boat tied to the dock down there. Now, the dock sat empty, reflecting the gray sky above the dark, rolling lake.

He didn't mind that his al fresco breakfast required a heavy jacket. He was out of the wind, there was no rain, and life was good.

Tony was in such a good mood because he was going to terminate Ricky Harris after forty years of letting him slide. He didn't like to think about how many times Harris could have caused trouble for him and Rocco. This late in life, it was not good to take chances. There was just too much to lose, however unlikely.

It had been some years since Tony had allowed himself the pleasure of a personal hit. That was a thing best left to the Roccos of the world. Tony was a businessman and a respected member of society. A man in his position could not be seen dirtying his hands with anything so mean and mundane as murder.

But the fun of the hunt and the intrigue accompanying the risk of getting caught were an intoxicating concoction that Tony had forgotten how much he enjoyed. The businessman in him had done the math. He knew that Harris was no threat and had not been for many years.

Still, he found that the more he envisioned shooting Harris right off that stage this afternoon, the better he felt. It was a good day for a hit.

He finished breakfast and his coffee and came into the welcome warmth of the house. Tony was prepared for stealth this day. He went to his bedroom and walked into a generous clothes closet.

Tony's wife, Donna, was visiting friends in New York. She would not be back for another week, so he felt secure that he would not be discovered. He was so excited to get on with it, that he felt a little guilty. It was as though he was cheating on her, though he would never do such a thing.

He changed into black slacks and a black turtleneck. He had black leather gloves which he tucked into a black balaclava and shoved both into a jacket pocket.

On the top shelf of the closet was a gun safe. He stepped onto a low stool, to get to eye level with the safe, and put in the combination. It opened, and he removed a little Glock 26. Behind it lay a suppressor, which he now attached, easy peasy. He also got a second clip, just to be safe. He did not intend to fire more than one shot, but he had not been to the range in some time, and he wasn't as sure of his aim as he'd once been.

By the time he got downstairs, Tony was humming a little tune. He really felt great. He didn't have to think about work. He didn't once think about his enlarged prostate—BPH the doc had called it. He couldn't remember the last time he felt this good.

Donna loved the theater and the Paramount was a fun

place to go. Back in May, he'd taken her to see a performance of *Rent* which turned out to be pretty good. Anything for his Donna. So, he knew the fastest route to get to the Paramount from his home on Mercer Island.

Tony had no intention of trying to stay hidden for eight or ten hours while act after terrible act did their tryouts. Staying hidden that long would be nearly impossible, anyway, and listening to the same songs over and over sounded like a good reason to swallow his gun rather than use it on Harris.

Instead, as soon as he learned the date and time of the auditions, he had contacted an acquaintance in The Seattle Theater Group. This non-profit owned the Paramount and a few other venues around the city. Because Tony was a generous donor to the arts, his acquaintance was more than happy to dig up a copy of the list of acts and their order of go for today.

It turned out that Harris's band was one of the last to audition. That gave Tony his relaxing morning and confidence that he could slip in and out undetected.

He parked four blocks away, determined to walk the rest of the way. It would make for some small issues upon leaving, but he had a big down jacket in which to stash the face covering, gun, and gloves. In Seattle, even an older gentleman dressed all in black would not raise suspicion or even warrant a second look.

There would be no one in the box office this time of day when there were no public performances going on. The front doors would surely be locked. Tony had decided that rather than risk being seen entering through a side door, which would possibly even be unlocked for the acts to go in and out, it would just be easier to use the box office as cover and pick the lock on the front doors.

He arrived at the theater and waited a few minutes as several people crossed the street. He pretended to be on the phone until all of them had passed. When it was clear, he positioned himself at the center set of doors, effectively hidden behind the box office booth.

The lock was easier to pick than it should have been. No alarm sounded, as expected. He reckoned that it would be shut off due to people coming and going out the back. He had counted on that. He entered and thought about locking the door behind him. He'd be able to get out either way, as public buildings are not set up to lock patrons inside. But nobody else was going to come in this way, so he left it.

He could hear music playing from the main hall and he entered on the right side. He stopped in the vestibule and carefully peered around the corner to make sure no one was close by. The few occupants of the theater were clustered on and around the stage. He was alone in the dark as he'd hoped.

He took off his coat and stashed it in the vestibule. He would grab it on the way out. He put on the gloves and balaclava, quietly picked up the gun, and took the aisle seat in the back row nearest the exit. When he left, he would barely have to get out of the seat before grabbing his coat and taking off.

His watch read 2:20 so he knew Dead Salmon had not yet performed. On stage were three scruffy-looking guys who couldn't have been old enough to remember Windy City, but there they were. He recognized the song they played, *Phoenix*.

Tony had never been much into rock. He was raised on Frank Sinatra, Dean Martin, and Tony Bennett. Even as a kid in New York, his tastes had mirrored those of his mother.

Still, in the seventies, it was hard to get away from the rock bands. He knew who Ricky Harris was when he and Rocco learned about the star's supposed death the day after it happened. He had heard some of Windy City's stuff—everyone had. So, these guys hacking away at *Phoenix* wasn't much of a surprise.

It's probably the millionth time they've heard it today, he thought. After that, those kids did another song which Tony didn't think was by Windy City, but he could be wrong. They sucked at that number too, or so Tony thought. Probably a good thing nobody would be asking his opinion on this fine day.

He waited for over an hour, having to sit through two more acts until he finally saw what had to be Dead Salmon take the stage. They were as old as the preceding acts had been young. They set up and there was some brief conversation between the tall guy in front who could be no one else but Thor Swenson aka Ricky Harris, and another man sitting in the front row with the rest of the judging panel.

A woman had come in with the band, and she was now sitting to the left of the stage, several rows behind the front row center people. She was in the dark mostly, but Tony saw her raise a cell phone. Catching some video, no doubt.

The band began to play, and it was not a song Tony was familiar with. It was pretty rocking, and after a few minutes, there was a great guitar solo. Tony found himself entertained. If there had been any doubt, it would be gone with this performance. That was definitely Ricky Harris up there, though quite a bit older than the last time Tony had seen him.

Before he realized it, they had finished the song, and he was no closer to taking out Harris. Shit. But he relaxed when he remembered that all the preceding acts had played two songs each. That meant that Dead Salmon would, too.

Harris took out a different guitar and seated himself on the edge of the stage. The others walked off and he was alone up there. *Oh, how perfect is that?* Tony thought. But then it got even better. The few stage lights and dim house lights were all brought down until only a single spotlight remained on Harris. Someone may as well have painted a bullseye on his forehead.

Tony waited until Harris began to sing and then slowly took aim. Just as he went to squeeze the trigger, the woman in the front row jumped to her feet shouting, "Ricky!" and ran out the door. Just like that.

He sat there, staring at the stage. What the hell? Should he take the shot while they are all in disarray like this or...? Before he could make up his mind, Harris goes running out after her.

Tony was dumbfounded. This was a most unexpected turn of events. He didn't know what to do. He could leave and forget the whole thing. It was possible he could still slip out without being seen, but maybe not. The people up near the stage were milling around for a few minutes until the lady with the cell phone came up to them and started talking.

Tony strained to hear what she was saying, but it was no use. He was just too far away. Without amplification, voices didn't seem to carry far in this cavernous room.

She talked to them for several minutes. Now and again a louder voice would arise, but she would gesture and keep talking. The three men who had left the stage for the solo returned and seemed as intent as anyone on what the woman was telling them.

After about ten minutes, Tony decided that the whole shit show was a bust, and he was going to have to give it up. He would wait until the woman who had been doing all the talking was no longer facing him, then skedaddle.

Then, all of a sudden, the woman who had run outside comes back in. A few seconds behind her is Ricky Harris. They join the group in front of the stage.

It's now or never, Tony thought. He stood, raised the gun, and squeezed the trigger.

Chapter 25

Mick parked across the street from the Paramount. It was a pay lot, which was a pain in the ass, but he dutifully pulled out a credit card and put it in the machine. As he got to the street corner and pushed the button for the Walk signal, Mick had an uncomfortable thought.

Was it at all possible that Thor and his band were trying out for this contest? Could a brilliant man like Swenson be that stupid? Mick thought that he could. After all, he was in a band, playing and singing just like Ricky Harris. Why wouldn't he have the hubris to try to pull off his disguise in front of the very people who had the most reason to believe him dead?

Mick didn't want to take any chances. He returned to the car, passenger side, and opened the door. He retrieved his Smith and Wesson 66 .357 revolver. It was old fashioned to be sure, but he loved that gun and had carried one until forced by the department to change to a semi-auto.

He put the gun in his coat pocket and relocked the car.

When he got to the box office, he realized that these were closed auditions, there was no audience. He'd have to go around back to get in. But even as he thought these thoughts, he continued on to the front doors just to give them a shake and make sure they were locked.

To his surprise, the right-hand door opened when he

pulled on it. He stepped in.

Mick expected to hear music, but instead, the theater was deathly quiet. He stood in the lobby for a few moments, listening. Perhaps he had arrived between auditions. No people were about, no conversations came from the auditorium, so Mick went through the door to his right.

It was pretty dark in there, and he didn't see what he stepped on at first. He bent down and picked up a men's winter jacket with a hood. It was black and had been virtually invisible in the darkness.

Now his cop senses started to kick in. He got a very uneasy feeling in his gut. There was still no sound coming from the theater.

Mick straightened up, setting the jacket behind him. He was reaching for his gun when he saw something reflect the meager light from the stage. It was a man's shoe. Someone was standing just inside the theater to Mick's left.

He moved a little farther to the right, careful to make no sound. Slowly, he leaned forward to take in more of the stage and get a better look at just who was standing there.

There was a spotlight on the stage, but no one was performing. A group of people stood clustered both on and in front of the stage. They seemed to be talking but he couldn't hear their words.

He glanced to the left and saw a man standing in front of the very last seat, not two feet from him. The man was dressed all in black and he had a gun. He was aiming it at the stage.

Without thinking, Mick jumped through the door and tackled the man with the gun. Even with the silencer, he heard it discharge.

They rolled and grappled in the close confines between the seats. As they did, the house lights came up suddenly. Mick had the other guy on the ground, and he shoved an elbow into the guy's solar plexus as hard as he could manage.

With his left hand, he pulled the gun from his gasping opponent's grip and tossed it aside. He had his own gun drawn now, and he got off of the man dressed all in black and stood over him.

"Don't move, asshole," he said. He was winded from the exertion and was gratified to see that his opponent, also not in good shape, was equally tired. He pulled the ski mask off the guy and was stunned to see Tony DiThomasso lying before him.

"Well, I'll be goddamned," Mick said. "Tony D if I'm not mistaken."

Tony D said nothing. With his left hand, Mick got his phone out and called Chuck.

"I don't have time to explain, just come to the Paramount Theater immediately and bring some black and whites with you!"

As Chuck ranted on the other end of the phone, Mick heard someone yell, "Somebody call nine-one-one!"

"Send an aid car, too!" he yelled into the phone and hung up.

Mick dragged Tony to his feet and then pushed him into a seat. He walked around to the row behind where Tony sat and kept the gun trained on the back of Tony's head.

"Don't move. The cops will be here shortly," he said. He finally was able to look at the people gathered by the stage and saw that one of them was on the ground. Tony's shot must have found its mark before he fell.

∽∾∽∾

Thor let the stage door close behind Angie before he followed her in. He had no idea where to take it from here. But it was a certainty that Angie had not expressed the happy reaction Barb predicted she would.

The theater was still dark when he went back in. The light guy must have been so fascinated by the unfolding drama that he never bothered to turn the house lights back on.

Tom, Roger, and Bert were standing together on the stage, looking down at Barb as she talked with Rufus, Craig, Don, and Ray. Angie was joining them as Thor entered. When the door clicked shut behind him, all nine of them turned to look at him at once.

Thor had never felt so exposed. He wanted to say something. It was clear Barb had finished letting the cat out of the bag. But again, no words would come to him.

It was Rufe who broke the awkward silence. "Is it really you, Ricky?" He sounded awestruck.

Thor sighed. "Yeah. It's me," he said.

"I can't believe it," Ray said. "After all these years…"

Everyone started to talk at once then, and Thor wanted nothing more than to just go home. He was about to walk out when he felt a sledgehammer hit him high up on the left side. He staggered, confused, then collapsed like a sack of rocks.

He lay on the floor, bewildered. He had no idea what had just happened. It was getting really hard to breathe. He turned his head and looked down at his chest, but all he could see was blood pouring out of a rather large hole.

It didn't make sense. He was struggling to breathe now and vaguely aware of people moving around him. A commotion at the back held their attention, then he saw Barb look at him on the ground. He heard her call his name just as pain that felt like a chainsaw began ripping through his chest.

కొకొ

"Oh my god, Thor!" Barbara cried. She looked to see him on the ground in a rapidly widening pool of blood. As she ran to him, he closed his eyes. "No!" she yelled. "Somebody call nine-one-one!"

She put her hands over the bleeding hole in his side. Angie and Rufus joined her. Rufus took off his jacket and created a pillow under Thor's head.

"You stay with me!" Angie cried. "I won't lose you twice!"

Barb leaned down and put her head on his chest. She could still hear a heartbeat, but it was slow. "Oh my God! Thor!" she cried.

The others had gathered around and were watching Barbara's feeble attempts at staunching the blood flow. Thor's labored breaths slowed and stopped.

"He's not breathing!" Rufe yelled. He began chest compressions.

After what seemed an eternity, four paramedics, two men, and two women entered the theater through the right-side door, carrying equipment and wheeling a gurney. They pushed the others out of the way.

"Gunshot," one of them said into the radio clipped to his shoulder. The other three took over chest compressions and began feverishly working on the unconscious Thor. It was another ten minutes before they got him loaded onto the gurney and out into the waiting ambulance.

Chapter 26

Mick was relieved when the EMTs arrived. He had been watching the frenzy down by the stage, wishing he could help. Tony D hadn't moved. It was as though he was resigned to this rather unfortunate end to his illustrious career. He hadn't spoken a word either.

After a few minutes, Mick had recognized some of the Dead Salmon band members and realized that the man on the ground had to be Thor Swenson. Logic told him who would have been Tony's target, although how Tony found out about this audition was a mystery. *Unless he heard about it on the radio like I did,* Mick thought. But if that was the case, then he didn't hear about it at the last minute as Mick had. DiThomasso was obviously well prepared for this little ambush.

Mick hated to see Thor lying there. He brought his gun in case Swenson tried to run, but he never intended to use it. It was purely coincidence that being armed turned out to be the right call. He hoped Swenson would survive, but when he saw the man at Thor's head begin chest compressions, Mick's hopes dimmed.

Soon after the paramedics got busy with Thor, Chuck and a gaggle of uniforms blew into the theater.

"Chuck, thank God!" Mick said.

Chuck motioned for two of the officers to take Mick's

prisoner into custody. One of them produced handcuffs, and soon Tony was on his feet again.

"Detective Wilson, let me introduce you to Mr. Anthony DiThomasso," Mick said formally.

"Are you shitting me?" Chuck asked. He stared open-mouthed at Tony D, who returned his stare with a smirk.

Mick turned to the arresting officers. "I personally witnessed this man shoot the gentleman down there," he indicated the rescue in progress at the front of the auditorium. "Please read him his rights. I will accompany Detective Wilson to give my statement." The cop with the cuffs nodded, and they led Tony up the aisle.

"By rights, I should take your piece, so we don't leave any procedure undone that DiThomasso's lawyers can pick apart at trial," Chuck said.

"Of course," Mick said. "It was not discharged." He clicked on the safety, turned the pistol butt-first to Chuck, and handed it over.

"Thank your lucky stars for that. We don't want any forensic tangles either. That is, assuming they can get the bullet intact out of our friend down there. Who is it that he shot?"

"Three guesses," said Mick. "And the first two don't count."

Chuck shook his head. "Dr. Swenson? Wow. Just amazing."

"Yeah. I hope he pulls through," Mick said with a sigh. "If not, it's going to be a shitty end to his long deception."

"Doesn't look like he's doing too well right now," Chuck added. They turned to go.

Mick and Chuck left the theater to find that the weather had turned grayer and wetter. The infamous Seattle drizzle was misting everything in its path.

"We'll take my car," Chuck said. "I'll have someone bring yours down to the station later. You can go home from there."

ⅇⅇⅇ

"May I ride with him?" Barb asked anxiously.

One of the paramedics, a petite young woman, came to her and put a gentle hand on her arm. "I'm sorry. There just isn't room. We are taking him to Harborview. The trauma team there is an expert with gunshot wounds. Do you know how to get there?"

Barb was crying and frustrated that she couldn't find a Kleenex in her purse. She focused on digging around for one to keep her from watching the ambulance speed away, lights and sirens blaring.

"I do," said Roger. "Barb, come with us in the van. We'll be right behind him." He carefully took her elbow and steered her in the direction of the waiting van that Tom had brought around to the alley where they stood.

Angie ran up to them. "Can we follow you?" she asked.

"Of course," Roger said.

Soon a small procession of the Dead Salmon band van and a rented Emerald City Limo was racing through the streets of Seattle, heading south toward the hospital. There was no conversation in either vehicle.

Chapter 27

Chuck parked his car in the garage, and he and Mick took the elevator to the fourth floor and the Homicide office. Mick followed quietly. It seemed so odd to be a civilian witness coming in to make a statement. This building had been his home for more years than he could remember.

"You want to go to an interview room?" Chuck asked.

"Not really," Mick said. "Is there anything wrong with your desk?"

Chuck laughed. "For you? Absolutely not!"

Chuck led him to the desk he knew so well. His own former desk sat adjacent to it, empty.

"They still haven't replaced me?" Mick asked.

"Oh, well not exactly," Chuck said. "They decided to use the reduction in headcount as a cost-saving measure. As if one less body in here doing the work is a good thing. Don't get me started." He snorted.

"Right," said Mick.

He waited patiently while Chuck booted up his laptop. He brought a form up on the screen and began to fill it out. About halfway down, the form had a large blank space for the witness statement.

Mick knew that Chuck could type almost as fast as he could talk. He would take the statement, proofread it, then print it out for Mick to review and sign. That would be such a great time saver for Mick. He was anxious to get to Harborview to find out if Thor survived.

Mick would not have been able to offer such a service. He would hand the witness a pad and a pen and have them write down their statement and sign it. He would then have the statement typed up by somebody else, dated, filed, and printed out. Chuck's was a much more twenty-first-century approach.

"Since I just saw you at lunch today, I know what you were doing prior to witnessing the crime in question," Chuck said. "Which crime is now in the system with an incident number, so it looks like they got him processed pretty fast. I'm sure his high-priced lawyer is already here too," Chuck said with a sneer.

"What I would like to know is, how the hell did you end up at the Paramount?" He looked as though he might add to the question, but he did not.

"I was on my way home after lunch and I heard the DJ on KZOK talking about a Windy City tour. That caught my attention so I turned it up and listened to it.

"The DJ was actually mentioning that the Ricky Harris replacement auditions or whatever they called it, were going on today at the Paramount." He shrugged.

"I wasn't that far away, so I turned around. I figured I might be able to convince one of the people in the band to come with me to meet Dr. Swenson. I thought they would see through his flimsy disguise immediately."

"Why were you armed, Mick?" Chuck asked.

Mick shifted in his seat. That was innocent, but it was going to be just a little harder to explain than his presence at the auditions in the first place.

"Chuck, you know I keep my gun in the car. I have a civilian CCP, as you know. I almost left the pistol in my glove box, too. But at the last minute, I realized that if Swenson is dumb enough to play in a band and essentially hide in plain sight, then he might just be dumb enough to try out for his old job!"

Chuck frowned. "And you needed to arm yourself against the possibility of Dr. Swenson being armed?" he asked. The sarcasm was quite thinly veiled.

It was Mick's turn to frown. "Of course not! But I thought it might give him second thoughts if he tried to flee. He already thinks I'm a crazy stalker. I'm sure I could convince him I would shoot if he took off."

"And would you have shot him if he took off?" Chuck asked. His voice was level and he watched the screen as he typed.

"Chuck, I know this is routine, but do you really need to ask me that?"

"I just have to put your answers in here accurately, Mick. I'm not implying anything. These are routine questions as you said."

Mick rubbed a weary hand over his face and took a deep breath.

"I know. Jesus, I just hope he isn't dead."

"Swenson?" Chuck asked.

"Yeah." Mick sighed again.

"Well let's get this over with so you can go find out, OK?"

"Yeah. Where were we? Oh yes, so the answer is no, of course, I would not have actually shot him. I think your guys will find that the gun isn't even loaded. The bullets are still in my glovebox."

"So, your intent in taking a weapon to the crime scene was to just use it to intimidate Swenson if you ran into him, correct?"

"Yes," Mick answered.

"Did you find Dr. Swenson at the audition as you feared you might?"

"No. In fact, I wasn't aware it was him who had been

shot until just before the police arrived."

Chuck nodded and typed away. "Did you know that Anthony DiThomasso was going to be in attendance at the auditions?" he asked.

"No," Mick said.

"How did you find DiThomasso?"

"As I entered the auditorium, I almost tripped over something. It was a winter jacket. I found it suspicious that a coat would be lying on the floor inside what I thought was a locked theater. All of the people who should have been there were down by the stage."

"Did you go into the auditorium to look for the coat's owner?" Chuck asked.

"I took a very slow, quiet, and quick peek inside the door," Mick said. "If someone had left the coat there and was still around, I didn't want to be seen by them."

"What did you see when you peeked in the door?" Chuck went on.

"At first I only noticed the people down by the stage. They were all standing around talking. There was no music, no audition going on that I could see.

"Just as I was about to step in, I saw a reflection on the floor. When I looked down, I noticed a man's shoe. I knew then that someone was standing right on the other side of the opening where I was."

"What did you do?"

"I looked over to see him. He was standing, aiming a gun toward the stage. The gun was equipped with a suppressor. At that point, I didn't have time to lose, so I jumped him and knocked the gun from his hand, but I was too late.

"I heard the gun discharge before I hit him. I didn't realize he had found his target. We wrestled for a few minutes until I could subdue him and train my own weapon on him. I removed his face covering and recognized him immediately."

"You say you recognized him," Chuck interjected. "And who had you just tackled?"

"It was Anthony DiThomasso," Mick said. "I pulled him to his feet and sat him in one of the theater seats to hold him until you arrived. That's when I called you." Mick finished.

"What happened while you were waiting for the police to arrive?"

Mick remembered the paramedics coming within two or three minutes of his call to Chuck. "While I was on the phone with you, I heard someone yell, 'Call nine-one-one!' so I asked you to send an aid car and hung up. Only after I got DiThomasso into a seat, where I could keep an eye on him, did I have time to see what was happening down by the stage.

"Medic One got there pretty damned fast. I watched them working on Swenson until you showed up. You know the rest," Mick finished.

Chuck didn't ask any more questions. He finished typing into the document and then printed it out. When he returned from the printer, he sat down again and handed the finished statement to Mick.

Mick skimmed over it. He had no doubt it was accurate, and he was comfortable enough with his confidence in Chuck that he just grabbed a pen and signed it. "Is that it?"

"Yes," said Chuck. "You're free to go. But do me a favor and call me when you find out how Swenson is, will you?"

"Of course," said Mick and he was out the door.

As he went past the duty sergeant's desk, the officer sitting there handed him his car keys. Mick smiled. "Thanks."

Just as Chuck had promised, he sent someone to pick up Mick's car from the Paramount parking lot.

"It's in the building garage on level 2 about halfway down as you exit the elevator," the sergeant told him.

"Thanks," he said again.

He found his car right, where she said it would be, and sped out of the garage.

Chapter 28

When the two cars full of senior rock bands arrived at the ER, Barb was leading the group. She marched straight to the reception desk and asked about Thor. The receptionist was a very large woman, impeccably dressed. She had a calm demeanor that didn't change as she picked up a phone and spoke quietly into it for a few seconds. When she was finished, she looked up at Barb and said, "The doctor will let you in those doors. Mr. Swenson is in the Trauma Bay."

There were ten people in their group, and the emergency doctor who came through the double doors was not about to let them all in. "Who is family out here?" he asked.

"Dr. Swenson has no living family," Barb said. "I'm his girlfriend." It felt funny to use that term, but she couldn't come up with a better one.

The doctor looked unsure. "Do you have medical power of attorney?" he asked sounding hopeful.

Barb was discouraged. "No," she said quietly.

The doctor thought about it for a moment more. He was tall, looked to be in his forties, and had wavy salt and pepper hair. His eyes were blue and looked as though they had witnessed their fair share of tragedy.

"The rest of you stay out here in the waiting area," he said. He turned to Barb. "You, come with me." He slid a card through a reader to the right of the double doors and they swung open.

Barb followed him down a hall that was filled with doctors and nurses rushing about. It smelled of alcohol and medicines and blood. She could hear someone moaning on the other side of a curtained-off area as they passed.

The doctor took her to an interior window that looked into a room full of doctors and nurses, medical equipment, telemetry, and other machines she didn't recognize. The emergency personnel were working fast and shouting information at each other.

Barb knew it was Thor they were working on. He was still alive then. She took what little comfort she could from that.

Before long, several of the people left the room. The two remaining pushed the gurney through the door and toward an elevator at the end of the hall. They were walking very fast.

The doctor that had stationed Barb at the window followed them out and came over to her. "We're taking him to surgery now. We had to get him stable after that blood loss. He's not breathing on his own yet, but he has a good strong pulse. You should probably join your friends in the waiting room. This will take some time. I'll come down when we're finished and let you know how it goes."

Barb was terrified. "Thank you," she said. She tried to remember the way back to the waiting area and when she found the double doors again, she hesitated to go through them. They would lock behind her. Would that be the last time she saw Thor?

She exited the trauma bay and began to cry again. Roger led her to a chair.

"What did the doctor say?" he asked.

Barb shook her head. "Not much, really. He said they had to get him stable before they could take him to surgery.

That's where they are taking him now. He said Thor's not breathing on his own!" She sobbed into her already saturated Kleenex.

❦❦❦

About an hour after Thor arrived at the hospital, Mick pulled into the parking garage across the street from it. He knew his way around Harborview after so many years as a cop. He parked and hurried to the Emergency Department.

When he arrived, he found Thor's big entourage filling the waiting area. The attractive silver-haired woman Mick had seen at all the Dead Salmon performances was there. He went to her. She looked extremely upset, as was to be expected.

She didn't seem to notice him as he approached. He knelt in front of her. "Are you Mrs. Swenson?" he asked.

She looked at him and smiled thinly. "Not yet," she said, "but I'm working on it." Mick patted her hand.

"Do you know anything yet?" he asked her.

She shook her head. "Not really. They just took him up to surgery."

Mick breathed a sigh of relief. So, he's still alive. Thank God. He knew the surgeons at Harborview were the best in the business. If Swenson had a chance of pulling through, the docs here would make it so.

"My name is Barbara," the woman said. Mick shook her hand.

"Mick Thorne," he replied.

"Of course!" she said. "You're the detective who's been coming to all his performances." She didn't sound surprised or even upset about that.

"Retired detective," Mick said.

"Well, I, for one, am very grateful that you showed up when you did," she said. "We had no idea there was a man with a gun sitting back there. I only wish you'd come in a few minutes earlier." A tear slid down her cheek then, and Mick got up. He looked around for a chair and saw there were none free.

Just then, the outer door opened, and Eric Jensen came running into the Emergency Department. The receptionist didn't even speak to him, she just pointed at the waiting area. He joined the rest, looking shocked and confused.

Mick recognized him as the rhythm guitar and backup vocal guy from Dead Salmon. He wondered why he had been absent from the auditions until he recalled that Jensen was the head coach of the Chinook University Cohos football team. He would have been at a football game on an October Saturday.

Barbara rose from her seat and ran to him. He hugged her. "Jesus, Barb, what the hell happened? Sheryl called me right after the game. She said Tom called and told me to meet you guys here. Somebody shot Thor?" Barbara only nodded.

Mick tapped Jensen on the shoulder. "I think I can fill you in. She needs to sit down. Come with me, I'm going to get a cup of coffee." He looked around. "Can we bring anybody else anything from the cafeteria?" None of them answered so Mick decided to just bring a whole bunch of coffee and snacks back. No doubt they were hungry after all this time, but they were too numb with shock to think about it.

"Mick Thorne," he said and offered Jensen his hand.

"Eric Jensen."

"I know who you are," said Mick.

"Hey! You're that guy that's been following the band around!"

"Yes, I am. Now let's go get some coffee, and I'll bring you up to speed." Mick steered Jensen toward the elevator to take him up to the second-floor hospital cafeteria.

They stepped off the elevator and Mick walked toward the waiting coffee pots. He paid for both of them, and they sat at a small table near the elevators.

"Mr. Jensen, you are in for a shock. The others found out the hard way today, too. I'm sorry to have to tell you this when your friend is upstairs in surgery, but there is no other way to explain why we're all here." Mick took a sip of his perfectly horrible coffee. Some things never change.

"I don't understand," said Eric.

"I know. You're going to get the Reader's Digest condensed version here I'm afraid. If Dr. Swenson lives, he can add his own color commentary."

"Okay..." Eric said slowly.

"Dr. Swenson has not been entirely honest with all of you. He is not who you think he is." Mick paused. That wasn't entirely true. He was the super-educated, brilliant mathematician he claimed to be. He just wasn't Thor Swenson.

"What are you talking about?" Eric said. "Of course, he is! He's been at Chinook for years. He's quite well known in academic circles."

"Yes," said Mick. "I know all of that. What you don't know is that he started life as Ricky Harris from Chicago."

Eric's eyes widened.

"Yeah," said Mick. "*That* Ricky Harris. And today at the audition, Angela Gardiner recognized him. Ricky faked his death all those years ago and assumed the identity of Thor Swenson. Thor was the deceased man they found in Ricky's car that night." Mick paused to let Eric take it all in.

"You can't be serious," Eric said.

"I'm completely serious," Mick replied.

Eric sat in the blue plastic cafeteria chair, his Styrofoam cup of coffee raised halfway to his mouth. After a long minute, he went ahead and took a sip.

"That explains why he was so against doing this contest at first!" he exclaimed.

"He was?" asked Mick. "I really thought he had convinced himself that no one would recognize him."

"Oh no, not at all. He was furious that I entered the contest without consulting him first. He wouldn't really tell me why. Then Barb talked him into it." A look of understanding crossed Eric's face then, and Mick knew he'd put the pieces together.

"She must have known!" he said.

"She certainly knew before today," Mick answered. "He must have confessed to her after you entered the contest, and she convinced him to do it."

"So where do you fit into all of this? Why were you stalking Thor? How did you know he would be at the audition today? Who shot him?"

Mick raised a hand. "Whoa! Slow down. One question at a time." He took another sip of coffee. It did not improve as it cooled.

Where to begin? "I worked on the original Ricky Harris accidental death case," Mick said. "I am recently retired, and I've long wondered about a lot of inconsistencies in that case, which I won't bore you with now. Suffice it to say that I never, in all these years, believed that Ricky Harris died that night.

"I've had time now to research my theory, and I have gathered enough evidence to prove I'm right. I confronted Dr. Swenson at your last gig at Parker's. Do you remember?"

"Yes, but he didn't share much about the conversation. He called you a stalker."

"He was very defensive as you can imagine," said Mick.

"The man who shot him today is the same man who killed the real Thor Swenson. Ricky witnessed the murder.

He put Thor's body into his rental car and pushed it into the canal."

"Unbelievable!" said Eric.

"I went to the audition today," Mick continued, "hoping to get one of the surviving members of Windy City to confront Dr. Swenson with me so that he would no longer be able to deny who he was. Believe me, I was stunned to find Anthony DiThomasso there planning to kill Ricky after all these years. There is still a lot we don't know."

"Did you arrest this DiThomasso?" Eric asked.

"He's in custody, yes." Mick didn't see any reason to repeat that he was retired and couldn't do any arresting. He changed the subject.

"My understanding is that Barbara filled in the rest of the band, and the rest of Windy City, too. That is about all any of us know. Your friend is still in surgery.

"Let's take some more coffee downstairs and see if we can't revive a few of those poor folks, OK?" Mick got up and headed back over to the coffee pots.

The two of them got on the elevator, both laden with coffees, cream and sugar packets, and a few sweet rolls in case anyone was hungry. Mick gladly paid for those too.

They arrived in the ED waiting area and passed out the food and drink. It was received gratefully, if quietly.

ୡ୬ୡ୬

After she finished eating, Angie tossed her coffee cup into the trash and went over to where Barbara was sitting. She motioned for Roger, who had never left Barb's side, to switch seats with her. She sat down and Barb slowly turned toward her.

"I overheard you talking to the doctor. I just assumed that you were Ricky's wife." She paused, knowing how using his real name might upset Barbara.

"I'm sorry," she said. "It's just that I only know him as Ricky. I can't get used to calling him Thor."

"I know. It's all right," Barb said.

"Have you been together long?" Angie asked.

"My husband passed away last January," Barb answered. "He and Thor were friends, but Thor and I didn't get to know each other until after Larry's funeral. We've been seeing each other for about six months.

"I just don't think I can go through this again!" she cried and buried her face in her hands.

Angie put an arm around her. She was not yet used to the idea that Ricky was still alive. The notion of losing him a second time seemed like such a cruel twist of fate. She could only imagine what this poor woman was going through.

The doctor who had first taken Barbara back into the trauma bay came through the double doors again. He looked through the crowded waiting area until he found Barb. Thor had been in surgery for nearly four hours.

Angie tried to read his face as he approached, but his expression gave nothing away. She helped the doctor bring Barb to her feet and followed them out of the waiting room.

It was good the doctor didn't object her to tagging along, because she really needed to know how Ricky was.

"Mr. Swenson is out of surgery and he's been taken to the ICU," the doctor said. "The surgery went well. We were able to recover the bullet, which I will turn over to the police. He was very fortunate in that it missed his heart. But it did some extensive damage to his left lung. It lodged in his sternum and caused that to fracture.

"We were able to repair the damage to the lung. He's breathing on his own again. He's not quite out of the woods yet, but we are guardedly optimistic. Mr. Swenson is not a young man, but he seems otherwise to be in good health. The next 24 hours will tell. I can let you see him if you'd like," he said.

"Yes, please!" Barbara said.

The doctor nodded. He was still wearing green scrubs. "Follow me."

They went to the elevator, and Angie returned to the waiting area. She repeated the news of the surgery and Thor's prognosis. She told them that Barbara had gone to the ICU to stay with him.

"I'd like to go back to the hotel if you don't mind, guys. It's been a long and stressful day for all of us. Rufe, I think we should stay in town until...you know, we hear how Ricky's doing," she said.

"I agree," said Rufus. He turned to Ray.

"I think we can agree the contest is at least suspended for now, right?"

Ray looked as though he'd rather be just about anywhere else. "Of course. Jesus Christ what a fuckfest! Are we supposed to spread the news that Ricky Harris is still alive?" he asked.

"No!" Angie said. "That is not our news to spread. It's entirely up to Ricky if he wants that made public. And he's in no condition to say right now, so we sit on it until further notice, got it?" She was looking directly at Ray.

"Don't you think a well-liked college professor getting shot will be reason enough not to continue?" she asked him.

Ray looked embarrassed. "Yeah," he said. "You're right. Let's get out of here."

Chapter 29

Angie, Rufe, and Ray remained in Seattle for three more days until they were assured that Ricky was out of ICU and on the road to recovery. Angie found herself liking Barbara more and more, and she felt good to know that Ricky had someone.

They sat in a departure area lounge and had a few drinks while waiting for their flight.

"I just got off the phone with Dale at the record company," said Ray. "They're pretty damned impatient, and they think we've delayed long enough. We have to get back to Chicago and finish the finals." He took a drink.

"That's bullshit!" cried Rufe. "Ricky almost died, for fuck's sake! They can't expect us to just say, 'oh well,' and go on like it didn't happen!"

Angie put her arm around him and smiled. "That's my boy," she said. "Unfortunately, my dear, we are under contract. They do expect us to go on like nothing happened."

Ray sighed. "She's right. It's just the way it is, Rufe."

"Yeah? Well that don't make it right," he said.

The TV over the bar was tuned to a local news station, and the bartender turned the volume up when the broadcaster announced that he had breaking news.

The three friends stopped talking when they heard the TV get louder.

They listened as the announcer said, "We have just

learned from a source at Harborview, that Ricky Harris, the rock singer who was thought to have died in a car accident here in Seattle forty years ago, is alive and currently being treated for a gunshot wound.

"We will have updates as soon as we get them." The news gave way to a commercial and the bartender lowered the volume again.

Angie, Rufus, and Ray all looked at each other, not speaking. Ray wouldn't have to worry about spilling the beans now. This revelation would be picked up on national news within minutes and after that, it would be common knowledge.

℘℘℘

When Mick walked into Thor's hospital room, he wasn't surprised to find Barb sitting there. She had never left his side except to go home to get a few hours' sleep, now and then, and to feed Thor's cat.

"Hey, Mick!" she said. He appreciated the warm greeting and squeezed her hand.

"How's our favorite patient?" he asked.

"At the moment, sleeping. But I think he's frustrated that he can't talk with that tube down his throat." She pointed to a second guest chair and Mick dragged it over.

"I brought you guys some news about DiThomasso. It's a little too early to tell where this will go, but the DA is talking plea bargain."

Barbara frowned. "How is that good news?" she asked.

"Because," said Mick, "it means that he'll get a lighter sentence for the attempted murder of Thor for helping the cops bring down his crime boss, Taglio."

"Oh. But won't that mean he'll get out sooner?"

"Normally, I would say it's possible. But DiThomasso will have to admit his involvement in the Thor Swenson killing forty years ago and that confession will get him locked up pretty much for good."

Barb seemed to consider this. "I think Thor will like that idea."

Thor raised his left hand in a thumbs-up gesture, and they saw that his eyes were open. He waived at Mick in lieu of talking. He rolled his eyes and pointed to the tube entering his mouth.

"Yeah, yeah, I know," Mick said. "Don't exert yourself, you'll get out of here quicker."

Thor gestured to Barb for a pen and paper, which she handed him, and he began to write. After a few moments, he tore off the top sheet of the little pad and handed it to Mick. Mick blushed as he read it.

It said, "I understand I owe you a big thank you for saving my life. If you hadn't come when you did, Tony's aim would have been better, and I'd be dead now. I can never thank you enough."

Mick looked at him, not sure how to respond. How do you thank someone for thanking you? He chose to just keep to the truth.

"We both got lucky, Thor. I'm just glad you're going to be OK. When you get out of here, let's take in a Cohos game! I'll try to explain football to you. It's played on a grid, there's a lot of math involved. I think you will actually enjoy it," he said.

Thor offered another thumbs-up.

"I'm sorry to say that by the time they let me take him home, the Cohos season will be over," said Barb.

Mick was disappointed. "Good point," he said. "Seahawks then! They're bound to make the postseason. I'll take you to a Hawks game." He smiled.

To Barb he said, "You take care of our boy, here. I'll stop by again."

She squeezed his hand. "Thank you for everything,

Mick," she said.

ↀↀↀ

Windy City and their manager, Ray Adler, barely had time to unpack their bags before they were back in the Chicago Symphony Hall conducting the finals of the Windy City Tour contest.

The original plan was to have netted 30 acts for the finals, ten from each city. But with Thor out of commission, and the Seattle auditions curtailed, they only had 28 acts to review.

Because all 28 were the best of their respective areas of the country, they all were expected to do well. The competition was fierce. The rules were the same as in the first round: each act would play two songs. One had to be a Windy City song; the other had to be by a different artist or an original composition. As the morning of the finals approached, Angie went to Ray with a rule change request.

"I think we need to stipulate that they can do any of our songs except *Phoenix*," she said. "Even if they didn't do it in their first audition."

Ray rolled his eyes. "Fine. Whatever you say. I'll get the word out to the contestants today. But no more extra rules!"

The band and Ray sat in the front row as they had on all previous occasions. Angie couldn't help but turn around to search the back of the theater once in a while. She knew it was silly. DiThomasso was in jail, Ricky was in Seattle recovering and there were no crazy men with guns after her and the guys.

The finals went quickly, and the general consensus was that their initial picks from each of the various cities on the contest tour were the right choices. They narrowed the field to the top three by the end of the first day. On the second day, each of those three contestants would play two songs with the band.

First to go was the young phenom from Chicago, their very first choice in the contest. Brent Caplan was only 18 years old, but he played the guitar like he was born with one in his hands. His voice was deep and gravelly, like Ricky's, and he had an amazing range. His stage presence was mature and confident, and the band got in synch with him right off.

The second of the three finalists was a heavy-set blues-man, from Philadelphia, Stan "Rumbling" Jones. He was in the same age group as Windy City and while his guitar style was uniquely his own, he could certainly play on the professional stage. He had been the only African American contestant in an otherwise lily-white field.

Last to go was another aging rocker, Norman Greene. Because the auditions were curtailed, Norman was the only contestant from Seattle that they chose and he definitely brought that Seattle grunge sound to the group.

After all of the final auditions playing with Windy City were complete, the contestants were sent back to their hotel for the afternoon. The judges would deliberate over dinner and then bring the three men back to Symphony Center to announce the winner.

The second and third place winners would each receive $5,000 and backstage passes for the tour in the city of their choice.

Angie, Rufe, Don, Craig, and Ray took the afternoon off, agreeing to reconvene over dinner at Exchequer Pub near the Symphony Center. Angie and Rufe went home to relax and talk over the day.

She poured a glass of wine. "You want one?" she asked Rufe who was leaning on the kitchen doorframe.

"Don't mind if I do," he said.

She poured him a glass and handed it to him. They both

went into the living room and sat.

"Who are you leaning toward?" she asked.

"You know, I enjoyed all three. I really did. They all have talent. They all seemed to blend right in with us and, if I'm to be totally honest, any one of them could easily go on the tour and be successful."

Angie laughed. "I love that you are taking this seriously enough to give everyone equal consideration," she said. "You know damned well that Caplan kid was the clear winner. I wanted it to be one of the older guys. I wanted them both so bad! But Brent just fits in the best and you know it," she finished.

Rufe smiled and coyly sipped his wine. "If you say so, my dear." She threw a couch pillow at him.

They relaxed for another two hours before it was time to get ready for dinner. They agreed that because they had been conferring together, an opportunity that the others didn't get, they would keep their choice to themselves until everyone else had weighed in.

After showering and changing clothes, they went down to the building's garage and retrieved their car. It was nice to be able to drive again and not have to rely on limos in strange cities. All too soon that was going to be the norm once again as they went on tour with their new addition.

Rufe chose valet parking rather than spend half an hour trying to stash the car someplace. When they entered the restaurant, all of the others were waiting for them. A gigantic pizza arrived about the same time as they did, and there were two pitchers of beer already on the table.

Once they were seated and properly fed, it was time for business. Everyone looked to Angie to begin the conversation. She just smiled, took another bite of pizza, and pointed to Ray.

"Oh no," Ray said. "You aren't going to drag me into any debates at this late date. You four are the judges, I'm just along for the ride; remember?"

Angie finished her bite. "OK," she said. "Then Don, what do you say? Did we get a clear winner today or not?"

Don laughed and Craig soon joined in. "You know we talked about it before you two got here," Don said. "If you guys chose anyone but that kid, Brent, you are off your rockers!"

Rufe slapped the table. "It's unanimous then!" He raised his beer stein. "To Brent Caplan, the newest member of Windy City!" The others joined in and enthusiastically toasted Brent. Now to deliver the good news.

After dinner and a few more beers, the group walked together back to Symphony Center. When they arrived at the concert hall, the contestants were there already. All three had changed clothes and they were nervously waiting up on the stage. The local press was there, as well as several record company executives to make the ceremony official and hand out checks to the runners up.

Young Mr. Caplan was as surprised as he was pleased to learn he was the winner. The second-place winner was Rumbling Jones, and he was thrilled to hear that if Caplan couldn't complete the tour for any reason, he would be brought in to replace him. In third place, grunge rocker Norm Greene was somewhat disingenuous after receiving his award.

"Did I ever have even the slightest chance of winning this when the real Ricky Harris auditioned right after me?" he asked. Angie was insulted by this remark and irritated that he had the nerve to tuck that five-thousand-dollar check into his pocket before making such a snarky comment.

"None of you had a snowball's chance in hell if Ricky hadn't been shot!" she retorted. Rufe put a hand on her shoulder and turned her away from the stage.

"Let it go, sweetie," he said.

Angie shrugged him off and mumbled, "dick" under her breath.

Chapter 30

Thor was released from the hospital just before Christmas, and Barbara moved into his house soon after. They decided to put her house up for sale after the first of the year to start their new life together.

Tim seemed happy to see his friend Thor again, but offered periods of aloofness too, as cats will sometimes do. With his new "mom" Barbara around all the time, Tim was quite happy to be her lap warmer any time she sat down. His twelve-cylinder purring motor was revved up and running whenever she so much as spoke to him. She could barely walk without that big old cat rubbing up against her legs. He reserved his head bumps for Thor though. It was the feline version of a fist bump and that suited Thor just fine.

Mick kept his promise about football, and the first Sunday in January found the three of them at CenturyLink Field to see the Seahawks play the Dallas Cowboys in the NFC title game. The winner would go to the Super Bowl.

"I cannot believe how loud it is in here!" Thor shouted. His lips were scant inches from Mick's ear and still, he wasn't sure Mick heard him.

Mick laughed. "The team hasn't even come out of the tunnel yet," he said. "Just wait!"

He had spent a few weekends teaching Thor about football and as he had predicted, Thor appreciated the mathematical aspects of the game. Eric had helped in that department, too. His Cohos had ended with a winning season, beating their rivals, the Western Washington University Vikings.

Thor was feeling much better and getting stronger by the day, but his lungs were a long way from being able to add to the raucous cacophony that was a cheering 12th Man crowd. He decided he would just enjoy the game as he put his newfound knowledge to the test. Mick and Barb would have to do the cheering.

Barb returned to their seats with three beers and Beecher's Flagship macaroni and cheese for the three of them. The men helped themselves, and Thor held Barb's beer until she sat down.

He took a bite of the steaming mac and cheese and washed it down with a gulp of beer. "Oh my god this is delicious!" he said.

"I know," said Barb. "I love this stuff, even though I'll have to spend a week on the treadmill to get rid of it." She laughed, and Thor felt a warm rush of love for her. They ate hurriedly to keep the food from getting cold. The temperature on the field was 29 degrees and the temperature in the stands wasn't much better.

Thor thought he had better get on with it before the teams came on the field and conversation was rendered impossible.

He put his arm around Barb and drew her close. "I think we should get married," he said in her ear.

She looked at him funny and only said, "Why?"

He pressed on. "Because then we don't have bureaucratic hurdles to clear the next time someone shoots me."

She pursed her lips. "Well, I can't argue with that logic!"

Thor kissed her just as the Seahawks started running out of the tunnel through flames and explosions and plenty of smoke.

സാരാ

One week after Thor watched the Seahawks barely miss a Super Bowl berth at the very first football game he'd ever been to, he and Barbara were on their way to the Paramount Theater. Windy City was in town on their Reunion Tour. Dr. and Mrs. Swenson had received complimentary backstage passes from Ray Adler for Christmas.

They arrived in the limo that the record company provided and were ushered backstage through a stage door on the alley. A loud party was well underway back there, and when Thor and Barb walked in, the cheer that met them gave the gathering a surprise party feeling.

Angie was the first to greet them. She thrust drinks into their waiting hands, but not before giving them both long, hard hugs of welcome. Thor kissed her cheek and she blushed like a schoolgirl.

"Introduce us to the new guy," Thor said after a moment.

"Oh yes, he's wonderful!" Angie said. "Rufe! Come here and bring Brent with you!" she called across the crowded room.

Rufe came over and hugged Barb. He looked at Thor. "Are you OK enough for a hug, my brother?" he asked.

"Fit as a fiddle," Thor said and offered Rufe a heartfelt bro hug. Don and Craig soon joined them and bringing up the rear was a shy, dark-haired young man. He stood politely to the side until Rufe finally turned to him.

"Thor Swenson, meet Brent Caplan," Rufe said.

"Brent," he continued, "meet Ricky Harris." Brent's brown eyes opened wide and he timidly shook Thor's hand.

Thor grinned. "Call me Thor," he said. "I've seen you

do some amazing stuff on YouTube. I respectfully bow to the master," he said and followed it with a bow.

"I don't know what to say, except thank you," said Brent, shyly.

Ray appeared then. "Thor and Barb, you two come with me. The rest of you, get your asses out there! Are you deaf or can you hear the crowd, and you're just ignoring them?" The crowd was indeed cheering and rhythmically clapping, and it was time for the show.

Ray led them to their seats, front row center. They would have the best view in the house.

Steve Slaton from KZOK came on stage and took the mike. "I know we've all been waiting a long time for this reunion tour," he said to thunderous applause. "But Windy City and KZOK have a surprise for us Seattle!" There followed more deafening applause and cheering. When it died down, he continued.

"As you may know, tonight, January 14, 2017, is the forty-second anniversary of the night Ricky Harris died, right here in Seattle. Or at least we thought he died." The crowd cheered, but more quietly this time so Slaton could continue.

The members of the band had come on stage behind him and were poised at their instruments. None of them spoke.

"We have a very special guest in the audience tonight," Slaton said. He looked directly at Thor. "Come on up here, Ricky!" The crowd erupted into the loudest cheering yet. Thor was stunned. This was completely unexpected. He looked at Barb and she just smiled a knowing smile.

"You had something to do with this?" he asked.

"Get up there!" she said and gave him a shove.

Thor walked over to the steps on the right side and climbed up on stage. Slaton welcomed him with a handshake and exited stage right. Brent came over and handed

Thor his old red and white Gibson Flying V. Thor put it on, strummed the opening chords of *Phoenix*, and stepped up to the mike.

"Hey, Seattle! Are you ready to rock?"

The End

About the Author

Vivian has been writing as long as she's been reading. She has previously published short stories in, *(mac)ro(mic)* and *The Scarlett Leaf Review,* along with several non-fiction pieces in *Horse Illustrated, Horseplay*, and *Washington Horse Breeder's Digest. Rock's Wages,* is her first novel.

A lifelong equestrian, Vivian divides her time between writing, riding her horse, teaching dressage professionally, and enjoying her day job as a Business Operations manager at Unisys. Her identical twin sons are adults now, but always the greatest joy of her life.

CPSIA information can be obtained
at www.ICGtesting.com
Printed in the USA
BVHW041400290522
638413BV00001B/5

9 781953 434432